MINE FOR THE WINTER

CARRIE ELKS

MINE FOR THE WINTER by Carrie Elks

Copyright © 2023 by Carrie Elks

231123

All rights reserved.

Edited by Rose David

Proofread by Proofreading by Mich

Cover Designed by The Pretty Little Design Company

"**M**om! Hey Mom!"

Kelly Fraser looked up from the bill she'd been staring at, to see her eleven year old son run into the kitchen, his cheeks flushed. He was holding his skates, the ones that had cost an arm and half a leg because his coach had told her that Cole had promise as a hockey player, but he needed the right equipment.

And she was all for that. Even if it meant making savings elsewhere. She loved that kid fiercely, and would fight to the ends of the earth for him.

"What's up?" she asked, turning the bills over so Cole couldn't see them.

"My feet won't fit in my skates."

"What?" She frowned. "Are they broken?" Did hockey skates come with a guarantee? They were only three months old.

He shook his head. "I think I've grown again."

Somehow she kept the smile playing on her lips, even though it was early in the morning and she hadn't gotten home from work until two a.m. and the bills she was hiding on the kitchen table were just some of many.

"Come here, let me look." She tried not to show her dismay. Her son didn't need to take on her adult worries.

Cole sat down on the chair next to hers and put his feet out. There were holes in his socks and she was pretty sure it was the same pair he wore yesterday, but she was learning to fight her battles.

And not to sniff when his feet were too close. He wasn't a teenager quite yet, but he was getting there. The mood swings would show occasionally, and he seemed to grow an inch every other week. And yeah, personal hygiene wasn't always at the top of his priority list, even if it was on hers.

He handed her the skate and she tried to slide it on his foot, but sure enough, there was no room. She let out a long breath.

"We're gonna need to buy some new ones," Cole told her. "I have a game on Saturday."

Kelly ran her tongue along her dry bottom lip. She hadn't had coffee yet. Hadn't had anything to eat, either. She'd grab something later that afternoon at work, probably, if she got the chance. And if she remembered.

"Yeah." She nodded, her lips pressed together. New skates didn't come cheap. And even if she could sell these on eBay, it would take weeks for the money to come in. She'd have to find some space on a credit card, or call Cole's dad, and if she was being honest, the credit card was her preferred option.

"What size are your sneakers?" she asked him. They'd bought those less than a month ago.

"Seven, I think." He wrinkled his nose.

"Okay." This time she was going to size up to give him room to grow. Another thing she'd learned in the past year. And if Cole needed some extra socks to fill the space so be it.

She couldn't keep buying skates every few months. Not if they wanted to eat.

"Oh, and Mrs. Grant reminded me about the trip," Cole said. "The one to the ski center in January. She said we need to get the form in and pay this week."

Kelly blew out a mouthful of air. She'd put the form in the kitchen drawer to forget about it for a while. "We have a couple of weeks before it's due, don't we?"

Cole nodded. "Yeah, but she likes us to be early."

"Don't worry about it. I'll drop it in the next time I'm passing," Kelly promised him. This one needed cash and that was a little harder to come by. She'd have to advance herself some wages.

Again. At least there were some bonuses to being your own boss. Or to your dad being your boss, technically, even if she was the one who ran the Winterville Tavern on a daily basis. Her dad had owned the place since she was Cole's age, and she'd been working there on and off ever since she could remember. Once she left school she took up half of the slack, and now she did almost all of the work.

Not that she minded. She was kind of attached to the place.

Cole stood and gave her his other skate, then ran out of the room in search of his backpack and shoes. Kelly put his skates on the table and stared at them for a minute.

Okay. It was going to be okay. She'd survived much worse than a cashflow problem. What was it her mom used to say? 'Never cry over money or men.' Well, at least she'd learned to follow part of her advice.

"Do you have my lunch money?" Cole shouted from his room.

"I made you a lunch today, honey." Kelly pushed herself up from the kitchen table and grabbed the brown bag from the refrigerator. Cole walked back into the kitchen, his sneakers and coat on, his bag dangling from his hand. "Cheese and ham. Your favorite."

"Thanks." He smiled at her and she couldn't help smiling back. Cole was a good kid. Sure, he didn't know the value of money yet, but he was learning, maybe too fast. She wanted to protect him from the realities for as long as she could. He was only a kid, he didn't need to worry about money or work or anything else. That was her job.

"No problem, kiddo." She ruffled his hair and he ducked away with a wrinkled nose.

"I just brushed that."

"I thought it needed a little zhuzhing," she told him, winking. And he rolled his eyes, but he was smiling again. "You have any after school activities?"

Cole shook his head, stuffing his lunch into his backpack. "Nope. Not today."

"Then head straight to the Tavern. I'll make you dinner there." And then her dad would take him home and Kelly would work all night.

That was their agreement these days. Ever since her dad's knees had started failing and he couldn't physically stand behind the bar anymore. She ran the place and he did the accounts. Between them, somehow they were keeping the business going.

"Gotta go," Cole said, looking up at the kitchen clock. She could remember taking it down from the wall to teach him how to tell the time when he'd just started kindergarten. It made her feel wistful.

"Come here." She pulled him close and kissed his cheek.

"Mom." Another eye roll.

"You're not too old for kisses from your mom," she told him as he pulled away. "I'll see you after school."

"Not if I see you first." He grinned and ran out of the backdoor, heading for the road where the bus would pick him up. She wasn't allowed to walk him there anymore. At the start of the school year he'd told her with a serious voice that he was too old for that.

And it hurt, but he was right. Her son was growing up. A few more years and he'd have bristles, an attitude, and a deep voice.

She wasn't sure she was ready for that. Maybe it was the time of year, or the fact that her son was growing up, but she could remember another boy turning into a man. Another voice breaking.

Her chest clenched.

She didn't have time for stupid reminiscences. Didn't have time for much except working, eating, and sleeping. Sighing, she pushed the memories away and grabbed her purse, walking down the hallway to the closed door at the front.

She put her ear against it but couldn't hear a thing. So she rapped on the door with her fingertips.

"Dad?"

There was no response for a minute. Then she heard the groan of the bedsprings followed by the slow pad of footsteps to the door. She'd had her dining room converted to a bedroom for him when he moved in with her a while back.

"Kelly?" Her dad frowned. His hair was messy, his face creased from sleeping. "What time is it?"

She smiled at him, because even though he was old and in pain he was still the man who'd brought her up single handedly. The one who'd been able to carry barrels of beer without getting winded and had made sure she had everything she needed, the same way she was trying to do for Cole.

"Just before eight. I need to head into town to pick up some things. Don't forget you have your appointment at twelve."

"I haven't forgotten." She could have swore he rolled his

eyes. "Don't see the damn point though. It's not like I can afford to have the surgery."

"You're having it," Kelly said firmly. "We'll work out a payment plan."

Her dad's eyes caught hers. He looked tired. And she knew he was constantly in pain. He couldn't even live on his own anymore, not when it hurt him to walk up stairs. Luckily her house was a bungalow and he had everything he needed on the ground floor. "Cole needs the money more than I do."

"Cole's absolutely fine. You don't need to worry about him." Her voice was firm.

"He needs new skates."

Ah, so he'd heard them talking. Not a surprise, this place was too small for the three of them, and the walls weren't exactly soundproof. "And he'll get them. The same way you'll get a new knee." She shot him a smile. "I'll see you at eleven-thirty to drive you to the doctor." He couldn't drive, either, thanks to his knees.

"I got a ride already," he told her. "Charlie Shaw's gonna take me."

"Isn't he working?" she asked. Charlie was one of her dad's oldest friends. He ran the Cold Start Garage in town. They were poker buddies, the kind of guys who shot the breeze together regularly but never talked about anything meaningful. But Charlie was always somebody they could rely on.

"Not today. That young kid has taken over most of the heavy stuff. He's a good worker, according to Charlie. He trusts him."

She opened her mouth to tell him she'd take him anyway, but then shut it again. She already had a hundred things to do, or a hundred and one now that Cole needed new skates. "Okay. But let me know how it goes."

"Will do." Her dad nodded. "And sweetheart?"

"Yes?" She gave him a soft smile.

"I appreciate all you do. Me and Cole, we both do."

Her stomach tightened. "I appreciate you, too." She gave him a hug and he looked surprised, because the two of them had never been the hugging type. "Cole's coming to the Tavern after school. I'll drop him home later." She lifted her brow at him. "You okay to take care of him tonight?"

"You know I am."

"Thank you." She blew him a kiss and headed to the front door. As soon as it was open, icy cold air enveloped her. She exhaled heavily, the vapor rushing out of her lips and dissolving into the air.

"It's gonna be okay," she whispered to herself. Because it had to be. She'd find the money the way she always did.

And if she couldn't? Well there was always OnlyFans. Or stripping.

And she was only half joking when she thought that.

The skies were gray overhead, heavy with the kind of snow you only got in the mountains of Winterville. Kris Winter kept his hands on the wheel, music pumping from the stereo of his rental car as he passed the old wooden sign telling him he was back in his home town, proper.

How long had it been since he'd spent any real amount of time here? He blinked when he realized it'd been more than a decade. He'd left under a cloud just like the one in the sky now, even though it had been summer back then.

A bird swooped down and he pressed the brake, slowing enough so it had time to fly back up before it hit his windshield. He had the driver's window open, the cold mountain air rushing in and clearing his lungs. He'd forgotten how it tasted different here, so very clean compared to the thick atmosphere of London where he'd made his home for more than a decade.

He took another breath, centering himself because this peace wouldn't last for long. Not when his family realized he was back. North, his eldest brother would probably mutter something about it being good to see him, and Gabe, his middle brother, would throw his arms around him in excitement, any questions about why he was here or why he'd stayed away so long wouldn't be vocalized by them.

They were as bad at emotions as he was. Three men who avoided them like they hurt to say out loud.

His cousins, however, would be different. Holly, Alaska, and Everley were all too free with their thoughts. Probably best to avoid being alone with them for too long.

He turned the corner onto the main road and wasn't sure whether to laugh or cry when he saw the town was already decorated for the holidays. Not that he should be surprised, from the moment his grandmother had founded the little town of Winterville she'd declared that it would be Christmas all year round.

Even now that she was gone, the family kept up the tradition. Or at least his brothers and cousins did. He steered the sports car he'd rented from the airport through the town square and past the huge tree in the center, that Kris knew had come from his brother's Christmas Tree Farm. The traffic was slow – the town was full of tourists at this time of year – so it took him a few minutes to make it past the Jingle Bell Theater and the Cold Start Garage, and then on to the Winterville Tavern.

The familiarity of it all felt like a kick in the gut. A reminder of easier, happier times.

Times when he hadn't been the black sheep of the family who never came home.

It was surprising how easy it had been to leave this place

behind. How quickly he'd ended one life and begun another, far away, where the memories couldn't find him. Sure, he'd kept in touch with his brothers. Sent gifts for their weddings, and to their kids when they were born. He'd even kept in touch with his cousins.

But he'd managed to forget about the visceral reaction this place and the people who lived in it gave him.

As though his thoughts were strong enough to conjure up a person, suddenly a woman walked around the corner. She was carrying two bags in her arms, her dark hair flowing out behind her. And the twist in his stomach turned into a knot that wouldn't go away.

He knew exactly who she was, even though it had been more than ten years since he'd last seen her. His mouth was dry, but he couldn't stop looking at her no matter how hard he tried.

Balancing both bags in one arm, she slid a key into the lock and opened the door to the Tavern, kicking it open and trying to step inside. But then one of the bags slid from her grasp and hit the ground, the contents – fruit and vegetables – spilling onto the sidewalk, apples and oranges rolling toward the gutter as she started hopping around and grabbing for them.

A better man would have gotten out and helped her. But Kelly Fraser had never been the kind of damsel who accepted assistance from a man like him. She opened her mouth but he couldn't hear what she was saying, though he could take a guess. She'd known all the swear words when they were kids and wasn't afraid of using them.

The woman still knew how to cuss like a sailor. Some things hadn't changed.

The guy in the car behind him honked his horn, making Kris startle. The road ahead of him had cleared. The jarring sound made Kelly look up, and he turned his head away, because he didn't want her to know he was back.

Not yet. Not until he was ready to talk to her. To beg forgiveness for what he'd done. But that wasn't now. He'd deal with his family first and Kelly second.

Her image was still seared into his brain, though. Her glossy mahogany hair falling down to her shoulders, her eyes as wide and expressive as he'd remembered. And those lips. Damn those lips. The ones that had teased him as a kid, the same way he'd riled her up every time they met for lunch in the school cafeteria. The ones he'd lusted after as a teenager.

The ones he'd kissed that fateful night.

Putting his foot on the gas, he stuck his hand out of the window and flipped the car behind him the bird, then pulled away, pushing the memories down because sometimes they were sharp as a knife.

He'd go to the Inn first, and see if his cousin Alaska, who ran it, could find him somewhere to sleep. Then he'd call North and Gabe and admit he'd come home without warning them, because he'd been in a mental debate about his return and wasn't sure he'd actually make it.

He'd almost got out of his seat before take off and walked back into the airport, after all.

But he was here now, and everything was about to hit the fan.

2

K *elly, age 11*

All the other girls were wearing dresses. Okay, not all of them, but the popular ones were. The ones sitting in the center of the cafeteria laughing with their friends, the ones who looked at her like she was a complete weirdo when she walked into class at ten this morning.

Holding her lunch tray tightly in her hands, Kelly squared her shoulders and walked over to a spare chair next to a blonde girl who looked kind of friendly. If friendly came with a wrinkled nose and narrowed eyes.

"That's taken," the blonde girl snapped. Okay, definitely not friendly.

The girl sitting next to the blonde chuckled, as though she'd told the funniest joke. She was a redhead who was wearing way more makeup than the dress code allowed. The blonde turned her back to Kelly and leaned in, muttering something to her.

Kelly took a deep breath. It was okay. First days were always bad. Especially when you didn't want to leave your old school in the first place. And especially when you left because your mom died and your dad couldn't cope with staying anywhere near the house you grew up in, so he bought a tavern in a mountain town where everybody stared at you like you weren't supposed to be there.

Another breath. This one felt more difficult. She wasn't going to cry, she just wasn't. There was an empty table in the corner. She'd sit there for the lunch hour. She had a book in her bag, it was all good.

She'd almost made it when somebody brushed past her, his shoulder bone sharp as it bumped against hers. He reached out for the chair she'd been aiming for and in her haste to walk somewhere else, she tripped over her beat up sneakers and flew into the air, sending her food and carton of chocolate milk flying.

As soon as her head hit the cold tiles she could feel the tears stinging at her eyes. She hated this school. Hated this town. Wanted to close her eyes and disappear so nobody was laughing at her.

"You okay?" Bony shoulders asked her.

"I'm fine," she muttered, even though she felt as far from fine as it was possible to be.

Ignoring her, the boy started gathering her food, putting her banana back on the tray, along with her milk carton, and the sandwich she'd chosen from the counter. He turned it over and she could see dust and hair collected on the bread.

"Yeah, you probably don't want to eat that," he said. "Come on, you can share mine."

"It's fine." She finally lifted her head, taking in his dark messy hair and black Green Day t-shirt. She was pretty sure the hand holding a grenade printed on the front of it wasn't dress code either, but he had a flannel shirt over the top. Probably buttoned it up when he was in class.

He put her tray on the table and held out his hand. For a moment she stared at it from her vantage point on the floor. It took her that long to realize he was offering to help her up.

"It's fine. I can do it myself."

"Do you know any other words?" Green Day asked.

"Like what?" She stood and brushed the dust from her shirt.

"Anything other than fine would be a start. I mean it's a good word, don't get me wrong. But a different one might be useful occasionally."

She looked at him carefully, not sure if he was being an ass or trying to be funny. He was half-smiling, his hair falling down over his eyes.

"Kris Winter," he said.

"I'm sorry?"

His smile widened. He had the kind of face that looked too young for his taller-than-her frame. Like his legs had grown but his face hadn't got the message. "My name is Kris Winter. What's yours?"

"Kelly."

He nodded, looking pleased at her answer. Like she'd given him more than she had. "Want to sit with me for lunch? I'll share my sandwich. Since it looks like you also like cheese."

"It's okay, I'll just eat my banana."

He pulled a chair out and she waited for him to sit down. Then he gave her a look and she realized it was for her. What kind of boy held chairs out? She frowned but took the seat anyway. And then he sat down next to her and put half of his sandwich on her tray. "Eat it. It was my fault you fell over."

Her stomach growled and she did as she was told, even though it bruised her pride some.

"You're new," he said.

"Yep." She bit into the sandwich and her stomach growled again. She'd been too nervous to eat breakfast. Too worried about having to meet with the principal and then meet kids she didn't know.

"That's a first. You didn't say you were fine." He was grinning now. He had these little dimples that puckered his cheeks. "So where are you living?"

"In Winterville." She put the half-eaten sandwich down and took a better look at him. He had a straight nose, the kind of nose she'd always wanted because hers had a bump on it and she hated it. His *eyes were blue, and his hair was annoying because it kind of dangled into them. She wanted to wipe it away.*

"Ah, you're the tavern girl."

She tipped her head to the side. "How'd you know that?"

"The tavern has a new owner. He has a daughter. It doesn't take a genius to figure out that's who you are." He was still smiling. And he'd spoken more words to her in the last two minutes than anybody else had all morning. Even the teacher in her first class had just pointed at a desk and then carried on with teaching the lesson. Any hope she'd had that she'd at least get somebody assigned to her as a buddy had drifted away.

When the lunch bell rang she'd followed everybody else, her purse clutched in her hand because her dad had given her exactly two dollars to pay for a sandwich. He'd looked hopeful when she left. As hopeful as he did since her mom had died.

Even if she had the worst day today, she'd tell him it was fabulous.

"Do you live in Winterville?" she asked Kris.

His grin widened. "Yeah. My grandma owns the town."

And now she felt stupid. He was related to Candy Winter. Of course he was with that last name. Her dad had bought the tavern from Candy, and he'd talked about her the whole drive here. Told Kelly about how famous Candy Winter had once been. How she'd moved back to her hometown after a Hollywood scandal and had purchased the whole town, throwing money at the place until there were jobs for everybody she loved.

Kelly opened her mouth to ask Kris about his grandmother when a voice from behind her interrupted her thoughts.

"What's the sitch?" She turned to see a sandy-haired boy grinning at them both. He sat down heavily next to Kris. Then he looked over at Kelly, his brows lifting. "Who's this."

"Kelly. Her dad bought the tavern," Kris told him. "And she's fine, so don't ask."

Kelly started to roll her eyes, but she stopped when she felt the smile tug at her lips.

"And this is Lyle. General asshole. My best friend."

"Pleased to meet you, Kelly." Lyle reached out his hand and she shook it. "So your dad bought the tavern. You think you can get us some free beer"

"No." This time she did roll her eyes. It made Kris smile.

"That would not be fine," Kris said, deadpan, looking at Lyle.

"Completely un-fine," Kelly agreed.

Lyle looked from Kelly to Kris and then back again. "You two are weird," he muttered, then grabbed his own sandwich and bit into it, still looking at her. "Wanna hang out with us after school? We're going to my place to play some Legend of Zelda.*"*

"Sure." She shrugged. "Sounds good." Her dad wouldn't mind. He'd told her she needed to make friends. She'd just have to call him from the payphone before she caught the bus.

"Excellent." Lyle stuffed the rest of his sandwich in his mouth and she peeled the skin off her banana.

It wasn't exactly paradise, but maybe school wouldn't be so bad. At least there were two people here that didn't hate her.

"Hey sweetie!" Dolores said to Kelly as she pushed the door to the Tavern open, bustling inside. Her face was flushed and she still had her apron on, Cold Fingers Café emblazoned across the front. She was wearing Christmas tree earrings, and there were gingerbread men printed on her apron. Dolores loved Christmas, especially when it brought in all the tourists.

Dolores had run the café for as long as Kelly had lived here. As a kid, she'd go in there with Kris and Lyle and they'd rifle through their pockets to get enough change to buy a hot chocolate with all the toppings. She could still remember their orders. Kelly had insisted on having it straight up, because the chocolate was sweet enough. Kris would have extra whipped cream and Lyle would get the whole hog. Whipped cream, marshmallows, and dustings of shaved chocolate.

The boy had been a sugar freak.

"What's up?" Kelly asked her, looking up from where she'd been scrubbing the counter with a spray and cloth. The Tavern had been busy all afternoon, and she knew it would be crowded this evening, so she was using the lull between services to make sure everything was spotless. She was still a little annoyed at herself for tripping earlier and spilling groceries everywhere. This took her mind off of it.

"I've been waiting for you to come into the café. Don't you want a coffee?"

Kelly hadn't been into the café for weeks. She was stashing the money for her daily caffeine injection into Cole's Christmas gift fund. "I've given up coffee," she told Dolores.

Dolores blinked as though Kelly had told her she was giving up on life. "You? Giving up coffee?" She shook her head. "Never thought I'd see the day."

"I'm trying to get healthy." Kelly shrugged. "I'm not getting any younger."

"You look pretty healthy to me," one of the guys at the counter growled. Kelly lifted a brow at him and he physically shrank back.

She'd worked at the Tavern before she was legal to be serving alcohol. First as a kid helping her dad out during the weekends and holidays. Then when she left school she started working here full time. It was her second home. One of the constants in her life. Like her dad and Cole, and Winterville itself.

And now she ran the place. And she didn't take shit from anybody. Even ones giving back handed compliments.

"Anyway, that's not why I'm here," Dolores said, breathless. "Have you heard?"

"Heard what?"

Dolores looked to the left and then to her right, as though she was a spy and needed to make sure the coast was clear. Then she lowered her voice enough that Kelly had to crane her neck to hear her.

"Guess who's back in town?"

"Who?" Kelly asked.

"I just told you." Dolores frowned.

"No you didn't. You said 'guess who's back in town?'" Kelly said, trying not to smile. Dolores loved to gossip and though Kelly loved it less – especially since she'd been the object of Winterville gossip for years – she still loved Dolores. Everybody did. She was the town's grandmother now that they no longer had Candy Winter around. She knew everyone and everything that went on here in town. The only thing she didn't gossip about was herself, or her supposedly secret relationship with Charlie Shaw.

Funny that.

"I said Kris is back in town," Dolores said pointedly.

Kelly stopped cleaning, her hand frozen as it grasped onto the cloth. She looked up, trying to keep her face expressionless. "I'm sorry?" She must have misheard.

"Kris Winter," Dolores said slowly, like Kelly was hard of hearing. "He's back in town."

Kelly's heart slammed against her chest. "He's here? Now?"

"Yes, now. He's at the Inn with his family. I heard one of the waiters talking about it when he came in after his shift for coffee."

Her heart wasn't slowing down. If anything it was faster now, a constant hammer against her ribcage. She hadn't seen Kris Winter in more than a decade.

Not since that day. The one she never wanted to think about again.

Her hand shook as she picked up the spray again, pressing the trigger to moisten the cloth. "That's nice," she said, keeping her voice even. "I bet North and his family are happy."

"You could say that. I hear there was a huge rumpus at the Inn when he walked in. The whole family rushed there, even though they're all crazy busy at this time of year."

That was true. North ran the Christmas Tree Farm, and Gabe ran the ski resort that had opened recently thanks to their first layer of snow. Kris' cousins were also immersed in the family business – Everley ran the Jingle Bell Theater, Alaska headed up the Inn, and Holly was the business woman who kept an eye on the whole town.

The door to the Tavern opened again, and this time it was Amber, Kelly's best friend and North Winter's wife. Amber looked at Dolores, her brow crinkling. She was huffing, as though she'd run from wherever she'd managed to park her car.

And when her eyes caught Kelly's, Kelly knew her friend was there for only one reason.

To warn her that Kris was back. But she was too late.

"Dolores," Amber said, walking over and putting a winter cooled hand on the older woman's arm. "There's a huge line forming at the café."

Dolores' mouth fell open. "Oh my. I should get back." She flashed a smile at Kelly. "Sorry, honey, gotta go."

As soon as she'd bustled out, Amber leaned on the counter, cupping her swollen stomach with her palm. She was pregnant with her second child, her stomach as round as a basketball.

"You okay?" Kelly asked her, concerned for her friend. She and Amber had become close friends over the past few years.

"I wanted to be the first to tell you." Amber's eyes met Kelly's. "Damn Dolores."

"It's okay," Kelly said, keeping her voice light. "We all know Dolores would run a four minute mile to spread some gossip."

Amber laughed softly. "North said he turned up this morning. Just walked into the Inn like he hadn't been away for over a decade. Alaska threw a fit, of course, and then called everybody and told us all to get there ASAP. North's kind of annoyed with him for not giving us notice, but he can't say anything because he's so happy to see Kris."

Kelly nodded and took a deep breath.

"Did he say how long he's here for?" Kelly asked her.

Amber shook her head. "No. I think everybody was too afraid to ask him. I never thought he'd come back." Amber hadn't known Kris well before he left. She knew he and Kelly used to be friends, but that was it.

"I guess we'll find out at some point," Kelly said. And she had no idea how to feel about that. He'd once told her he would never come back. Promised it, even.

Although back then it had felt more like a threat than a promise. And now? It just felt a little sad.

The door to the tavern opened for a third time, and for a second Kelly's heart rate shot up. But this time it was Cole, his backpack slung over his shoulder, his jacket nowhere to be seen.

"Hey sweetheart," Kelly said, lifting a brow at the way he wasn't wearing a jacket despite it being freezing outside. When had kids stopped wearing coats in the depth of winter? She'd never left home without being warm when she was younger, but now they walked around like it was the middle of summer in December. "How was school?"

"Boring." Cole shrugged his backpack off and put it on the stool next to Amber. "Hey Auntie Amber."

"Hey Cole." Amber ruffled his hair the way that Kelly had this morning. This time his cheeks pinked up. He was too polite to protest when Amber did it, unlike when Kelly annoyed him.

"I'm gonna have to love you and leave you," Amber said, shooting Kelly a look. "I'll call you later." She ruffled Cole's hair again and this time he wrinkled his nose. "Be good for your mom."

"I will."

Kelly watched her friend leave, then looked back at her son. "You got homework?"

"Yep." He wrinkled his nose. "Math and English."

"Grab the table in the office," she told him, lifting the counter for him to walk behind the bar. "You can start working, and I'll bring you some dinner. Grandpa's expecting you home at six."

"Thanks Mom." He smiled at her, and she felt herself relax. Cole was the important one here. Nothing else mattered. Not her memories, not her emotions.

And definitely not Kris Winter. Any feelings she had for him were in the past. If she saw him around town she'd nod and walk on by.

She was certain he wouldn't want to talk to her anyway.

❧ 3 ❧

"To Kris," his brother North said, holding up a glass of champagne. Everybody repeated North's words, beaming at Kris with pure happiness. Kris tried to smile back at everyone, but he felt like an asshole.

As soon as he'd walked through the door of the Winterville Inn, it was like he'd climbed into a rollercoaster car that was never going to stop. Alaska had been at the reception desk and it had taken her a moment to recognize him, but then she'd squealed and run over to him, insisting on introducing him to everybody.

Before he knew it, North had arrived from the Christmas Tree Farm, along with his other brother Gabe, who ran the ski resort on the outskirts of Winterville.

And now his whole family was here. The ones of his generation, anyway. His cousins and their husbands, his brothers and their wives. And kids. So many kids. The last time he'd been here they were the youngest generation, and now there were little people everywhere.

He felt like Rip Van Winkle. He'd gone to sleep for years and when he woke up everything had changed.

North had insisted that they have a party to welcome him home that evening, so here they were. *His family.* The ones he'd run from. And they were welcoming him home with open arms.

"I still can't believe you're here," Everley said, hugging his waist. She'd arrived late because she wanted to make sure the revue at the Jingle Bell Theater had started without any problems. Her son, Finn was asleep in the corner in a little chair, his thumb stuck in his mouth. Next to him was North's daughter, Willow, who was as cute as a button. "How long do we get to keep you for?"

Kris swallowed a mouthful of champagne. He'd been expecting that question all day. But it was like they were all too scared to ask except Everley. "A few weeks." Truth was, he wasn't sure. He didn't want to make promises he couldn't keep.

He'd learned that much over the years.

"Are you staying for Christmas?" she asked, looking hopeful.

"Maybe." It depended. He wasn't exactly popular around here. Especially with certain town residents.

"Oh, please stay. Imagine us all together for Christmas." Everley's hug got tighter. "When was the last time that happened?"

"When Grandma was alive." He lifted a brow. He'd been back since, once, for the funeral, but that was in the summer, nowhere near the holidays.

The funeral had been a big enough affair to get lost in. An ex-Hollywood darling, Candy Winter's name brought in the crowds from all around. It was easy enough to avoid *her* then.

But not now.

"Gabe, tell Kris he has to stay for Christmas," Everley called out to his middle brother. Gabe walked over, an easygoing smile on his face. His four month old son was in a papoose on his chest. Gabe looked pleased as hell to be carrying him.

"You are staying, aren't you?" Gabe asked.

"He says he's not sure." Everley pouted. She always had been the drama queen of the family. She took after their grandmother that way.

"I'm just gonna play things by ear," Kris told them. Gabe gave him a look. The kind of look he used to give Kris when they were kids and he knew he'd been up to no good.

They'd all had their roles to play growing up. North was the strong one, the leader. Gabe was the chilled out middle son. And Kris was the black sheep. The one who always caused problems and got into trouble.

"It'd mean the world to us all if you were here," Gabe said, stroking his son's downy head.

"How's he doing?" Kris asked, nodding at his nephew.

"Ah, he's having a ball. Sleeps when he should be awake, screams when we all want to sleep, and shits as soon as we put a new diaper on him."

Kris bit down a smile.

"We got your gift by the way," Gabe continued. "Wyatt loves it."

"I know." Kris nodded. "Nicole sent a thank you card."

"She did?" Gabe looked surprised. "Well okay then. Thank you again."

Kris smiled. "You're welcome."

Wyatt snuffled against Gabe's chest, then turned his head, his pale blue eyes looking at Kris. Kris lifted a brow at him and Wyatt tipped his head, tiny lines appearing in his brow.

"He likes you," Everley whispered.

"Of course he does. I'm eminently likeable." And he'd had some experience with babies. Been a stepdad to one for as long as you could blink an eye. But he'd messed that up the way he messed up everything.

23

Leaving a trail of broken lives behind him.

"And you're staying for Christmas," Everley said firmly. "Or I'm going to chase you to the airport and drag you back."

His eyes met Gabe's. His brother gave a shrug which Kris knew well. It meant just go with it. Be chill. Everything's going to be okay.

"I'll probably stay until Christmas," Kris told her and Everley let out a squeal of pleasure.

"Yes! I'm so happy." She hugged him even tighter. "This is going to be the best Christmas yet."

Kris woke up at a stupidly early hour the following morning. He'd stayed in one of North's guest rooms at his brother's insistence, while Alaska arranged for his cabin at the Inn to be ready.

Pulling some clothes from his suitcase on, he tiptoed into the kitchen, being careful not to wake up North or his family, because Amber was pregnant and she deserved some sleep. Grabbing his coat from the hook by the door, he slid his feet into his engineer boots and decided to walk into town to grab some coffee.

It had snowed overnight. Enough for his feet to make imprints in the sidewalk as he passed the Cold Start Garage. There was a guy sitting in his car outside the garage drinking a coffee and eating what looked like a breakfast burger. He glanced up at Kris and looked away, uninterested. That made a change, at least.

A few cars passed him as he made it into the town square. And then his phone buzzed and he grabbed it out of his pocket, his brow lifting when he saw who was calling.

"Hey. You're up early."

"I'm on the first shift," Alaska said. "Just wanted to let

you know your cabin should be ready by lunchtime. The cleaners are already in this morning, and the electrician will go in later to make sure that everything's in working order."

"You didn't need to do that," Kris protested. "I could have done it."

"I know, but you're our guest. And I have a vested interest in making your stay as cosy as possible," Alaska told him.

"How did you know I was awake anyway?"

"Amber called. She said your coat and boots were gone. Just wanted to make sure you didn't skip town while everyone was sleeping."

Of course. You couldn't do anything around here without somebody noticing. He wasn't sure if he liked that or not yet.

"I'll pay you back," Kris promised. He'd always had time for Alaska. The quietest of the cousins, she was the kindest, too. And they'd once almost lost her as a kid.

It was hard to forget that.

"Actually, I was hoping you'd say that. We could use some help on the Christmas Trail."

"The what?"

She laughed. "We're building a trail around the Inn for the kids. Lots of twists and turns and things to find. A little bit of fun. It opens soon but we need some extra hands to get everything set."

"Happy to help," Kris said. "You can tell me all about it later.

"It's a deal." She sounded happy, and that made him kind of happy too. "I'll see you later."

"Yes you will," Kris promised. "And thanks. For everything."

"It's a pleasure," Alaska told him. "I'm just glad you're home."

When she ended the call, he pushed the phone back into his pocket and walked into the warmth of the Cold Fingers

Café. The place was decorated for the holidays, garland and ornaments covering every surface, with a large tree adorned in sparkling lights in the corner.

He headed straight to the counter because he needed caffeine like he needed oxygen right now.

"Kristopher Winter," Dolores said, a huge smile splitting her face. "I heard you were back and I was wondering how long it'd take you to come by to say hi. I was about to pull your scrawny behind out of North's place and demand a hug."

A smile quirked his lips. "Dolores, you look more beautiful than ever." He had no idea how old she was, though she had to be past sixty. But she had one of those smooth faces that never really aged.

Before he could say anything else, Dolores lifted the counter flap and bustled through to pull him into her arms. At six-three he towered over her. He could remember a time when they were all scared of Dolores.

Now it felt like cuddling a teddy bear.

"What can I get you?" she asked, patting his cheek. "You look tired, honey. Don't they make good coffee in London?"

He shook his head and that made her smile again.

"I'll have an Americano, please."

"Cream, no sugar, right? Or have you changed your order since you left?"

"You remembered." He needed the caffeine hit. Just in case he decided to do what he'd come here to do.

"You drinking here or would you like it to go?"

"I'll take it to go."

While Dolores filled the machine with coffee, he looked around the café. There were a few early birds at the tables. And a few more workers who'd come in behind him to get their start-of-the-day caffeine hit. He knew from experience that the tourists wouldn't arrive until later. Those who were staying at the Inn would be eating breakfast in the restaurant, and the ones who came for the day wouldn't arrive for a few more hours.

This time of day was for the locals. The ones heading for work, clearing the roads, and serving food to the tourists. He used to savor it when he was a kid.

It was funny how quickly the memories came back. He'd spent the last decade trying to forget this place existed.

But it had been here all along, waiting for him.

Five minutes later he was walking into the square, a Styrofoam coffee cup in one hand, a bag with a muffin in the other — courtesy of Dolores, even though he insisted he didn't want anything. He reached a bench and dusted the snow off of it, shrugging off his jacket and putting it between his ass and the wooden slats so his jeans wouldn't get wet.

A car pulled up about twenty feet away from where he was sitting. He looked over, taking in the rusty hunk of junk that was coughing out exhaust into the cold air, and his heart slammed against his chest because he knew exactly who it belonged to.

It was the kind of death trap Kelly had always driven.

The door opened and sure enough she climbed out. She was wearing a cream padded coat and brown boots that hit just below her knee. Her hair was flowing out over her shoulders, tamed only by a wool hat she'd pulled over her ears.

She hated being cold. He could remember that. All those times he'd built a fire in his cabin to stop her from shivering. Or leant her his coat because her own wasn't enough.

He shifted, lifting his cup to his lips and checked the time. It was almost seven. Too early for her to be opening. But she pulled a set of keys out of her pocket and slid one into the lock on the tavern door, but instead of turning it she suddenly froze.

And slowly turned to look at him.

Had she sensed he was there? Was it weird that he hoped she had?

Her eyes caught his, but there was no expression of surprise on her face. So she knew he was back. That wasn't a surprise. The grapevine worked hard in Winterville.

Her lips parted and he could see her breath hit the air. She was even more beautiful than he remembered. Creamy skin and doe eyes that he hadn't been able to forget no matter how far he'd run. He couldn't see the color from here but he could pick it out from a chart if you asked him to.

Brown with hazel flecks. And just one blue fleck in her right eye.

Sure, she was older. He was too. But she wore it better. Keeping his gaze steady, he took another sip of his coffee.

Then instead of opening the door, she pulled the key from the lock and turned on her heel, her eyes narrowing as she hurried across the road toward him.

Damn, she looked furious. And she should. He took a deep breath, readying himself for the onslaught.

4

"So, you're back." The words escaped her lips before she could appreciate the stupidity of them. He was lounging on a bench drinking coffee and watching her. But she had to say something because she wasn't going to let him win this staring match.

And if he was here for a while she needed to set some parameters between them.

Because this was *her* home. She didn't care that it bore his family's name or that along with his brothers and his cousins he owned a share of the land here. He was the one who left without taking a backward glance.

She was the one who'd stayed and paid the price.

"Looks like it," he murmured. His gaze lifted to hers again. She was shocked at the intensity of her reaction to him. Her body felt tight, on edge. Like her muscles had memories of him that her mind had tried to forget.

Anger rose up inside of her and she let it, because it stopped her from feeling the pain.

"Are you planning on spending your days stalking the tavern?" she asked, her voice tight.

His mouth twitched. Was he finding this funny?

"I'm not stalking the tavern. I'm sitting on a bench drinking coffee. You're the one who's disturbing the peace."

She crossed her arms over her chest and it made him smile more. Which made the fury inside of her heighten.

And then he slowly stood and she found herself having to tilt her head to look at him.

Had he always been this tall? Yeah, he had, but somehow he'd grown into his height. In his early twenties he'd still had a leanness to him, but now he looked muscled and strong. She was sure he could still lift her without losing his breath.

"But while you're here, I'd like to talk to you," he said. She tried not to stare at his mouth as he talked. It was too easy to remember how it once felt against hers.

"No." She shook her head. "That's not happening." She'd spent way too long getting over Kris Winter to give him an opportunity to hurt her again. It had taken her years to build the wall around her cracked heart.

She wasn't going to let him sledgehammer it apart.

"I have to go," she told him. "Have a great stay."

"I'll see you around."

She shook her head, even though she knew it was true. Winterville was too small not to bump into him while he was here.

Hopefully he'd be gone before she knew it.

She turned on her heels and started to walk away, because she couldn't stay close to him.

Couldn't bear to look at the man who'd broken her in every way.

"How's your dad?" he shouted out when she was a few feet away.

"He's fine." Another lie.

"I heard about his knees. I'm sorry."

She turned back around to look at him. He hadn't moved

from his spot next to the bench. He was wearing a hoodie and a pair of jeans, his thick hair lifting in the winter breeze. And for a moment he looked like the boy she'd loved so much it had consumed her.

And suddenly she was remembering the day they'd borrowed North's boat and had zoomed around the lake, chasing otters and fish, the three of them – her, Lyle, and Kris – laughing out loud. He'd held the tiller, the breeze rushing through his hair, a grin on his face as she'd squealed every time he'd sped up.

They'd all been browned from the sun, but his nose had peeled to reveal pink flesh. How young they'd been then. How hopeful. How happy.

So different to now.

She blinked the memory away and concentrated on the man standing in the square, not the boy she'd once loved.

Because they weren't the same.

He'd leave again. Because if anybody was good at leaving, it was Kris Winter. He'd perfected running away to an Olympic level.

But this time he wouldn't take her heart with him.

Kris, Age 13

"You need to keep a grip on the tiller and keep it steady," North said, pointing to the stick jutting horizontally from the outboard engine. They'd been begging North to let them take the boat out all summer. His older brother hadn't had time to take them until now – he'd been too busy working at the Inn for their grandmother and hanging out with his friends to pay much attention to three thirteen year olds' desperate need for adventure.

It was a blistering hot day, the sun was shining down on the lake, the surface dappled with diamonds as he looked out on it. He was wearing an old t-shirt and some jersey shorts – Gabe's hand-me-downs because his mom was annoyed that he kept growing too fast – and Lyle was in a basketball tank and shorts that his dad had bought him for his birthday.

Kelly was in cut offs and one of Kris' old t-shirts. His Green Day one. She'd always loved it.

And now the three of them were hanging on North's every word, barely able to hide their excitement at being allowed to take the boat out on the lake.

"If you want to go forward you pull this arm forward," North continued. "Push it into the middle for neutral and back for reverse."

"Got it," Kris said, nodding. North had to be at work in an hour and he'd ridden his bike down to the lake with them, so he didn't have long to show the kids what to do. Beside him, Kelly was listening intently. Lyle, on the other hand, was throwing stones in the water, already bored with North's lecture.

"And don't forget to push the tiller in the opposite direction you want to go. Left for right, right for left."

"Port," Kelly said. "Isn't that the right word for right? And star-board is left?"

North turned his attention to her. "Yeah, that's right. But I thought this lumphead wouldn't know those."

"I didn't." Kris shrugged. "Right and left are fine."

"This is the engine cut off." North pointed at a curled plastic pull attached to a switch. "Use it if you need it. And clip the front end to your shorts."

Kris took a deep breath. He knew all these things. But North was an annoying older brother who liked to show him up in front of his friends.

"And don't go too fast," North said.

"We won't," Kelly assured him. And North smiled at her.

"*Thank God one of you is sensible,*" he said, and Kelly beamed like the sun above them.

"*Can we go now?*" Kris asked, rolling his eyes.

"*Yep. I'll keep an eye on you from here for a minute. Once I think you've got it I'll head off. Make sure you tie it up when you're done, okay?*"

"*Sure.*"

"*And don't tell Mom and Dad I let you do this. They'll kill me.*" North caught his gaze.

Kris nodded. They barely told their parents anything. Even if they did, they probably wouldn't listen. They were too busy playing bridge with their friends to pay attention to the boys.

The three of them clambered onto the boat, Lyle putting his arms out to steady himself as he headed for the bench seat in the middle. Kris took the low seat next to the engine at the back and Kelly sat next to him, watching as he started it up the way North showed him.

He slowly pushed the tiller forward and the engine hummed as they moved forward slowly.

"*Kel, come see this,*" Lyle called from the front of the boat.

"*What?*" Kelly asked, scrambling forward. Kris kept his hand steady on the tiller.

"*That's an otter, see?*"

Kelly shaded her eyes with her hand, following the direction of his pointed finger. "*It can't be. Otters don't swim in lakes.*"

"*It is,*" Lyle insisted. He put his hand on her back and for some reason that pissed Kris off. Maybe it was because his two friends were having fun while he had to carefully steer the boat.

"*Otters swim in rivers,*" Kelly pointed out.

"*Not this one.*"

Kris steered the boat closer, but the otter noticed them coming, diving beneath the surface and swimming away.

"*Chase him,*" Lyle urged.

"*I can't. North will kill me.*" If he sped the boat up now his brother would never let him drive it again.

"Spoilsport," Lyle muttered. He'd shaved his hair off that summer. They both had. Kelly had told him he looked like a thug. He was probably going to grow it back out again, because he preferred it long.

And he kind of missed the way Kelly tugged it to annoy him.

Like she knew he was thinking about her, Kelly turned to look at him. The hot summer sun caught her hair, making it look golden and sparkly. His throat felt tight, which was weird because this was Kelly, his best friend along with Lyle.

It was always the three of them. Had been since that day he'd tripped her in the school cafeteria. North called them the three muske-teers, always doing things they shouldn't be. And yeah, he liked that a lot.

So why did he keep looking at Kelly's hair?

"North is waving at you," Kelly said, her eyes catching his.

"He is?"

"Yep. You better see what he wants."

Kris turned around to see his brother standing on the deck, gesturing at him.

"What?" Kris shouted, but North couldn't hear him over the engine. Sighing, he carefully turned the boat around and headed back to the pier. Lyle reached over the side of the boat and scooped up some water and threw it at Kelly.

She screamed and slapped his arm. Lyle grinned hard.

"I gotta go," North told him. "Remember our agreement?"

"Yep."

"Good. Come see me at the Inn when you're done. So I know you're alive."

"Sure."

North looked at Kelly. "Keep an eye on them for me."

"Why don't you ask me to do that?" Lyle said. "I'll keep an eye on them."

"Because you're an idiot like my brother." North lifted a hand in goodbye. "Have fun, kids."

*As soon as he turned around, Lyle pulled Kelly into a headlock.
"Just so you know, you're an idiot, too."*

"Shut up," Kelly said, but she was grinning.

*Kris pulled the boat away from the pier, feeling the air rush
against his face, determined to ignore the twist in his stomach that
still wouldn't leave.*

*He was lucky. He got to spend the summer with his two best
friends, playing in a boat on a lake.*

He wasn't going to let anything spoil that.

5

Kelly was in the middle of a dream about the Tavern running out of beer when the sound of Cole's voice cut through. For a moment her brain tried to bring him into her reverie, but it gave up the fight, forcing her eyes open.

"Mom?"

Cole was looming over her, his brows pulled down. She opened her mouth to talk, but it was so dry. It felt like she'd just spent ninety days in the desert. "What time is it?" Her voice was low and raspy.

"It's almost nine."

"Sh—Oh holy moly." She sat up. "Why didn't you wake me up?"

Cole shrugged. "It's Saturday. No school. And I was watching YouTube. But we probably need to go soon."

Oh damn. Cole had a hockey game today. She was supposed to drive him there and his friend's mom would drive him to the Tavern later, dropping him off so Kelly could give him dinner before it started to fill up.

Grabbing her robe, she jumped out of bed and pulled it

around her. According to the clock by her bed, they had twenty minutes before they had to leave.

It took every one of those minutes to shower and make herself look respectable, and apply a slick of make up on her face. She had to open the Tavern for the lunchtime customers as soon as she'd dropped Cole off at the rink, and wouldn't have time to get herself ready in between.

"You got everything?" she asked, bustling out of her bedroom, sliding her watch onto her wrist.

"Yep." Cole's bag was already slung over his shoulder, his new skates dangling from the straps.

"And you've eaten breakfast?"

"Grandpa made me some."

Her dad was sitting on the easy chair in the living room, watching some kind of animal documentary on the TV.

"Good. Come on then, let's get out of here." She blew a kiss at her dad, then rushed Cole out of the door, ten minutes later than she'd planned. Luckily, he was in as much of a rush as she was to get to the hockey rink, so he pretty much hurled himself into the backseat, along with his bag, and had already done his seatbelt up before she'd climbed inside.

"Can you put your foot on it, please?" he asked.

She looked at him, amused. "I'll be keeping to the speed limit, thank you very much."

"I hate being late."

"Should have woken me up earlier then." He got his fear of being late from her. She ran her life on such a tight schedule and he'd been swallowed up in her need to be every-where early. "It's fine. You won't miss anything. Maybe just a little warm up."

The roads were busy as they headed through town. The tourist traffic was increasing week to week as the holidays approached, and she hit her first set of taillights before she'd made it to the main road out of town.

"Mom..." Cole's voice was plaintive.

"It's okay," she told him. "I know a shortcut."

It wasn't one she particularly liked, because it went through the country backroads that could get blocked up with snow in the winter. But they hadn't had any for a few days, and if it was a choice between putting her big girl pants on and driving down narrow country lanes or having Cole miss his hockey game she knew which one she'd chose.

A few cars honked as she turned around, but she rolled her eyes because it wasn't as though she was stopping them from moving. Then she took a left past the theater, and a right onto a steep incline, gritting her teeth because the road surface wasn't the best and her car's suspension was non-existent.

Cole leaned forward. "Mom, what's that noise?"

Kelly blinked out of her thoughts. "What noise?"

A loud clunk came from the engine.

She swallowed hard. "I'm not sure. Probably needs some oil or something. I'll get Charlie to look at it next week."

"I hate this car," Cole complained.

So did she. "Yeah, well it's the only one we've got."

As soon as the words escaped her lips, she saw the smoke rising from the hood. Damn it! She hit the brake and pulled to the side of the road, her tires hitting the piles of snow that edged the forest beyond.

"Mom?" Cole said, his voice high.

"Get out of the car, honey." She took a deep breath, trying not to sound like she was panicking.

"What's happening?" Cole's voice was tremulous. "What's wrong with the car?"

"I don't know. Please get out." Kelly unclasped her seatbelt, trying not to panic. She had visions of the whole thing blowing up with them inside. "And go stand by the trees."

"But it's cold. Can't we stay in here?"

"*No!*" It came out more vehement than she intended. A mixture of fear and urgency sending her voice sky high. She scrambled out of the car and wrenched his door open, and Cole stepped out.

"Go stand by the trees," she said again.

"But why?"

Kelly took a deep breath. "Because if the car blows up I don't want you anywhere near it. And if another car drives by they may swerve and hit us if we're too close to the road."

Her words must have hit home because Cole nodded, his questions forgotten. "Can I bring my bag? I don't want my hockey stuff to blow up."

She exhaled heavily. "Yeah, I'll bring it over."

A moment later she put both of their bags by the tree she'd insisted Cole sit by. His brows were pinched. "I'm not gonna get to play today, am I?"

She pressed her lips together in sympathy. "I don't know. I'm gonna call Charlie and see if he can help us. Then I'll call one of the other moms and ask them to pick you up."

Cole nodded, but said nothing. She felt the ache of his disappointment as she dialed the Cold Start Garage, muttering a curse when it went straight to voicemail. She left a quick message explaining what had happened and where she was, then tried Charlie's cell phone.

"I'm over in Marshall's Gap," he said after she'd apprised him of the situation. "Everybody's car is failing today. I can probably get to you in an hour."

Cole's game would be half finished by then. But that wasn't Charlie's fault. It was hers. "Okay, no problem. I'll be waiting." It wasn't as though she had anywhere else to go.

Cole's lip wobbled, but he said nothing.

She called three different moms from the team but none

of them answered. They were probably all driving right now. Then she called her dad, but he didn't pick up either.

Kelly gritted her teeth with frustration. Why did nobody answer their damn phones anymore?

Cole's teeth started to chatter.

"Put on your jersey, honey," she suggested. "An extra layer will help." She was feeling damn cold herself, but she pushed it out of her mind. She needed to think.

Cole hunkered down to rifle through his bag. But then he suddenly stopped, looking up from his bag to the road ahead of them.

"Is that a car?" he asked.

Kelly looked in the direction that Cole was pointing, further up the foothills. A little tiny blip was moving in their direction, disappearing around a curve then reappearing again. Getting bigger. Closer.

Yep, it was definitely a car. Thank the lord.

Cole stood. "We need to stop him."

"Or her," Kelly said because she was damned if her son was going to show any unconscious bias.

"Either way they could help us."

She gave him a soft smile. "Don't get your hopes up, honey. Could be a lost tourist. They don't tend to stop."

But Cole was already up and running toward the road. "Hey!" he shouted, even though the driver was way too far in the distance to hear them. "We need help. Mayday! Mayday!"

"Keep back," Kelly called out to him, running over to where he was jumping up and down. Their car had stopped smoking but there was still a danger that this approaching driver wouldn't see them. Reluctantly, Cole took a couple of steps back, and Kelly walked firmly in front of him. If anybody was going to get hit it would be her.

As it got close she saw the car was sleek and dark, the

windows tinted in the way only an expensive car would be. Cole was still shouting, and she started to wave her arms.

The car slowed to a stop. And she finally allowed relief to wash over her.

"He stopped!" Cole shouted, his cheeks pink with excitement.

"It could be a she," she pointed out. *Again.*

"I don't care if it's a dog. They stopped!" Cole sounded so excited she hated to dampen his fervour. But Kelly grabbed her phone because she'd seen enough true crime shows to know that a woman and a boy on the edge of the road were vulnerable.

The car door opened and two long, muscled legs climbed out.

Not a she, then.

Then her heart almost stopped because she recognized who those legs belonged to.

"Hey!" Cole called out. "Our car is on fire."

Kris' eyes caught hers and she swallowed hard.

Of all the damn people who could be here to help, it had to be him. Although he was the one who'd showed her this shortcut, back when they'd been little more than kids with their drivers' licences so fresh the ink would still smudge.

"You need some help?" He was wearing a dark leather jacket and a beanie, his jeans clinging to his thighs like they were in love with them.

She swallowed hard. "It's okay, Charlie should be here soon to tow us back to town."

"You said he'd be at least an hour," Cole said, frowning. Damn the honesty of kids. "I've got a game to get to."

"What kind of game?" Kris asked.

"I play hockey," Cole told him, looking proud. "I'm the center."

Kris smiled at Cole and it made her feel weird. "I used to play center, too."

"You play hockey?" Cole's face lit up.

"Yeah. Used to play with your dad in high school."

Cole's mouth dropped open. "You know my dad?" He turned to look at Kelly, his eyes shining. "Mom, this guy knows Dad."

Kris' eyes darted from Cole to Kelly. "You're Cole, right?"

"Yeah."

All those lectures about not talking to strangers had clearly not worked. Kelly put her hand on her son's shoulder. "Honey, go back to the trees."

"Why?" Cole shook her hand off. "He knows Dad. He's a friend. He's here to help. Can you get our car going Mister..."

"Winter."

Cole blinked. "Your last name's Winter?"

"Yep." Kris nodded.

"Like Auntie Amber and Uncle North?"

Kelly felt like she was going to throw up.

"Yeah. North is my brother."

Cole tipped his head to the side. "Isn't Gabe his brother?"

For the first time Kris smiled. She hated how handsome this man was. "Yeah, Gabe's my other brother. I'm Kris." He held out his hand and Cole shook it, looking pleased as punch to be treated like an adult.

"You have two brothers? Cool." Cole let go of his hand but was still looking at him hopefully. "Can you fix our car?"

Kris shrugged. "I can take a look."

"It's overheated," Kelly told him. "It's not going anywhere. The last time Charlie looked at it he told me it was on its last leg."

The hope on Cole's face faded.

"It's okay," she told him. "I'll get another car." Somehow.

Damn, this really was the last thing she needed. Especially in front of *him*.

Kris looked at his watch. "What time's your game start?"

"In half an hour," Cole said. He was still staring at Kris like he was fascinated.

"Is it at the new rink?"

Kelly nodded.

Kris shot her the smallest of smiles then looked back at Cole. "I think if we leave now we can just about get you there on time."

Cole's face lit up like it was Christmas morning. "You can?"

"No," Kelly said firmly, and they both turned to look at her.

"But Mom..." Cole whined.

"I have to wait with the car. And you're not going to the rink with a stranger." Her voice was firm.

"You can come with. I'll leave you guys there and I'll come back and take care of the car," Kris said, and she wanted to scream. He wasn't supposed to be nice. And Cole wasn't supposed to be looking at him like he was Thor and Superman all tied up into one lovely package.

She was supposed to be able to sort out her problems on her own.

"I have to get to work after I drop Cole off," she said.

Kris' eyes caught hers. "Then we'll drop him off and come back here, sort your car out, and you can work. Or I'll drop you off at work then come back here." He tipped his head to the side, still looking at her. "It's easy if you want it to be."

"Please, Mom." Cole tugged her hand. "I want to play in the game."

Her heart was racing. It was one thing to see Kris in the street, another thing to sit in his car.

And something even more terrifying to have him help her

like they were friends. But Cole was still looking at her with those wide eyes and she knew she was going to have to ignore the stubbornness inside of her. For her son. For his game.

"Okay then," she said, her voice tight. "A ride would be great. Thank you."

"Yes." Cole pumped his fist. "Let's go."

6

Kelly was sitting stiffly in the passenger seat, her lips closed as Kris followed the GPS in the direction of the new ice rink. He'd tried to make small talk for about half a second, but the expression on her face had silenced him.

Luckily Cole had kept up a steady stream of conversation, asking Kris about his hockey playing past, about how he knew his dad, whether he'd won any trophies and if he'd gone to the same school that Cole did.

Kris answered easily, keeping his foot on the gas to make sure they got to the rink on time. And when they arrived, Cole grabbed his bag and jumped out of the car. "I'm going straight to the locker room," he said excitedly. "Thanks for the ride. You rock."

Kelly opened the door and climbed out, pulling him in for a hug. From the corner of her eye she could see that Kris had climbed out of the driver's side and was watching them both.

"I gotta go, Mom."

She nodded and let him go. "Good luck!" she told him. "Don't break a leg."

"Mom..." Cole shook his head.

"And Riley's mom's bringing you home after the game. Come straight to the Tavern."

"I will. Now can I go?"

"Yes. What do you say to Mr. Winter?"

Cole looked up at him. He had the same eyes as Kelly. Wide, expressive, brown with those damn flecks. "Thank you, Mr. Winter."

"It's Kris. And you're welcome. Good luck with the game."

"Thank you." Cole grinned and turned on his heel, running across the parking lot.

Kris brought his attention to Kelly. She was wearing a thin jacket, her hair pulled into a messy bun. She had hardly any make up on but she'd never needed it. Kelly had always been naturally pretty.

"Don't you want to go in and watch him?" Kris asked.

"I can't." She shook her head. "I have to go to work." She glanced at her watch, her jacket rising up her arm with the movement, revealing her slender wrist. "Damn, I should already be there."

"Then get back in. I'll give you a ride."

Kelly didn't move. Just looked at the car and then her mouth did that little twist he could remember she always did when she was undecided about something. It was coming back to him now. The memories of how she'd waver between an egg salad or cheese sandwich on the days she bought lunch in the school cafeteria.

He opened the passenger door. "Get in, Kelly."

"It's fine. I can get a ride back to the car. I have to wait until Charlie gets there anyhow. The Tavern will have to wait."

Fine. He opened his mouth to tease her about the word then shut it again, because now wasn't the time.

But she wasn't fine. He knew her better than that. Or at

least once he had. She'd want to get to the tavern as soon as possible. The place was everything to her, the same way it was to her dad.

"Will you just get in?" he asked.

"No."

Kris sighed. Long and loud enough for her to hear and give him a dirty look. "Are we going to do this again?"

"Do what? I haven't seen you in years." God, she was cute when she was frustrated.

"Do the whole *'you don't need any help because you're a kick ass independent woman'* and then we'll fight until you finally let me do something?"

She folded her arms across her chest. "I don't want any help from you because I know what happens if I get it."

"What happens?" His voice was tight.

"You take off and leave me to mop up the pieces."

He ran his hand through his hair. "Jesus, Kelly."

"Jesus, Kelly what?" she asked, her brows pinching.

"Jesus, Kelly can you get in the car and we'll have this argument as I drive you back to town?" He shook his head. "You haven't changed a damn bit, have you?"

She took a deep breath, the action lifting her chest. "How would you know? You haven't been here."

She said it softly, but he felt the accusation deep in his gut. And it twisted because she was right. He *hadn't* been there. Hadn't wanted to. He'd walked away and she'd paid the price.

He was supposed to be making amends, not causing more problems.

"Please get in the car," he said, his voice quieter now. "I'm driving back anyway."

She paused for a moment. Then nodded, not looking at him as she finally climbed back into the passenger seat. He closed the door behind her and walked around the car, pressing his lips together because dealing with Kelly was like dealing with a wild cat.

She bit, she scratched, but deep down she had a heart of soft wool.

Even if she never admitted it.

"I'm sorry for snapping. Thank you for the ride," she said, her voice tight. "And for getting Cole to his game. I think you have a new fan."

Well that was something at least. If only the mom was as easy to make happy as the kid.

Ah well. He never shied away from a challenge.

Her phone rang right as Kris joined the traffic heading into the main square. Seeing her dad's name on the screen she accepted it and lifted the phone to her ear, glad to have a distraction from the man sitting next to her in the driver's seat.

"Hi Dad."

"I just heard your message. Sorry I missed you. Are you still with the car? Have you called Charlie? Is Cole okay?"

Her lips twitched. "It's all good. Cole's at his game and Charlie is gonna get there as soon as he can. I'm heading to the Tavern now."

"How'd you get Cole to the rink?"

She glanced at Kris from the corner of her eye. They'd barely spoken since she'd gotten into the car. He'd asked her if she was warm enough and she had said she was. Then the space between them filled with silence she wasn't sure how to break.

She felt exhausted and she hadn't even dealt with the lunchtime rush yet, let alone the Saturday night one.

And she was more than a little annoyed with herself

because Kris had come to the rescue and she had bitten his head off. She knew better than to behave like that.

"I wish I could help," her dad said, breaking the silence. "I hate that I can't even drive a damn car."

"You'll be able to soon. Just gotta get you that new knee." They'd made it into the town square but of course there was nowhere to park. "Dad, I gotta go. I'll call you later, okay?"

"Okay, sweetheart. Take care."

She ended the call and looked at Kris. "I'm sorry about all the traffic."

He shrugged. "What are you apologizing for? It's my family's fault."

The ghost of a smile pulled at her lips. "And I'm sorry for being a pain earlier. I'm really grateful for your help."

Kris turned to look at her. Up this close she noticed a scar right above his lip. That was new. Or at least it had happened in the last twelve years. She wanted to ask him about it, but she thought better of it.

"I'll drop you off and go back to your car. If you give me the key I'll wait for Charlie up there."

"It's okay. I can—"

"Kelly." It wasn't a question. Not a command either. Just her name and enough to make her realize she was doing it again.

Trying to find a way not to be a burden. Trying to make her needs small because everybody else's were bigger. She'd always done that. "Sorry."

His lip twitched. "It's okay. Key please?"

She passed it to him and grabbed her purse. "Thank you. For everything. You're going to be Cole's number one hero now." She leaned in and gently kissed his cheek.

Kris didn't move, though she could hear the rumble in his throat.

"Thank you," she whispered again.

"You're welcome."

She pulled the car door open and hopped out. Her lips were burning like the car engine had been earlier.

When she looked back at him, Kris was touching his cheek where she'd kissed him, and she lifted her fingers to her mouth.

It felt like it was burning.

It was only as she walked into the Tavern that she realized they'd just touched for the first time in twelve years. And she wasn't sure how she felt about that.

"Hey Kris!"

Kris looked up to see Cole running toward him, his sports bag slung over his shoulder. He'd spent the last hour in the garage with Charlie Shaw clucking his tongue over Kelly's car.

He was just on his way to the Tavern to give her an update about the car. Not a good one either. "Hi." He gave Cole a big smile. "How was your game?"

"We won." Cole's smile was huge. "I scored a goal. It was game changing, you should have seen it."

"Congratulations." Kris wanted to reach out and ruffle his hair or something, but Cole wasn't his kid and it would have been weird. Even though Cole was beaming up at him like he was some kind of friend.

Funny to think that if things had been different, he and Cole would probably have been like nephew and uncle. He shook that thought away because the past was a different country and he wasn't going there.

"My friend's mom took a video of it. She sent it to me. Wanna see?" Cole got his phone out, his face flushed with excitement. He tapped the screen and held it up to Kris, who leaned over and watched as the kid skated toward the goal, his stick gently touching the puck until he had a clear line of sight to the net.

And then wham. It was in.

"That's fantastic," Kris said, meaning it. "Great goal."

"You think?" Cole looked at him like he was some kind of hockey expert. "I was so scared I wasn't going to get it in."

"But you did."

"Yeah." Cole nodded. "I wish Mom could have seen it."

Kris' mouth dried. "I bet she does, too. You heading into the Tavern?"

"Yep." He looked up, his eyes shining. "You coming?"

"Yeah. I'll follow you in. Just gotta do something first."

It was a lie, but Cole believed it anyway. Let the kid have his glory with his mom, before Kris walked in and put the damper on things.

He waited a couple of minutes before he pushed the Tavern door open, and the warm air washed over him as he headed toward the bar where Kelly and Cole were talking. The tavern was only half full – the lunchtime rush was over, and he figured the evening one hadn't begun yet, though give it an hour and everybody would be coming in for their pre-theater drinks.

Kelly looked up, her face expressionless as he walked toward her.

"Hey."

"Hi." She nodded at Cole, who pushed through the door at the back of the bar, presumably to the office at the back of the Tavern. Cole gave Kris a wave and Kris waved back.

Weird how much he liked that kid.

"Thank you for all your help earlier. I owe you one," Kelly said as he reached the bar.

"You're not going to thank me when you hear what Charlie has to say."

She laughed but there was no humor in it. "I already called him. He told me it's time for the junk yard."

"I'm sorry," Kris said, because he hated this. "Repairs would cost way more than it's worth."

"Yeah, I get that." Kelly nodded. "I guess I'll just have to get myself another car." She didn't meet his eye. He had to push down the urge to reach out and touch her chin. He wanted to look into her eyes. Read her emotions.

But it wasn't his place to do it.

"Can you use your dad's?" he asked her.

She shook her head. "He sold it last month."

Kris wanted to ask why, but she'd already picked up a couple of dirty glasses from the bar, trying to end the conversation.

"You can have my car." The words escaped his lips before he could think them through.

She stopped what she was doing, holding the glasses in mid air. "What?" Her brows pulled together.

"You need a car to get to work. To drive Cole around. You can have mine."

"It's a rental," she pointed out.

"I'll put you on as an additional driver."

Kelly put the glasses back down on the counter and turned to look at him. "It's okay. I can figure it out on my own."

"Or you can take my help."

She blinked, her lips parting and he had the strangest urge to reach out and touch them. "I can't afford a car like that."

"I didn't ask you to pay."

"And I can't take your generosity either. You've already done too much. It's fine, I'll work something out."

She was *fine* again. And he still couldn't tease her.

"Can I have two beers?" a man called out over Kris's shoulder, interrupting them.

"What time do you finish?" Kris asked her.

"One, two in the morning."

"Okay."

Kelly glanced over his shoulder at the customer, then back at Kris. "What does that mean?"

"It means if you won't take my car I'll give you a ride home."

"No." Her voice was firm. "That's not happening."

He shrugged. "That's funny. Because I think you'll find it is."

❄ 7 ❄

"How're things going?" North asked. Kris was hammering the nail into a sign cut into the shape of a pointing finger, with *Christmas Trail This Way* painted onto the front. After he'd left the tavern he'd come straight here, having promised Alaska he'd help with the final preparations for the trail.

It was due to open tomorrow at lunch time. They just had the tree to set up and a few last minute checks to do in the morning light, because right now the sky was darkening and there were a few rogue snowflakes dancing around in the breeze. He had a lamp set up, but they wouldn't be able to turn the floodlights on until the electrician checked them in the morning.

"Almost there," he told his brother. After the day he'd arrived to town, he hadn't seen so much of North. He was busy at the farm, managing everything because Amber was pregnant and he didn't want her to work so hard.

"I heard you rescued a damsel in distress today." There was a half smile on North's lips.

"I helped Kelly out, yeah."

North nodded but said nothing.

"Come on, if you want to say it, say it." Kris shook his head, a smile playing at his lips. "If you want the full details, I rescued Cole. Kelly just kind of came along for the ride."

"That's not how I heard it," North said mildly. "From what I heard, you stayed with her car until Charlie came with his pickup, then helped him back at the garage. And that's why you're still working here in the dark."

Kris stepped back to make sure the sign was straight. Yeah, it would past muster. Or in this case, Alaska's scrutiny.

"Just helping out a friend in need."

"So you and Kelly are friends again?" North asked.

Kris' mouth felt dry. "Not quite." But he wanted to be. Wanted a lot of things. Mostly to make up for all the mistakes he'd made. Wasn't that why he was here, to mend all those fences he'd trampled?

"Hey," Amber called out, walking over to where they were standing. "Alaska has some hot chocolate in the foyer. You guys coming in?"

"Where's Willow?" North asked her.

"Already drinking hers. Although in her case it's warm chocolate. And mostly whipped cream and marshmallows." Amber smiled. "Alaska spoils her."

"Everybody does," North agreed, not looking perturbed at all. He glanced at Kris. "You coming in?"

"I just want to check a few things out here first."

"We'll be inside in a sec," North told Amber. "Get inside before you freeze."

He watched her walk back into the Inn then turned to Kris. "Let's finish up for the night. I want to make sure Amber takes it easy. She's too pregnant to be doing so much."

"You looking forward to being a dad again?" Kris asked.

"Yeah, I can't wait." North beamed. "Willow's so excited to be a big sister, too."

"You're a sap," Kris teased, but he liked seeing his brother so happy. There was a time he never thought North would settle down.

"You wait until you find the right woman. And have a kid..." North trailed off, suddenly realizing what he'd said. "Sorry, man. I didn't mean—"

"It's fine," Kris said quickly, because he didn't want to get into this discussion right now. Another mess he'd made, this time all the way in Europe.

"You ever see her?"

"Yeah. Last time I saw them, they're both doing fine." Without him. He'd thought he could be a good husband and stepfather. Turned out he couldn't.

North touched his arm. "It's good to have you back. Whatever your reasons for being here."

"Yeah, it's good to be back," Kris said. And it was true. He just wished everybody felt the same way.

Kelly really thought she'd gotten away with it and that Kris had forgotten or thought better of coming back to the Tavern. She'd locked the door after the last customer left, then spent the next half hour cleaning the tables and the bar, before starting the dishwasher as she pulled on her coat and picked up her purse to walk the mile and a half home.

Stepping outside and turning to lock the big oak door behind her, the quietness of the town square overwhelmed her. It had snowed again, the soft layer of white glistening in the moonlight. Everybody was asleep, all the lights in the surrounding businesses were out. She fished into her purse to find her phone to turn the flashlight on when she heard a voice that made her jump.

"You ready?"

"Dear God." She put her hand on her heart. "You scared the heck out of me." When she turned to look at him, Kris was biting down a smile.

Damn, that man knew how to smirk. It made her heart twist a little. Like it was yearning for things it used to have.

"You don't need to do this. I can walk home."

"I just happened to be driving past. Saw you standing here." He shrugged.

"Liar."

His smile widened. A breeze danced through his thick hair.

"Why are you doing this?" she asked him.

"Doing what?" He looked genuinely confused.

"Being nice to me. I don't understand."

"You don't understand people being nice to you?" His eyes scanned her face and she felt her body warm up at his scrutiny. "It's just a ride, Kelly. Nothing else. I want to make sure you get home safely. I don't want your thanks or your undying affection. Just a good night's sleep knowing you're safe."

She swallowed. "You won't talk to me?"

"What?" He looked amused at her question, his eyes crinkling. Or maybe more bemused than amused. She wasn't sure.

"Last week when I saw you in the square you said you wanted to talk to me. I said I didn't want to talk. Is this a ruse to corner me so I can't escape?"

This time he laughed. "No, but I wish I'd thought of it." His expression turned serious. "I'll drive you home and I won't say a word. Scout's honor."

"Okay then." She nodded. "Thank you."

"No problem."

She followed him to his car and he held the passenger door open for her as she climbed in. The seat was still warm, as though he'd had the heater on just for her a few minutes ago. He walked around and got into the driver's seat.

For the next five minutes he did as he promised and didn't say a word. And it felt weird. A couple of times she went to break the silence but stopped herself because this was what she wanted.

Wasn't it?

She was so confused. He was being so nice after years of complete radio silence. And the way he'd left. The pain she'd felt. It was too much. She'd spent years forgetting about him, but now that he was back it was like everything had come up to the surface. Her memories, her feelings. The way she'd loved him so much.

From the corner of her eye she took in the dark shadow of his jaw, the razor sharp shape of it, the way his nose was perfectly straight and strong in profile against the light of the street lamps as he drove her home. He held the wheel gently, his thick hands curled around the sleek leather.

And now she was remembering the way they curled around her for the last time that night.

He pulled up outside of her house.

"How did you know where I live?" she asked, suddenly realizing she hadn't told him.

"North told me."

Of course he did. People around here loved to talk.

She unclasped her seatbelt and reached for the handle, emotions spilling over her like a rainstorm. He was too close, close enough for her to smell the familiar masculine scent of him. Enough for her to be overwhelmed.

"Thank you," she whispered.

"Kelly."

The sound of his voice cut through the turmoil of her thoughts. She turned to look at him. "Yes?"

"Cole is amazing. You're a great mom." His words were so unexpected they winded her for a moment.

Oh God, she was going to cry. A few words of comfort

and she had no idea how to deal with them. "Thank you," she said again, her voice thick and husky. Kris held her gaze for a moment, and she felt her whole body shiver.

He nodded and she gave him the smallest of smiles back. "Good night, Kris."

"Good night." She could feel the heat of his gaze on her as she pulled the door open and stepped onto her driveway, closing it behind her as she grabbed her keys and walked to the door. He didn't back out – he was too chivalrous to leave without making sure she was inside safely, and she took one last look at him before she opened the front door and walked inside.

He was still staring at her. She swallowed hard and smiled at him. He smiled back.

It was enough. It had to be. Hastily she stepped inside and closed the door, leaning back against it as she tried to catch her breath.

"That you, Kel?"

She exhaled heavily. "Yeah. Why are you still up, Dad?"

"Couldn't sleep."

The light was spilling out from beneath the living room door. She pushed it open to see her dad sitting in his chair, his legs extended on the footstool, an ice pack on his knee.

"Are you in pain?"

"Just a little." He was in his pajamas. The television was on, but he must have muted the sound when she walked in.

She walked over to him, grateful for the distraction from her thoughts. "You taken some pain meds?"

"All the ones I got."

She hoped he was joking. "Want me to make you a cocoa?"

"No, honey. You go to bed. You must be exhausted."

"I'm fine." She put her hand on his shoulder, trying to

show him some solidarity. "We need to get this surgery booked."

If they had the money he could have the surgery in early January. That's what the doctor had told him at his last appointment.

"You know we can't." He gave her a pained smile. "It's okay. The pills will kick in soon."

She sat heavily on the sofa next to him. "We can take out a loan to pay for it."

"No."

Damn, he was as stubborn as she was. There was no guessing where she got it from.

"Dad..."

"Who's going to give me a loan?" he asked her. "I'm a bad bet."

"We can use the Tavern as collateral."

"No!" He was vehement this time. Enough to make her flinch. "That's not happening."

She caught his eye. "We're going to lose it anyway."

"No, we're not. The Tavern is safe. It's the only thing that brings us money. This is the end of the conversation, Kelly. I'll be okay, just let it be." He picked up the remote and switched the sound back on.

"Is Cole okay?" she asked, because she knew better than to push her dad when he didn't want to talk about something. It was like knowing herself.

"He's fine. Still excited about his win." Her dad smiled. "That kid is a goodun."

Yeah, he was. "Thank you for looking after him."

Her dad's gaze lifted. "Thank you for looking after all of us."

It was weird how raw she felt. How emotional. "I'm going to head to bed. Another early start tomorrow." And she needed to think of a plan. To talk to somebody about a loan.

Because her dad couldn't go on like this. "Night, Dad. Try to get some sleep."

She kissed him softly on the cheek and he patted her arm. "Night, honey. I'll be fine. Now go to bed before you fall asleep on your feet."

———————

Kelly – age 16

"You got your ugly boots on again," her dad said as she walked into the Tavern. It was almost empty – no surprise since it was four o'clock on a weekday at the start of fall. There was a guy holding up the bar at the end, and a couple whispering furiously in the corner, but that was it.

"They're called Ugg boots, Dad." She smiled because he knew that. And to be fair, they weren't genuine Uggs either. Who the heck could afford those? They were pretends, fakes, knock offs. And since she'd bought them last week, nobody had let her hear the end of it.

Not her dad, not Lyle, and definitely not Kris. He told her she looked like she was half woman half horse.

The idiot.

"How was school?" her dad asked.

"Boring." Truth was, it was horrible. Most of the class was away visiting colleges, including Kris. It had just been her and Lyle hanging around and it felt like her arm was missing or something.

A little taste of what it would be like next year when Kris went to college and left her and Lyle behind. Lyle already had a job offer from Walker Woods in Marshall's Gap, and she was going to sign up for some community college classes while she spent the rest of her time working at the tavern.

She wouldn't be able to serve alcohol, but she could do everything else. And let's face it, when people weren't watching she'd probably sneak behind the bar to serve, too.

"It's college day, right?" he asked.

"Yeah." She nodded. He must have overheard her talking with Kris about it last week.

"Must be hard watching your friends leave."

"They'll be back," she said, her voice thick. They would, tomorrow at least.

But next year they'd be gone for good. The thought made her heart hurt.

"It's not too late for you to go look at some colleges, too, you know?" her dad said. "We can make it work. I've got some money saved. We can take out loans."

She gave him a smile. "It's all good. I've got community college. And this place." She looked around at the empty tavern. "Anyway, you trying to get rid of me or what?"

Her dad looked at her carefully, not smiling at her teasing. "I just want you to be happy, Kel."

"I am. Real happy. I promise." She leaned forward to hug him. "It'll all be fine."

He didn't tease her for saying the word like Kris did. She'd miss that, too.

The same way she'd miss him. He hadn't even left yet and it already hurt.

But she'd get used to it. She'd have to. She had no choice.

8

When she got up the next morning, Cole was already shoveling cereal into his mouth and watching morning cartoons on the television. Her dad's door was closed and she walked softly past it, not wanting to wake him.

"You're up early," she said to her son. "It's Sunday, you could have slept in."

"A few of my friends are heading to the Inn. They're opening the Christmas Trail at lunchtime. We want to be the first ones there to try it out."

The Christmas Trail was a new thing, planned by Alaska, who ran the Inn. During the day you could walk around and see Santa and all his elves, and by night it would be lit up into a magical walk.

"Aren't you too old for that?"

He shot her one of those looks. "There's free candy," he said.

"Ah." She nodded. *Of course*. He was still at the age where sweet things trumped anything else. "Make sure you keep your phone with you. And if anything happens..."

"I'll call," he promised.

She was still getting used to him going out with his friends on his own. The first few times she'd hated it. But he was growing up and she knew he was slowly pulling away from her.

But only slowly, thank goodness.

"Once you finish at the Inn, you can all come to the Tavern and I'll make you hot drinks," she told him. She liked his friends, and she never got to host them at home. But at least she could spoil them there.

"Sounds good. Thanks, Mom." He finished his cereal and carried the empty bowl over to the dishwasher, half an eye still on the television. "Did you hear about your car?"

"Yeah. It's kaput. But I'm working on getting another."

"Oh. That's sad."

"Right? Come on, we can walk into town together if you're ready."

Cole wrinkled his nose. "I was going to take my bike. We're all meeting in the square and riding to the Inn."

Ah. If only she had a bike. But her legs would get used to walking until she worked out how to get another car.

An hour later, she was at the Tavern. She'd deliberately arrived early, because she wanted to go through the old filing cabinet in the office to find the last insurance valuation they'd had done.

She knew her dad didn't want to secure a loan against the business, but they had no choice. She'd go to the bank and find out what they could borrow and give it to him as a fait accompli.

There was no way he could go on without that surgery.

"Knock knock."

She looked up to see Amber in the doorway. "Hi." She closed the filing cabinet. "I didn't hear you come in."

"Will let me in." He was one of her barmen. "I heard about your car," Amber said.

Kelly wrinkled her nose. "Of course you did. Who spilled the beans this time?"

"Charlie Shaw told Dylan, who told Everley who told Alaska who told Gabe who told North."

Kelly started to laugh. "That's one hell of a grapevine."

"Right? And I started to wonder why my best friend didn't tell me herself." Amber gave her a pointed look.

"I would have if I saw you. Anyway, yesterday was a mess. I had to get Cole to his hockey game and then work a double shift. I didn't have a chance to think let alone call you."

Amber looked mollified. "Okay then. But I could have helped."

"It was fine. Honestly, I had it covered."

Amber rolled her eyes.

"I did," Kelly protested. "I kind of got some help."

"You got help? And the world didn't blow up?"

"Haha." Kelly wrinkled her nose. "You're supposed to be my friend here."

"I am. I just know what you're like." Amber was grinning at her. And for a moment Kelly wondered if Amber knew that Kris had been the one to help her.

Luckily at that moment, Will shouted through the door.

"Kel? You want me to open up?"

"Yes please. I'll be there in a minute." She shot Amber an apologetic look. "I gotta go."

"I know." She stood slowly then walked over to Kelly, hugging her. Amber's stomach pressed against her hip. "Take these," she said, placing something metallic into Kelly's hand.

Kelly glanced down at her palm. "Why are you giving me your car keys?"

"Because I don't need them and you do. I put you on the insurance this morning. I prefer driving North's truck anyway, and you need a car, so don't you dare start protesting."

"I wasn't going to," Kelly said. "I was just going to say thank you."

"You're welcome." Amber smiled warmly at her. "I hate this time of year. We never get to spend any time together."

"How's work?" Amber ran the farm with North, her husband. And from fall until the holidays they were constantly busy, the same way that Kelly was at the Tavern.

"Stupidly busy. North left to go over there before the sun came up. And Willow's with Everley. We're taking her, Finn, and Candace to see the new Christmas Trail."

"Cole's over there. Let me know if he misbehaves."

"Cole never misbehaves." Amber shook her head, smiling. "He's a good kid."

"So everybody keeps telling me." She liked that. Maybe too much. She'd made a mess of so much, but not Cole. She was thankful for that.

"Well I gotta go." Amber kissed Kelly's cheek. "Keep the car as long as you need."

"It won't be long." If she got this loan they could pay for her dad's surgery and a car for her. Nothing fancy, nothing new. But maybe something more reliable. "And thank you so much. I owe you big time."

"No you don't. You do a lot for me, too. Remember how you took care of me after Shaun?" Amber asked.

Kelly winced at the name of Amber's ex. The one she'd run from on their wedding day after Amber had found out about his infidelity. Biologically he was Willow's father, but he'd ceded his rights to North.

"You're my best friend. I'd do anything for you."

"Ditto." Amber blew her a kiss. And Kelly couldn't help but smile. Because things were looking up.

For now she had a car and next week she'd get that loan, then everything would be okay. She was back in control and it felt good.

"Okay, you can plug it in," Kris shouted. He was halfway up the large Christmas tree at the end of the trail. The lights had shorted out ten minutes before the trail was due to open and Alaska had run to find him and Gabe, panicking. The Inn's electrician was working on another problem in the Winterville Inn itself, leaving Kris and his brother to locate and change the bulb that had shorted the whole lighting system.

They'd always been the ones to troubleshoot problems when they were kids, and their grandmother employed them to work at the Inn over weekends and holidays. Kris had been a fast learner, shadowing all the tradesmen as they worked through their job lists. It came in handy any time he had an issue at his own home.

Truth be told, he'd forgotten how much he enjoyed this kind of good, honest work with his hands.

"Hey, Mr. Winter!" Cole appeared at the end of the trail, his face flushed.

"He talking to you or me?" Gabe asked.

Kris wrinkled his nose. "I always think people are talking to Dad when they call me that."

Gabe laughed. "Right? We're too young and hip to be called Mister anything."

Kris lifted a brow. "Young and hip, right." A smile pulled at his lips as he jumped to the ground, dusting his palms off as Gabe flicked the switch and the lights flooded the tree. "Hey, Cole, you okay?"

"Sure am." Cole gave him the widest smile. "What you doing?"

"I got a list of jobs from my cousin." Kris pulled Alaska's list out. It made him smile because his grandmother, Candy, always used to write him lists. "Gotta go change some bulbs in the Inn next."

"Can I come?"

Kris blinked. "Ah, I don't think so."

Cole's face fell. "Oh. My friends are supposed to be meeting me here but they're gonna be late. I don't know what to do."

And now he felt bad. "Tell you what, you can come help me get some tools out of the attic if you'd like."

"Why are your tools in the attic?" Cole frowned.

"I guess that's where they got stored when I left town." Alaska had told him they were there. Most of them were probably useless by now but he wanted to look at what he had before he used the newer tools the Inn had in the workman area. "

"When did you leave town?" Cole asked. "And why?"

Kris chuckled softly. The kid was full of questions, the kind nobody else around here would ask. Not even his brothers.

"It's a long story. You coming?" Kris inclined his head at the Inn and started walking.

"Of course." Cole's feet thudded against the ground as he chased after him.

The foyer of the Inn was bursting. They had to brush past guests and staff to get to the banks of elevators. Everybody was waiting for the official opening of the trail. Alaska was at the front desk, along with Holly who caught his eye.

"Ready?" she mouthed.

He nodded and she grinned.

"Ladies and gentlemen, please follow me outside. We're about to open the Christmas Trail."

"You sure you wouldn't rather go do the trail now?" Kris asked as they reached the elevator.

Cole shook his head and leaned forward to press the button.

Well okay then.

The elevator car arrived and more people spilled out, talking excitedly as they followed the crowd out of the Inn toward the trail. Kris stepped into the elevator car and Cole followed as Kris hit the button for the highest floor. And then a thought pushed into his mind.

"You should probably ask your mom if it's okay to come with me to the attic," he said.

Cole shrugged. "She doesn't mind what I do. She trusts me."

"But I'm a stranger. It's not good to be with strangers."

"You're not a stranger. You know my mom and my dad. You're a trusted adult."

The car pinged as they reached the top floor and they walked out. The attic was at the end of the hallway, through a door marked 'staff only', and he let out a relieved sigh when he saw his cousin Everley walking toward them.

"What are you two up to?" she asked, her lips pulling up into a grin.

"You got a few minutes?" Kris asked her.

Everley glanced at Cole and then back at Kris. "Sure. What do you need?"

A chaperone because I'm here with the kid of the woman I hurt who won't take no for an answer.

"I want to find my old tool box. Alaska said it's in the attic."

Everley's face lit up. "I know exactly where it is. Candy stored all your stuff together up there."

"What do you mean?"

"When you left, she got all your things and put them together. Said you might want them one day when you're older."

Kris's throat tightened. He'd left town with little more than two suitcases and the biggest chip on his shoulder, assuming all his things would be thrown away by his parents.

"All my things?" he repeated. Was she serious?

"A lot of them." Everley nodded. "Wanna come see?"

He wasn't sure whether he did or not. He'd left them behind the way he'd left everything else. And now it felt like he was stirring up the hornet's nest of his past.

She hit the entry code on the pad beside the attic door, and the three of them walked up the gloomy stairs. Dust motes danced in the air, making Cole sneeze twice.

"I've never been in an attic before," he said.

"Well you're gonna love this one," Everley told him. "It's like a treasure trove. My grandmother never threw anything away."

When they reached the top she hit the switch and light flooded the room. There were boxes and trunks everywhere, along with old chairs and tables and dressers that once graced the rooms of the Inn.

"Your pile is here," Everley said, when they reached a stack of boxes. "I think your tools are at the bottom."

"Of course," Kris said dryly. He lifted the first box off of the stack and to add to the joy of it all, the bottom fell out, picture frames and clothes falling to the ground in a loud cacophony.

"Is that your hockey shirt?" Cole asked, leaning down to pull a red jersey from the pile. "Cool."

"Careful," Kris said gruffly. "Let me check if there's any broken glass."

But Cole was too busy looking at the shirt. It was one of Kris' old high school ones. He'd played varsity during his senior year. Cole lifted it and turned it around, to see Winter and the number eight on the back.

"That's Ovechkin's number," Cole said, with what sounded stupidly like awe.

"Yeah. I kind of liked him as a kid."

"You should give it to him," Everley whispered.

"What?" Kris frowned. He'd forgotten she was there.

"Give the kid the jersey." She nodded her head at Cole who was still staring at the old top like it was the damn holy grail.

"Did your dad ever give you his jersey?" Kris asked Cole, remembering how Lyle was kicked off the team during senior year. Had he even kept it?

Cole shook his head. "He didn't give me anything."

And fuck if that didn't make Kris want to sob. "It's yours."

Cole's mouth dropped open. "Seriously?"

"Yeah. If you want it you can keep it. I'd forgotten I'd even left it."

Cole held the top against his body. It swamped him, looking more like a dress than a jersey. But Kris had been fifteen when he'd first worn it and Cole was a good few years short of that.

"Oh my God, look at you here," Everley said, picking up a photograph. "I'd forgotten how long you'd grown your hair after you shaved it off. Man, it was pretty."

"Is that my dad next to you?" Cole asked.

"Yeah." Kris nodded. "I think it was taken at prom."

"And that's my mom?" The jersey was momentarily forgotten. He was staring at the picture of the three of them, standing together, laughing. Kris and Lyle in their tuxedos, Kelly in a dress she'd made by hand because money was tight and it didn't extend to buying prom gowns back then.

"Can I have this, too?" Cole asked, his voice soft.

Kris and Everley exchanged glances. "The glass is broken," Everley said. "Why don't I fix it and then see if it's okay?"

See if it was okay with Kelly. Kris should have probably asked her before agreeing to give Cole the jersey, after all.

He blew out a mouthful of air, making the dust dance in front of him. "That's a good idea," Kris said gruffly. "Take the jersey now, and we'll see about the photograph."

"Were you and my dad best friends?" Cole asked.

"Something like that." Kris lifted the next box, and luckily this one stayed intact. It had 'trophies' written on it. So his grandmother had gone to his parents' house to box everything up and bring them here.

He had no idea why that made him feel so emotional. Guilty, too, that she'd loved him so much to keep his stuff when he'd left town without a backward glance.

Just like Everley had said, his toolbox was at the bottom, making him think that his nosey cousin had probably rifled through these boxes herself. That made him feel calmer. She never meant any harm.

She just liked knowing everything that was going on.

Cole's phone beeped. He pulled it out of his pocket. "My friends are here." He looked at Kris again, still clutching that jersey. God only knew what Kelly would think when he came home with that.

"Tell your mom I gave it to you," Kris told him. "If she asks."

"Okay." Cole nodded. Then a moment later he spoke again. "Can you come watch me play hockey next week? It's a big game and nobody else can come."

Everley bumped her shoulder against his arm.

He wanted to. He hated that Cole had nobody there to support him. Hated that Kelly wanted to be there but couldn't because she had to keep the tavern open.

"Ask your mom," Kris told him. "If it's okay with her, it's okay with me."

"Thank you!" For a moment it looked as though Cole was going to hug him. But then he rolled his shoulders, as though remembering he was way too cool for that. "Gotta go. Laters."

He ran for the stairs and Kris yelled after him to wait,

because he couldn't let him wander around alone. He'd at least make sure he met his friends and was safe.

"Somebody has a little hero crush on you," Everley whispered in his ear.

Yeah. That's what he was afraid of. And maybe what he wanted, too.

❧ 9 ❧

K RIS – AGED 17

Lyle was smoking again. He'd started last year, but Kelly had reamed him out about it, so he'd stopped for a while. But he'd started again and gotten more stealthy about it, but not stealthy enough because coach had caught him and thrown him off the team.

Kelly didn't know about that yet. She would have already reamed Lyle out if she did. Of the three of them, she was the one with her brain screwed on.

Sensible. Grown up. Pretty as hell. That's what she was like. She'd spent most of this year studying like crazy to try to get her grades up because she'd selected the courses she wanted to take at Marshall Gap Community College next year.

So the two of them had started studying together, while Lyle hung out with some older guys he knew who already worked at Walker Woods.

But Lyle was here, now, as they stood outside the Winterville Inn, on Kris' break from working in the kitchen. Lyle wasn't working yet, said he was enjoying his last bit of freedom before he became a full time employee at Walker's.

Kris' grandmother insisted on all of her grandchildren working at the Inn, and in exchange she gave them a fair wage and let them each choose their own cabin on the grounds. Over the summer and holidays when they had early starts or late finishes they stayed here rather than going home. North still worked here sometimes, even though he was about to graduate from college, and Gabe did during his breaks from snowboard training.

"So, have you asked anybody to prom yet?" Lyle asked, throwing the end of his smoke to the ground and extinguishing it beneath his feet.

"Nope. Have you?"

"I'm thinking of asking Caroline."

"Bennet?"

"Yeah." Lyle nodded. "Marina hasn't got a date yet either." Marina was Caroline's best friend.

Kris shrugged. "I'll probably take Kelly."

Lyle turned to look at him, his brows pinching. "Why would you take Kelly?"

"Because we're friends. And..." Kris trailed off. "I don't know. I just thought I would."

"But that's not fair."

Kris tipped his head to the side. Lyle looked pissed, which was unusual for Lyle. Except when he was drinking out of his dad's whiskey bottle. It was weird how mean a drunk he could be.

"Why's it not fair?" Kris asked.

Lyle ran his hand through his hair. It had grown back since he'd shaved it, thick and blond. "Because neither of us should ask Kelly. It'd be breaking up the group. Like Yoko Ono."

"What?" Kris laughed. "How do you mean?"

"I just think you should leave it. If you take her to prom she might think you want more."

"More than what?"

"Friendship," Lyle said.

Kris swallowed. Lyle didn't look happy about that thought. "Would that be wrong?"

"Yeah it would be wrong. You're leaving for college. She's staying. You're gonna be surrounded by girls. Don't leave her pining for you. And anyway, we're all meant to be friends. The three musketeers, remember?"

"Yeah." Kris nodded. "I remember." Though he hadn't heard it for the longest of times. He couldn't remember the last time the three of them hung out like they used to. Life was getting busy. He was always working here, Kelly was at the tavern, and they all had piles of school work to do.

"Let's make a pact," Lyle said, looking serious. "Kelly's out of bounds. For both of us."

"You're interested in her, too?" Kris asked. He was shocked. Lyle was always teasing Kelly. Making her laugh. But he'd never shown any interest in her that way.

"It doesn't matter. Neither of us should be. She's one of the guys." Lyle put his hand out. "Promise me we'll all just stay friends. For her sake."

Kris knew she was upset he was leaving. Hell, he wasn't exactly looking forward to it either. Maybe Lyle was talking sense for once.

"Okay. It's a deal. Just friends." Weird how that made his chest feel tight. Like somebody had put an elastic band around it.

They shook on it like it was some kind of business deal. And as Kris pulled his hand away there was a bad taste lingering on his tongue.

But maybe Lyle was right. He was leaving and Kelly and Lyle were staying. It was best not to change anything else. Even if every time he looked at her all he wanted to do was bury his face in her hair and smell her sweet shampoo.

The three musketeers. That's what they'd always be. And everything would be okay.

"Mom, can Kris come watch my hockey game tomorrow?" Cole asked, shoveling spoonfuls of cereal into his mouth. It was Friday morning and there were five minutes until the bus was due. She looked up from the email she was reading from the bank.

They had made an appointment for her to meet with the loan officer the week after next. Attached to the email was a list of documents she needed to bring, including the deeds to the tavern.

"What's that, honey?" She looked up from her phone.

"Kris wants to watch my hockey game tomorrow but he said I had to ask you. I kind of forgot." Cole lifted the bowl to his mouth.

"Don't do that." She pulled it away from him. He had a terrible habit of drinking the leftover milk. "If you want some milk pour it in a glass."

"This tastes better. It's sugary." Cole shrugged. "So can he?"

"When did you ask Kris?" she asked. She'd managed to avoid him all week, thanks to busy nights – and days – at the tavern.

"On Sunday. At the Inn."

"You didn't tell me."

"You didn't ask." Cole carried his bowl to the sink and emptied the milk down the drain, then pulled open the dishwasher and loaded it up. "I gotta go."

"Wait a minute," Kelly said, her email forgotten. "Did he ask you if he could come?"

"I asked him." Cole's jaw jutted out. "Now can I go to school or what?"

The clock ticked over, he had two minutes. "Yes."

"And can Kris come watch me tomorrow?"

"I'll think about it." She felt like she was back at square one now.

"Mom!"

"Go." She gave him the look. The one she knew would have the desired effect of sending him running with his bag slung around his shoulder. When she heard the door slam, she put her coffee cup into the dishwasher and sighed.

There used to be a time when Cole told her everything. Hell, there was a time when she'd been with him constantly so he wouldn't have to say a thing, she just knew it all. She was so happy he was growing up to be such a lovely, kind young man, but she missed those days, dammit.

His bedroom door was open, and the clean clothes she'd left outside after doing the laundry yesterday were still piled on the carpet. Sighing, she walked inside to put them on his chair.

And that's when she saw the jersey.

It was like being slapped in the face by a thousand memories. She knew before she even lifted it that it would have Kris' name on the back.

She turned it over and there it was. Winter. Number eight.

How many times had she watched him as he glided across the ice wearing that damn jersey? How many times had she screamed his name? She could remember the way he'd grin up at her and her heart would clench.

It was easy to be secretly in love with Kris Winter. Half the girls at school suffered from that particular affliction.

It was harder to be his friend. His circle was tight, he didn't let many people get close to him.

But she and Lyle had been allowed in. They were the three musketeers. Just friends – back then, at least.

She exhaled heavily. Because she was supposed to be

heading to the Tavern early to find those damn deeds she'd need for Monday's meeting.

But instead, she needed to see Kris, because he was stirring things up she'd rather keep forgotten.

And she needed to protect Cole from the fallout.

Kris was in the shower when he heard the rap of knuckles against the cabin door. He rinsed the suds from his hair and put his head around the shower door.

"Just a minute," he yelled. But whoever it was knocking didn't hear him, and knocked again, so he turned off the shower and grabbed a towel, wrapping it around his waist. He left wet footprints the whole way across the wooden floor and yanked open the door, his skin immediately hit by the ice cold air from outside.

"What is—oh." He swallowed, seeing Kelly standing there.

Her eyes widened as she took in his pretty-much-undressed state.

"Kel?"

Her mouth opened, but no words came out. Another gust of wind hit him, making his damn nipples contract almost into his body.

"Can you come in so I can close the door, please?" he asked, because he was in danger of getting frostbite exactly where he didn't want it.

Kelly didn't move. So he reached for her wrist, his fingers circling her delicate skin, then pulled her in and closed the door behind her. Kelly leaned back against it, her eyes darting all over like she was a scared animal and he was about to eat her up.

"Kelly?" He couldn't remember her ever being lost for words before.

"Can you put some clothes on," she rasped.

He looked down and his brows lifted. "I wasn't exactly expecting company."

"I can see that."

"So what can I do for you?" he asked her, confused at her sudden arrival. She was standing right in front of him because with the bed and the dresser and the easy chair there wasn't exactly a lot of space in the cabin.

"Put some clothes on," she said again, and he bit down a smile.

"I was going to do that. I do that most days. But thanks for coming over and checking on me. Is there anything else?"

Her eyes rose to his. "I need to talk to you about Cole."

Ah, so that's why she was here. He'd expected her to come on Sunday or Monday. By the time Wednesday had arrived, he'd almost forgotten about the whole thing. Assumed she didn't care.

He was her old history, why should she care?

"Take a seat. I'll put on some pants," he said, nodding at the torn easy chair by the fireplace, about two steps away.

"And a shirt," she told him. "You definitely need a shirt."

He couldn't stop the smile from pulling at his lips once more. "I remember when you told me I should never wear a shirt."

"That was in the summer. And a long time ago."

Yeah, it was. But he could remember it like it was yester-day. It was the summer after they graduated high school and they'd been at the beach. He'd caught her looking at his bare chest and it had made him feel weird inside.

Like he wanted things he couldn't have.

She'd joked about him getting all the girls on campus if he walked around without a shirt on and that had been that.

It took him two minutes to pull on his jeans and a Henley, running his fingers through his damp hair to get it into some kind of order. When he walked back out of the bathroom she was still standing by the front door, looking like she was about to bolt.

"You're not sitting down," he pointed out. The easy chair remained empty.

"No. This won't take long." She shook her head and stayed exactly where she was. "Did you give Cole your hockey jersey?"

"Yeah." He nodded.

"Why?"

"Because he asked for it. And it's not like I'm planning on going back to play for the high school team. I figured his need was greater than mine."

"He didn't tell me you'd given it to him," she said, her brows knitting.

Kris blinked, because he'd been expecting her to shout at him. Get angry, the way only Kelly could. Truth was, he'd quite looked forward to it back on Sunday after Cole had left.

He liked her fire. Or he had back when she'd had enough for all three of them.

"I didn't know that," Kris said. "He should have. I told him to talk to you."

"When did you see him on Sunday?"

There it was again. That strange wobble in her voice. She looked vulnerable and it touched him. Way more than it should. "It was only for a minute. I went to the attic at the Inn to dig out my old toolbox and Cole wanted to come along while he waited for his friends." He swallowed. "Everley came with us. It's all above board."

"I wasn't accusing you of anything." Her eyes caught his.

"I know. And I also know you have to be careful. He's your kid and he's precious. I get it."

She nodded. "Thank you."

"The jersey was in one of my boxes. Along with a photograph of us at prom."

Kelly blinked. "Of us?"

"The three of us. You, me, and Lyle. Cole was interested in it. Asked if he could have it. Everley told him she'd fix the frame first because we didn't know if you'd want him to take it."

"He wanted a picture of us at prom?"

It was Kris' turn to shrug. "I guess he wanted a picture of you and his dad from when you were young. I'm guessing he's not that interested in me."

Her lips twitched. "That dress I wore was terrible."

"It was beautiful." His eyes caught hers. "You looked beautiful that night."

She didn't move her gaze. Just stared right back at him with those soulful eyes. And it was like they were kids again, communicating by a roll of the eye. He'd loved her when they were kids and he'd loved her when they were adults.

He missed that feeling. Of knowing somebody who knew you so well they could almost *be* you.

"Do you hear from Lyle at all?" he asked her.

She didn't seem surprised at his question. "Not much. A phone call to Cole once in a while." She ran her tongue along her bottom lip to moisten it.

"He doesn't come back?"

She shook her head.

"Why didn't you tell me when he left?" The question he'd asked himself a thousand times.

"Because you'd left, too. And I didn't need either of you. Cole and I were – we are—fine."

"I know that." He nodded. "You were always fine. And I never doubted you would be anything else. You were always the strongest of us."

Her lips parted. "I had to be. But I'm not sure that I am anymore."

He frowned. "Why not?"

"Because I'm afraid my kid is getting attached to you and I don't know what to do about that."

"Cole?"

"Yeah. He told me about the game. That he wants you to come watch him. I said I'd talk to you about it."

Now he understood. "He asked me to come. I figured every kid needs somebody cheering for them in the bleachers. I know I did. But if you don't want me to, I won't."

Their gazes clashed again and he knew she was remembering the same thing he was. All those times his parents didn't come to watch him play. Of course Candy would be there, and his brothers and cousins.

But it was Kelly he'd always wanted to see yelling for him and Lyle.

"I don't understand why he asked you." She swallowed and he watched the way her neck bobbed. "He doesn't know you."

"Maybe he just associates me with his dad."

Her face blanched.

"Or maybe not. I don't know. But if you're okay with it, I'd be happy to go watch him."

"I don't want you driving him," Kelly said.

"Okay." Kris nodded.

"Or doing anything that gives him false hope," she added.

"What do you mean?" His brow crinkled.

"Don't make him promises you can't keep. Lyle does enough of that. Promises to stop by and see him for

Christmas or on his birthday, and then nothing. He doesn't even call. Please don't break my kid's heart. Or I'll have to twist your balls until you become a soprano."

His lips twitched, mostly because she was back. The ball-busting woman he'd grown up with.

"I would never hurt him," he told her. "I promise."

Her mouth twitched. Silence filled the air, punctuated only by the soft sound of her exhalations. "Funny," she said, shaking her head. "I remember you promising me the same thing."

And then she turned and grabbed the door handle. "His game is at twelve. Don't let him down."

"I'll be there." It was a solemn vow. He'd meant every word he said even if Kelly didn't believe it.

He wasn't here to hurt anybody. He'd learned from his mistakes. And now it was time to start making some reparations.

Kelly's face was flaming in spite of the icy cold breeze that lifted her hair as she walked away from Kris' cabin. Had he really answered the door wrapped in only a towel?

And did he have to look so damn fine? Her mouth dried at the memory of the sculpted rise and dips of his chest muscles. The way a droplet of water wound lazily down his pectorals to his stomach, hitting the tight band of ridges that led to the towel he'd wrapped around his hips.

She'd thought they were both grown up when he'd left. But he'd grown some more, in all the best ways. The boy she'd known had disappeared, replaced by this adonis. And now she couldn't get that image out of her brain if she tried.

Heading for the parking lot, she passed the Christmas

Trail that Cole had been so excited about last Sunday. Not that he'd talked a whole lot about it, and now she knew why.

He was hiding things. She didn't like it. He'd seen a photograph from her prom night and hadn't mentioned a word.

"Hey!"

She looked up to see Amber walking across the parking lot.

"Hi." She smiled softly. "What are you doing here? I thought you'd be at the shop."

"Pregnancy yoga." Amber rubbed her stomach. "It's the only thing that calms this little one down. How about you?"

"I had to see Kris."

Amber's eyes widened. "You did? Why?"

Kelly let out a long breath. "It seems that Cole has a thing for him. Keeps following him around. Took his old hockey jersey."

"Without asking?"

Kelly shook her head. "Oh no, he asked, and Kris said yes. Apparently he also saw a photo of me, Kris, and Lyle at prom."

"Oh." Amber pulled her lip between her teeth. "Did the three of you go together? I can't remember."

She and Amber hadn't been friends back in those days. Amber had probably been away at college then, anyway. And for some reason, even though she told Amber everything else, she hadn't given her the full details of what went down before Kris left.

Maybe she didn't want her friend to think badly of her.

"Yeah." The same way they always did everything as a trio. Except play hockey. The coach wouldn't have let Kelly get away with that, even if she maintained that she could easily have whooped half their opposition teams.

"I guess it's only natural," Amber said.

"What is?"

"That Cole's curious. He never sees Lyle and that must be hard on him. He's getting older, becoming a man. He wants to know where he's from."

"He could have asked me." Kelly swallowed.

"Yeah, but maybe he doesn't want to upset you. Kris is removed from the situation. He's not related to Cole, and he doesn't have an emotional reaction to Lyle."

Kelly blinked. There was a truth to Amber's words that made her chest ache. "He wants Kris to watch his game on Saturday."

Amber's eyes softened. "And is he going?"

"I think so." Kelly's chest felt tight. "I don't know if it's the right thing to do."

"That's the problem with being parents," Amber said, her gaze full of understanding. "None of us really know what we're doing. One minute we're kids without a clue, the next minute somebody's putting this tiny human life in our arms and telling us we're responsible for keeping it alive for the next eighteen years."

Kelly chuckled. There was a truth in Amber's words. "Do you ever hear from Shaun?" she asked. Like Kelly, Amber had an ex and a mutual child.

"Not since he signed the adoption papers. He was pretty stoked at giving up his parental rights to North."

Lyle had never given up his rights to Cole. He'd just disappeared and left them to it. Loved the bottle more than he loved them.

Though sometimes she wondered if he'd ever loved them at all.

"Kris wants to talk to me about the past." It came out in a rush, like she'd been storing it for too long and it had grown too big to keep inside of her.

For a moment Amber said nothing. Just looked at her

with compassion in her eyes. And then she reached out and touched Kelly's shoulder. "Maybe you should. I don't know what's going on but you've been strange ever since he came back."

Amber didn't say anything else. That was one of the things Kelly loved about her. She didn't pry, she was just there when you needed her.

Kelly's phone beeped and she pulled it out, seeing a message from her dad. And it reminded her that she needed to get to the Tavern before they opened. She had some documents to find.

"I gotta go," she said, leaning forward to kiss Amber's cheek. "Thank you. I love you."

"I love you, too." Amber winked at her. "Now stop worrying about things you can't control."

❧ 11 ❧

K*elly, Age 18*

"Have you heard from Kris?" She felt stupid asking Lyle, but if anybody had, it would be him. Kris had left for college two weeks ago, and she hated him being away.

Lyle started working at Walker Woods a month ago. He got his first pay check and he'd told her he was treating them both to dinner in Marshall's Gap. He'd picked her up from her house in his beaten up Ford truck, and was playing country music as he drove through the winding streets.

"No. But I didn't expect to." Lyle had his arm resting on the open window of the car door. The AC in his truck had broken long before he'd bought it, but she didn't mind. She preferred the breeze anyway.

"Why not? He said he'd call."

Lyle glanced over at her. He had a smirk on his lips.

"What?" she asked, confused.

"He's busy, Kel. Getting some, if you know what I mean."

"Getting some?" she repeated, not understanding.

Lyle shook his head, that smile still playing on his lips. "Sex. He's getting a lot of sex. He's probably constantly orgasm drunk so that's why he hasn't called."

"How do you know he's having sex if he hasn't called you?" Her throat felt tight.

"I saw his brother the other day." Lyle shrugged, then leaned forward to turn up the sound. "I just hope he doesn't settle down too soon."

"You think he likes somebody?"

"I dunno. But guys who go to college tend to go one of two ways. They become man whores or they get pussy whipped."

She hated the sound of both of those. Made her feel a little sick, if truth be told. It was stupid, because she knew that it couldn't always just be the three of them.

But she was here and he was gone and she missed him like crazy.

Lyle pulled into a dimly lit parking lot. "Stay here," he told her.

"Why? I thought we were going for dinner." The lot was surrounded by trees on three sides. On the fourth was a ramshackle bungalow. Music was blasting out from the open door.

"We are. I just gotta get something from a friend. I lent him something at work and I need it back." Lyle jumped out of the car. "Seriously, don't move, okay?"

"Okay." She rolled her eyes.

He left the keys in the ignition, so the country music he'd been playing clashed with the low beats escaping from the beaten up house. She twisted in her seat and grabbed her phone, checking to see if Kris had responded to the message she'd sent him.

To her surprise, he had.

Sorry. Been busy. Will call you soon. – Kris.

. . .

Well okay then. She turned her phone off and looked back at the bungalow to see Lyle emerging from the front door. He hopped in the car and switched the ignition back on.

"Where's the thing you got?" she asked him.

"What?" He frowned.

"Whatever you needed to pick up. You said you'd lent them something."

His face relaxed. "Ah. They didn't have it. I'll get it at work. No biggie." He reversed out of the driveway and pulled back onto the road.

Maybe she should have asked him more questions. But she already felt like she might be losing one best friend. She didn't want to lose another.

North put three cans of soda on the table and sighed. "Remember when this used to be beer? Or whiskey?"

Kris and Gabe were sitting around the table with him. Amber was out and North was in charge. It was boy's night in.

Or three boys and a girl, if you counted Willow who was sleeping in her nursery.

"Who needs whiskey?" Gabe asked. "With the lack of sleep I feel like I'm constantly drunk anyway."

"You sure you don't want a beer?" North asked Kris.

"Yeah, you should be drinking enough for all of us," Gabe said. "The only one without any kids to keep you awake. "You sure you don't want a beer?"

"I'm driving," Kris pointed out.

"Yeah, but Amber said she'd drive you home

Kris shrugged. "I have things to do tomorrow." And he'd never been a big drinker. Not after he'd seen the effects close up.

"Like what?"

Kris laughed. "What are you, my parents? I'm going to watch Cole's hockey game."

"Cole as in Kelly's Cole?" North asked. Kris had forgotten that North knew her really well these days. She and Amber had been tight for years.

"Yeah. I think he's missing his dad. He asked if I could come watch and I said I would."

Gabe gave him a sideways glance.

"What?" Kris asked his brother. "Is that illegal now?"

"I didn't think you and Kelly were talking. That's all." Gabe shrugged. "Last thing I knew you had a huge fight and left town."

Kris ran his finger around the rim of his bottle. "It was more complicated than that." And he didn't want to talk about it. Not with them.

There was only one person he wanted to talk to and she was as closed up as they came. Not that he could blame her.

"We can do complicated," North said. "We've lived it." He exchanged a glance with Gabe, and Kris knew exactly what he was talking about. Growing up with parents who argued. A dad who used his fists way too often.

Parents who tried to sell the town their grandmother had built from the ground up as soon as she died.

"I don't know what to tell you." Kris shrugged. "You know what a mess I left behind." His chest felt tight. They didn't talk like this to each other. Or they didn't used to. But he'd noticed his brothers had changed.

They were more open. They showed their feelings to their wives.

And now it looked like they were turning him soft as well.

"I know you and Kelly argued," North said carefully. "But I always figured you'd make up. I was surprised you left for so long."

Gabe took a sip of his soda and nodded. "I thought you'd come back when she had the baby. Or once Lyle left."

Kris' throat tightened. "I'd burnt my bridges by then." It was weird how much he wished he was like his brothers right now. He wanted somebody to talk to. To let out the things he'd kept inside for too long.

But he couldn't. That wasn't who he was.

"You know we're always here if you want to talk, right?" North asked, his gaze fixed on Kris.

"I know. And thank you." Kris' voice was thick. "I'm sorry I haven't been around for so long."

North's expression softened. "It's okay. Nobody said you had to stay here the way I did."

"Yeah, but I could have visited more often. Been there for you both." He hated the way he'd kept himself so disconnected. "My therapist told me I should come here and stop feeling so guilty."

North's eyes widened. "You have a therapist?"

"Well hell." Gabe sat back in his chair. "I never thought I'd hear you say that."

Kris shrugged. "We all got allocated somebody at work. We finished a huge deal that caused us a lot of stress, but made us even more money and the CEO insisted that we all have somebody to talk to."

"Really?" Gabe frowned. "Like mandated therapy?"

"Not really. We got six sessions. I booked some more after." Kris shifted in his chair. "It's not a big deal."

"Of course it is," North said. "You're the brother who never talks to any of us. And now you're talking to a stranger?"

"Laura isn't a stranger. She's a licensed psychotherapist."

"Your shrink is a she?"

Kris rolled his eyes. "Yes. And she's excellent at what she does."

"And she told you to come here?"

"Not in so many words. I just kind of talked and talked and she pointed out the pattern to what I do. I realized I needed to do something about it."

"What kind of pattern?"

"That I can't hold down a relationship. That I avoid people to stop from being hurt."

"But you got engaged. Nearly adopted a kid." Gabe frowned.

Kris swallowed hard, because that episode wasn't one he was proud of. It had happened years ago, when he thought it was time to settle down. He'd moved in with his girlfriend and her daughter.

And yeah, he didn't hold down that relationship either.

"I've apologized to Melissa. She's married with another kid now." And he was happy for her. When he'd seen her last month she'd been glowing.

"So now you're here because your therapist thinks you should be. Why?" Gabe ran his finger around the top of his soda can.

"To see my brothers for a start." Kris gave them a sheepish look. "I shouldn't have left you like I did. Or stayed away so long. I shouldn't have left so fast that you could barely blink and I wasn't here anymore. And then I wasn't here when Grandma died and you needed me."

Gabe and North gaped at him, surprised. But they weren't as surprised as he was. Maybe their newfound ability to tap into their feelings was rubbing off on him.

"Don't be an idiot. You've always been around. You help out when you can. There's no rule that says just because your last name is Winter you should stay in this town for the rest of your life." North shrugged.

"He's right," Gabe said. "You get to live your life any way you want it. I'm just glad you're here now."

He should have known they'd forgive him. Damn, he loved these two lumpheads. "Thanks," he muttered.

"It was never us you needed to talk to," North said. "Was it?"

"What do you mean?" Kris asked, his brows pulled tight.

"I mean it was always Kelly. She was the reason you left. The reason you didn't come back, right?"

Gabe looked from North to Kris. "You're not Cole's dad, are you?" he asked, "Because that'd be whack."

Kris frowned. Where the hell had that come from? "No I'm not. And if I was his dad, I would have never left the way I did. He's Lyle's."

A cry came out from the nursery and North stood and rolled his shoulders. "Duty calls," he said. "I'll be right back."

When he left, Gabe turned to Kris. "I don't really get what you and North are talking about."

"It doesn't matter." Kris shook his head. "It's old history. You were probably off snowboarding or something."

Gabe grinned. "Probably. But take it from me, whatever's bothering you, you need to sort out. I learned that the hard way. I nearly lost Nicole because I wouldn't tell her how I felt."

Kris had heard the story of Gabe and his wife. How she'd moved in with him to get over a bad relationship, and how neither of them had wanted to be attracted to each other.

Yet here they were, married with a kid.

North walked back into the kitchen, Willow in his arms, her face buried against his chest. "She says she had a night-mare," he said, lifting a brow.

"I did, Daddy," Willow whispered against his shirt.

"It's okay." North gently stroked her hair. "Daddy's here now. Let's get you a drink and you can go back to bed."

"I'll grab her cup," Gabe said, standing and walking over to the cupboard by the sink. And for the next few minutes he watched as the two grown men he'd always looked up to treated North's daughter like a princess and they were her slaves.

He'd never thought he'd see the day they were both brought to their knees by their kids. It made him feel wistful. And maybe a little sad he'd never had that for himself.

It also made him think things he shouldn't. What if he'd stayed? Would he have held Cole the same way his brother was holding Willow?

He had no idea. And he'd never get that time back again.

And it was always the what-ifs that killed him.

Kris, Age 20

It was strange being back in his home town after a year at college. Sure, he'd come home last Christmas but he'd been working nonstop at the Inn. Luckily, business was quieter in the summer. He'd dropped his bags off at his cabin and popped into reception to say hello, then headed straight to the town square and the Tavern. Pushing the door open he could see it was as quiet here as it was everywhere else.

Kelly didn't see him at first. She was behind the bar with her back to him. She wasn't supposed to serve alcohol because she was under twenty-one, but people around here turned a blind eye.

Her dad was the first to spot him. Paul was in the corner, leaning over some papers, his brows pinched in concentration. Then he looked up and his eyes caught Kris' and he lifted a hand. Kris waved back then strode to the counter.

"What does a guy have to do to get a drink around here?" he asked. Her shoulders tensed, then she slowly turned around, her face lighting up when she saw him.

"Oh my God! I thought you weren't coming home until next week." She practically ran around the counter and jumped into his arms. He caught her easily. She put her palms on his back and her eyes widened. "Where the hell did you get all these muscles from?"

"Hockey practice."

She'd changed, too. She was wearing makeup, and her hair was straighter than he remembered. Like she was using an iron on it. She was wearing cut-offs and a low black top. If he looked down he could see her cleavage.

And yeah, he looked down. But only for a moment.

"Wanna go for a walk?" he asked her. She was still clinging to him like a koala. He liked it. She was so much happier to see him than his parents had been.

"Yeah." She looked over his shoulder. "Dad, is it okay if I take my lunchbreak."

"Go." He sounded amused. "Have fun."

Paul was no stranger when it came to Kris. They'd spent half their teenage years hanging out at his house or in the tavern. Kris liked that he trusted him with his daughter.

Instead of putting her down, he carried her out of the bar as she laughed, her head back, her hair looking red as they stepped into the sunlight. She smelt good, too. Like flowers. The sweet kind his grandma grew outside the Inn.

He put her down and she was still smiling at him.

"I've missed you, you idiot." She slapped his arm. "You've got to learn to use a phone."

He'd called her every few weeks, even though he'd wanted to talk to her every day. Tell her about how difficult he found the course work and how he enjoyed going out with his friends but it wasn't the same without her. But he'd made a pact with Lyle and calling her more often felt wrong.

And in a stupid way he missed her so much he knew it would be worse if they were constantly talking.

"Well I'm here now."

"For how long?"

"Until the end of August."

Her face lit up. "Well in that case, you're forgiven. And I have two months to teach you how to use a phone."

❧ 12 ☙

Kris pulled into the parking lot at the hockey rink at the same time as Kelly and Cole arrived. She was driving Amber's car and Cole leaned forward and kissed her before jumping out of the back seat, his eyes lighting up when he saw Kris getting out of his own car.

"You came!" Cole shouted, grinning as he walked over. Kris couldn't help but smile back at his enthusiasm.

Kelly got out of the driver's seat, shooting him a wary look. "Hi." She was a little dressed up, in jeans and a pair of furry boots, and a short jacket that did nothing to hide the curve of her hips. She had lipstick slicked across her bow-shaped lips and it made him swallow hard.

"Hi." He nodded at her. "You sure you don't want me to bring Cole home after?"

"He's got a ride," she said, her voice tight. "But thank you for coming to watch him."

This woman was going to kill him with faint praise. "It's a pleasure."

One of Cole's friends shouted his name and he ran over, leaving the two of them alone.

"I told him not to get used to it. That you're a busy man," Kelly said. "So you don't have to worry that this'll be a regular thing."

He looked at her carefully. Wanted to ask her who hurt her but he already knew. He had. Lyle had. The whole damn town had.

They'd hurt her but she'd come back punching.

"I'm happy to watch him play whenever he wants."

"That's what I was afraid of," she said, though there was no rancor there. Just an honesty that touched his heart.

"That's not what you're afraid of." He shook his head and she frowned.

"What's that supposed to mean?"

"You're not afraid of me. You never have been," he told her.

"Then who am I supposed to be afraid of?"

"Yourself." His lip quirked. "And you shouldn't be."

"What makes you think I'm scared of myself?" she asked, her tone torn between curiosity and annoyance.

"Because if you weren't, you'd agree to talk to me about the past."

She laughed. "What is this? Reverse psychology?"

He smiled at her. "Something like that. Is it working?"

"Nope. Now go in and watch some hockey." The smile still lingered on her lips. He liked it because it felt like he'd had to fight to see it. "And I have to go to work."

"Have a good day, Kel."

Her eyes met his. "You, too. Shout for Cole like I used to shout for you."

He grinned. "I will."

Cole ran back, and gave his mom a quick hug. "Can we go in now?" he asked Kris.

"You want me to go in with you? Or be cool and walk around the front?"

Cole shrugged. "Come with me. Some of the dads come in and say hi to the coach." He blinked. "And friends," he added quickly. "They're allowed in, too."

Kris looked at Kelly and she shrugged. "Okay then, let's go."

He let Cole lead the way, not looking back when he heard the bang of the car door and the start of the engine as Kelly left. Cole was pointing out some of his team mates, the main entrance, and the door at the side where the teams walked in.

"Did you used to play here?" Cole asked, his face flushing as they walked into the warm hallway.

"No. This place wasn't built when I was a kid. There was an old rink in Marshall's Gap we used."

"You and my dad," Cole said, nodding.

"Yeah, that's right."

"Was my dad good at hockey?" A couple of kids ran past him, but Cole was too busy looking at Kris to notice.

"Yeah. He was good." Kris nodded. Truth was, they'd both been okay. Good enough to shine in a small town high school, at least until Lyle had been thrown off the team.

"You think I take after him?" There was a hopeful note in Cole's voice. It made Kris' stomach tighten.

"How about I tell you after I watch you play?" Kris said, his voice gruff. Cole's face lit up at the reminder he'd have somebody there for him in the stands.

"You'll be here after?"

"Yeah. I'll make sure your mom's friend takes you home safely."

"Can you come back to the locker room like the other dads do? The coach likes us all to be congratulated before we go home."

Like the other dads do. He heard it but he wasn't sure what it meant. Didn't know how to handle the answer. "Sure."

"Thank you."

"Now go get ready. Good luck." Kris held his hand up and Cole high fived him, his smile big as he walked toward the locker room, and Kris followed the signs for the bleachers.

He was doing a good thing here, wasn't he? Making up for the past, making memories for the future.

So why did his stomach feel like it was twisting in two?

"You're new," one of the parents said as Kris slid onto the bleachers at the side of the rink. There were only ten rows of seating. This place was mostly used for skating, not hockey, and there was no local team that required seating for thousands of supporters.

Kris gave her a quick smile, then turned to look at the rink. Funny how it all came back. The painted lines, the positions. The Zamboni that came out in the middle of every game.

He and Lyle had taken a joyride on one during senior year. They'd been fascinated by it for years. Lyle had managed to start it up without a key after they broke into the rink. They'd laughed their heads off as they drove around and around the ice.

Until the cops showed up and his parents were called to pick him up. He remembered his dad being furious, pushing him up against the kitchen wall as soon as they got home.

Good times.

"Who are you here for?" the woman asked. He turned to look at her. She was smiling at him, and he felt bad for brushing her off.

"Cole Fraser."

She blinked as though surprised, and tipped her head to the side. "Are you his dad?"

"No. A family friend." Kris shifted his legs. They were too

long for the gap between the benches. If he wasn't careful his knees would end up in somebody's spine.

"You know Kelly then." She smiled. "She's a character, right?"

"I've known her since we were kids. We grew up together." The three musketeers. Fighting for justice.

Then fighting each other.

The woman chuckled. "I'm Carrie-Ann. Stanley's mom." She pointed at a kid that looked exactly the same as all the others.

"Kris Winter."

Her mouth dropped open. "Are you related to the Winters who run Winterville?"

"Yeah, that's my family."

He willed the game to start. Small talk and him weren't exactly best buddies. Maybe that was his problem. Couldn't do the small stuff, couldn't do the big talks.

Although at least he was trying to rectify that one, even if Kelly wasn't playing ball.

It was strange how the woman's demeanor changed once she knew his name. She sat up straighter, touched the back of her hair. Pushed her tits out.

Christ.

"Are you here to visit?" Even her voice sounded lower. Like she'd just smoked a pack of fifty and was channeling Lauren Bacall.

"Yeah."

"And your wife?" She looked over his shoulder as though expecting to see his imaginary spouse appear.

"Is not here," he said, deadpan, because he didn't want to encourage any more questions. He was here to watch Cole play hockey.

"Oh."

Before she could shoot any more inane questions at him,

the home team skated onto the ice. Despite their armor and helmets, plus the inch or so their skates gave them in height, they still looked tiny.

He also couldn't tell who was who. They all looked the damn same. It was only when he read the back of the jerseys that he realized which one was Cole.

The kid was scanning the bleachers, then his face turned to where Kris was sitting and he started to wave. Kris couldn't help the smile from pulling at his lips as he waved back.

And that was why he was watching Kelly's kid. Because Cole deserved having somebody here for him. Even if it was the guy who'd left town before he was born.

"He's a cute kid," Carrie-Ann said. "He looks happy to see you."

"Yeah. I'm happy to see him, too."

"How long are you in town for?"

Any answer he could give was blasted away by the sound of music rocking through the loud speaker. The away team slid on, and the kids all lined up in their positions, the rest skating to the benches on the side. Cole was in center, just like he'd told Kris, and he looked up at him again.

Kris gave him the thumbs up and Cole gave it back.

"Are we allowed to record them?" Kris asked Carrie-Ann.

"Yeah, just don't put it on social media."

He bit down a smile because he didn't have any social media. He just didn't do that kind of thing. Still, he held his camera up as the puck was dropped and Cole got possession, his head down as he skated then passed it to the right.

And then he sent the video to Kelly. Because if she couldn't be here, she still deserved to see her son.

A minute later he got a message back from her.

. . .

Did you scream his name yet? – Kelly.

It was weird how good it felt to see her words on his screen. He smiled as he tapped out a reply.

Not yet, I'm waiting for the right moment. He's good. You should be proud. – Kris.

Thank you. I am. And thank you for being there. – Kelly.

Okay, it wasn't a breakthrough. She still didn't want to talk to him. But it felt like something more than they had before.

A chink in her armor. A gap in the clouds. Whatever it was, he wasn't going to mess it up this time.

Cole's team lost 2-1 but it had been a close run thing. Kris could see the dejected slant of Cole's shoulders as he skated off into the tunnel. He didn't look up at the bleachers this time, even though Kris called out his name.

He wanted to pull the boy into a bear hug. Tell him it was just a damn game. But he'd been that age once and nothing was a game.

It was serious. It was dog eat dog. And he had no idea how to make a boy Cole's age feel better.

The parents filed out and Kris followed them, feeling distinctly uneasy at going into the locker room when he wasn't related to anybody there. The team was sitting silently on benches, their helmets off, their hair mussed up. Some of the parents walked over to their kids and ruffled their hair or murmured words of consolation. A couple walked over and told their kids they needed to do better.

That kinda pissed him off.

Cole looked up and his gaze caught Kris'. Then he looked down again, his fingers intertwined as he rested his arms on his legs.

Go over there and talk to him. You're the one who wants to have big conversations.

Yeah, but not with a kid who's just lost a game.

Ignoring his misgivings, Kris walked over anyway, squatting down in front of Cole. "You played good."

Cole lifted his gaze once more. "We lost," he said, his voice monotone.

"Yeah you did, but sometimes that happens. You've won before and you'll win again. And you'll lose again, too. It's part of life."

Cole's brows furrowed. "I wanted to win." His gaze flickered up. "Do you still like me even though we didn't?"

Kris met the kid's eye. "Of course I like you. I don't care if you win or lose."

"That's what mom says, but she has to. Does this mean you won't come watch me again?" Cole asked.

He swallowed hard. "Of course I'll watch you again. Anytime."

"Thank you." Cole pressed his lips together, as though he was expecting the worst. And that was the killer. The kid didn't expect anything from anybody. He was like his mom in that way.

He didn't know you could have more. That you *should* have more.

"Okay, team, we lost this week." The coach was standing in the center of the room. The talking between parents and kids hushed down to nothing. "But next week is a whole new game. Fraser, you did good out there. Richards, you couldn't stop those goals but nobody could. And Markham, that was a good goal you hit into the other net."

Kris winked at Cole. He lifted a brow back.

"Now get yourself changed, go home, and enjoy the weekend. I'll see you at practice on Tuesday."

"You still got a ride home?" Kris asked Cole.

"Yeah." He nodded. "My friend Daniel's mom is taking me."

"Okay. Well I guess I'll see you next week." He high fived Cole, although the kid was only half-hearted in his hand slap. "Have a good weekend."

"Thanks for coming, Kris."

"It was a pleasure, kid." He pushed himself to his feet and followed the other parents out. Then he heard the boy sitting next to Cole speak to him.

"Is that your dad?"

"No. But they're real close, so he's kind of like a dad to me."

Kris felt a shiver snake down his spine. He was nowhere near a dad. He hadn't met the kid until the other week. Hadn't seen Lyle since Kris left town before Cole was born.

But he knew that need to belong. That urge to be the same as everybody else. To have something that the rest of the world seemed to take for granted.

But still, he needed to say something to Kelly, because he'd promised not to break the boy's heart.

And now he knew exactly what she was afraid of.

❧ 13 ❧

The Tavern was half full when the door opened and her dad hobbled in. He was using his cane all the time now, and she could tell by the way his face was crumpled up that the pain was getting to be too much.

"Hey." She gave him a big smile. "I wasn't expecting you today."

"You messaged me."

Kelly rolled her eyes. "I know, but I expected you to reply with a message. Not come here. Who gave you a ride?"

"Charlie Shaw was coming this way. Wanted a coffee if you know what I mean." He winked and Kelly shook her head. The garage owner's supposed relationship with Dolores was becoming a big talking point in town, especially for her dad's generation.

"I told him it might be time to rename the coffee shop," her dad said, his eyes twinkling. "I don't think any part of Dolores will be cold after he's done with her."

"Dad!" Kelly widened her eyes.

"Just saying what I see." He shrugged. "So what's up with this urgent message anyway?"

"I told you, I need to find some documents."

"Why?" Her dad leaned heavily on the bar.

She'd spent an hour going through the filing cabinets, but there was no sign of the deeds that the bank manager wanted to see. Everything was a mess. Her dad's filing system consisted of throwing paper into the nearest folder.

When the holidays were over she was determined to go through it all and clean it up.

"I just need them for something."

He tipped his head to the side, his eyes narrow. "You know when you're evasive you look just like your mom."

"Don't say that." Kelly frowned.

"Doesn't mean anything." He shrugged. "She was a beautiful woman.

"I know she was." Kelly couldn't remember her mom being evasive, though. It was funny how your memories shifted and morphed as you got older. Her recollections of her mom were hazy, dappled in summer sun and turned brown at the edges. She could remember her smile, her laugh.

The way she always smelt of lavender.

But she couldn't remember her mom avoiding anything. Or getting angry, even though logically she knew her mom must have at some point.

One of the things nobody ever told you when you lost your mom was that you lost your terms of reference, too. When Kelly had brought Cole home from the hospital, his body still curled up like he was in utero, his face scrunched up and angry, she'd longed for her mom's calm advice.

Longed to have her warm voice in her ear, telling Kelly that it would be okay. That Cole wouldn't scream forever.

That she wasn't doing it wrong.

She still longed for that. Because every day it felt like she was making bad decision after bad decision.

"So what documents do you want then?" her dad asked, interrupting her thoughts. "And why do you want them?"

Kelly let out a long breath. He was going to find out anyway. She couldn't get a loan without him agreeing to it. But she'd wanted to hand it to him as a fait accompli. That way he wouldn't argue.

Because every day the pain was getting worse and she couldn't stand to see it.

"I have an appointment at the bank on Monday," she told him. "They want me to bring the deeds in."

Her dad blinked. "What kind of appointment?" There was a low note to his voice that reminded her of when she was a kid and had been acting up. He would walk in from work, his bar t-shirt still on, and give her the riot act.

"For a loan. For your surgery."

He said nothing. Just looked at her and she knew he was pissed.

But she preferred that to him being in pain.

"No."

"Dad, this can't go on. We have to do something. You can barely walk right now. It's not fair to you, and it's not fair to anybody else."

"What does anybody else have to do with it?" he said, his brows knitting. "Keep your nose out of it. This help isn't wanted."

Her mouth fell open. "You think your knee doesn't affect anybody else?"

"I'm the one in pain."

"And I'm the one trying to run a house, a business, and bring up a kid all on my own. So maybe you could think about me and how much easier my life would be if you'd just have this damn surgery." She stopped for a moment. She shouldn't be angry at him. It wasn't his fault his body was breaking down. Softly sighing, she took his hands in hers. "I can't worry about you and everything else as well."

"Then don't worry about me," he told her.

"Well I do. So tell me where the deeds are and let's get this done." She looked at him imploringly.

He swallowed then looked away. "I don't have them."

Kelly blinked. "Then where are they?"

"Not here."

She exhaled heavily. "Okay then, we'll get some copies made. I'll explain to the bank manager on Monday. I'm sure it will be fine as long as they know."

He looked up, his eyes slowly lifting to hers. "I don't have them because I don't own this place."

His words were like a slap in the face. For a second she thought she'd heard him wrong. She had to have. He wouldn't sell the tavern without telling her.

Still frowning, she looked at him, waiting for him to laugh. It was a joke, of course it was. Some kind of sick twist of humor.

"Of course you own it," she said, her voice tight. "You've owned it for years."

He shook his head. "I've been *running* it for years. Had to sell it about six years ago. Remember when the roof needed replacing?"

"You filed a claim with the insurance for that." Her head felt light. Dizzy.

"I lied. There was no insurance. I hadn't paid it. It was sell the building or close the tavern."

Her hand shook as she lifted it to cover her lips. She'd spent the last god knew how many years keeping this place going, because she thought it belonged to them.

It was the one thing they owned. The thing they could rely on.

She was going to be sick.

And then another thought came over her. One that curled around her brain until she could think of nothing else. Slowly, she removed her hand from her mouth.

"If you don't own this place, then who does?"

Her dad shifted his feet and winced because he'd obviously forgotten his knee hated sudden movements.

"It doesn't matter," he said gruffly, not meeting her eyes." Just leave it, Kel."

She hated the way tears stung at her eyes. She rarely cried. She'd learned from experience that tears did nothing but made you look weak. And yet here she was, about to cry over a stupid building, because it was the one constant in her life.

She'd grown up here. Come here after school every day for years and sat in her dad's office while he served the customers upfront.

Even worse than that, she'd fought to keep it open. Believing it was the one thing they had.

And it wasn't. She'd worked so hard and given up so much and it wasn't theirs.

"Who owns it?" she said again, her voice lower. Her stomach was twisting like two hands were holding it tight. Wringing it out until she had nothing left.

"I had no choice. Believe me, honey, I tried everything I could. The bank wouldn't listen to my pleas. Back then Winterville was failing, you remember that, right? There was no money left anywhere."

He still wasn't telling her. Which meant it was bad. Lifting her chin she looked him in the eye, her brows raised because she wasn't letting this one go. She was as stubborn as him. She always had been. He used to tease her about it.

He didn't look like he was teasing any more.

Folding her arms across her chest she looked at him and he sighed loudly.

"You're not going to like this," he warned her.

"Of course I'm not." That's why he hadn't told her. He avoided sharing bad news like the plague.

He took a deep breath, like he was about to plunge under water, and finally looked her in the eye. "Kris bought it," he said, his voice low.

It felt like a cold gust of wind had washed over her. Her skin prickled, her stomach turned over again. "What?"

Her dad's brows furrowed. "He must have heard through the grapevine. Maybe Dolores told him, I don't know. North had tried to help but he had all his money invested in the farm, so that was no good."

"Kris Winter owns this place?" Her ears were ringing.

"Until I pay the loan back, yes."

"And when do you pay the loan back?" she asked, her voice tight.

Her dad paled. She'd never seen him look so old. So gaunt. And she had to remember his pain, too. She shouldn't put him through an interrogation like this.

And yet she had to know it all. So many questions were rushing through her brain.

He shook his head, looking defeated. "I can't pay it back. We never make enough money."

"Have you paid back anything at all?" she asked, her voice low. She needed to know how bad it was. If she didn't know that how could she solve the problem? And yeah, she might be kidding herself but she had to do something.

Kris Winter couldn't own this tavern. Her tavern. He just couldn't.

He slowly shook his head.

"How can that be? Loans have to be repaid. You agree to a repayment schedule, otherwise the interest kills you."

"He's not charging interest."

Kelly blinked. "Why wouldn't he charge interest?"

"He wanted to help. I think he wanted to give me the

money but I couldn't take it, Kel. I have some pride. We agreed to a loan. On favorable terms. He owns the title until I pay him back. Like putting a ring in a pawn shop or something."

"This place isn't a ring," Kelly said. "And you have to pay more to get something out of a pawn shop. That's how they make their money. Why wouldn't Kris charge you interest?"

"Maybe it was for old time's sake. I don't know." Her dad shrugged but there was no nonchalance in it. No bravado either. He looked as defeated as she felt.

"How much do you owe him?"

He swallowed. "A hundred thousand."

The wind escaped from her lungs. This time she really did feel sick. "A hundred thousand dollars," she repeated. "How did you ever think you were going to repay it?"

Her dad looked down at the floor. "I'm not smart like you. Maybe I didn't think it through. I just did what it took to keep this place going." He blew out a mouthful of air. "Kris and you were always friends. I thought it would be okay."

"So why didn't you tell me?" She tried to keep the hurt from her voice. But that's what she really wanted to know. If he thought it was okay to keep her in the dark.

"Because I didn't want to be another man who's let you down." He'd muttered it, still looking away, and it just about broke her. She inhaled raggedly, a sob catching in her throat.

"You've never let me down," she whispered. "You've always been there."

He was the one man she'd always known she could rely on. The one person, maybe, apart from Amber. He'd stayed steadfast when her mom had died, then took care of her when Lyle left her and Cole high and dry.

Sure, in recent years their roles had reversed, but she'd fight wars for her dad. Do whatever it took to protect him.

The same way he'd do for you.

"I wish you'd told me. I could have helped." She leaned on the counter. It hurt that he'd kept her out of the loop. It was so frustrating. She could have done *something* to change things. She knew that. Anything but this.

"What could you have done? The bank wouldn't listen, nobody would. Then Kris called me and told me he would help as long as I didn't tell you."

"He said that? Not to tell me?"

"I think he didn't want to worry you. The same as me."

Or he knew she would have refused his help. And then they would have lost the tavern and her dad's heart would have been broken.

Maybe hers would have, too. If an already broken heart could snap into pieces again.

She was so used to pushing her emotions down she didn't know what to do with the cocktail of them swirling inside her. Disappointment, fear, anger. And yeah, there was gratitude, too. Because Kris had done something she couldn't.

He'd saved the thing her father loved the most.

They were staring at each other again. Her dad looked old. Upset. She needed to find a way to make this better but she couldn't.

"We lost."

She'd been so busy concentrating on her dad that she didn't hear Cole come in. Taking a deep breath to center herself, she turned to her son, her face warm with compassion.

"I'm so sorry, honey."

Cole gave her a tight smile. "It's okay. Kris says he'll come again. I'm gonna play so hard that we win next time."

"I know you will." She stroked his hair softly, and he didn't flinch away. He had to be feeling down. "You want something to drink?"

"Can I have a soda?" Cole asked, hope lifting his voice.

"Yeah. But just one. And you have to promise to brush your teeth extra well tonight."

"It's a deal." He grinned and her heart contracted. She was going to concentrate on him and the tavern today. But tonight?

Tonight she needed answers. "Dad, will you be able to watch Cole this evening?" she asked him.

"Of course." He nodded. "Movie and pizza night?" he asked Cole.

"Yes!" Cole gave him a fist bump. Funny how easy it was to cheer him up. If only a pizza could do the same for her.

"I'll get you that soda." She grabbed a glass and the soda gun, filling it up. And after she gave Cole his drink she quickly whipped out her phone and sent off a message.

Can you meet me at the Tavern at closing time? I need to speak with you. I know about the loan you gave Dad. – Kelly.

A few moments later his reply appeared.

I'll be there. – Kris.

14

Kris glanced at his phone screen and then back at the Tavern. It was just past midnight, but light was still glowing from the windows and pooling onto the street. It had started to snow again, dusty flakes that made the sidewalk look pretty but didn't cause any problems on the road.

Still, Charlie Shaw would be out first thing with his plow to make sure the streets were clear.

When he pushed the door open and stepped inside, there were only a few patrons left finishing their drinks. It made sense. This close to Christmas, Winterville was full of families who went to bed early, not the kind of bachelor and bachelorette parties that came in during the summer and drank until late.

Christmas music was playing. He recognized the song. George Michael had always been one of Kelly's favorites.

Kelly looked up from the counter, a cloth in her hand, a glass in the other. She nodded at him and he nodded back.

"Want some help?"

"I've pretty much cleaned up around them," she said,

giving him a ghost of a smile. He couldn't read her face at all. Was she pissed at him?

She should be. He'd gone behind her back, after all. And it didn't matter if he had good intentions, he knew Kelly hated that.

One of the many reasons he'd asked Paul to keep the loan agreement between them. Not that he blamed Kelly's dad for telling her, any man would probably crack under the intensity of her questioning.

He might have left town years ago, but he still knew how stubborn she could be.

Leaning on the counter, he watched Kelly empty the dishwasher, deftly replacing the glasses on the shelves before reloading it with another dirty rack of glasses and plates. He'd always liked watching her work. When they were younger and he was home from college he'd come in at closing time and shoot the breeze with her and Lyle. And then more often when Lyle wasn't there, Kelly was worrying about him.

His stomach tightened at that memory.

"How's Cole doing?" he asked, to break the silence if nothing else.

"He's getting over the loss. Dad helped – they had a pizza and movie night."

"Carbs never fail to make a kid feel better." He gave her the softest of smiles.

To his surprise, she smiled back. And it felt like fireworks were going off in the room. Damn she was pretty. Even more so than when they were kids. She'd grown into her looks. Owned them. Every time he looked at her he felt a pull in his gut.

"Thank you for going to watch him. He was so happy. And for agreeing to go again."

He was surprised at the soft tone she was using. He'd come in expecting her to scream at him. To throw things.

And yeah, he could have dealt with that. The soft, almost hurt tone though? It made him want to run.

"It's not a big deal." He shrugged.

"It is to Cole." She ran her tongue along her bottom lip. "And me."

The words hung there for a minute. Their eyes caught and he felt the connection deep in his chest.

"Good night!" one of the customers called, walking out of the tavern with their friends. Kris could see a bunch of bills on the table.

"Want me to get that?" he asked her.

"Please."

"Give me a cloth and I'll clean the table, too."

Kelly lifted a brow but did as he asked, passing him the cleaning spray and a clean rag. Walking past the only other customers left – who looked like they were about to leave, too, he grabbed the cash, and cleaned the table, then carried the money back to Kelly.

She took it silently, pressing some buttons on the register that opened the cash drawer, putting all of the bills in except one. That last one she folded up and put in the tip jar.

"Thank you."

Then the last customer left. Kris took the spray and cleaned their table, too. By the time he'd gotten back to the bar Kelly was turning off the main lights, one by one.

"We gonna talk in the dark?" he asked her.

She rolled her eyes. "We're going to talk in the office. I just need to lock up."

"I'll do it." He wasn't sure if he was trying to keep himself busy or trying to get in her good grace. Either way, he flipped the locks and turned the key, pulling it out to join Kelly behind the bar. She'd already opened the door to the office and he bit down a smile when he saw how messy it was.

As though she could read his thoughts, Kelly lifted her gaze to his. "You want a drink?"

"Do I need one?"

"I don't know." She tipped her head to the side. "Do you?"

He chuckled softly. "I'll take a whiskey."

She disappeared out of the office, coming back a couple of minutes later with two glasses filled with ice cubes and a finger of whiskey. Passing him one, he felt the thrill of her fingers touching his.

Her eyes widened and she stepped back. "Take a seat."

He sat on the chair in front of her desk, as she walked around and took the other.

"This feels like an interview. Do you want me to tell you why I've applied for this position?" He leaned forward, a smile playing at his lips.

"Why did you lend my dad so much money?"

There it was. The crux of it. Her question didn't sound angry, though. Just confused. There were two little lines pinching her brow and he wanted to reach out to her and smooth them away.

"Because he needed it and I didn't," he answered truthfully.

"Do you go around giving money away like that all of the time?" She took a sip of the whiskey, her eyes on his.

"Nope. Just to people I like."

"Yeah, well Dad always did have a soft spot for you."

"Your dad liked both me and Lyle. He liked that we took care of you."

"Until you didn't."

"Yeah." His voice cracked. "Until we didn't." He picked up his whiskey glass and swallowed some down before looking her in the eye. "You want to talk about that now?" He was ready for it. Waiting for it even.

Kelly shook her head. She looked tired. But still so damn

beautiful it made his chest hurt. "I want to talk about the loan. Why didn't you ask for repayment."

He tipped his head to the side. "You know why."

"Because you never wanted it."

The corner of his lip quirked. "Something like that." He'd tried to give Paul the money, no questions asked, but he wasn't having any of it. So he prettied the money up as a loan with the most favorable terms anybody could get. Got a lawyer to sign off on it despite his advice that Kris was being an idiot. He didn't care. As long as it was legal he was doing it.

Kelly ran the tip of her finger around the rim of her glass. "So what was it then? Guilt money?"

"Also something like that." His voice was thick. "I guess more than anything I just wanted to make your life easier." Especially after he'd made it harder by leaving. It really was the least he could do.

She looked at him through thick lashes. He could see the hurt there again. Hated that he'd been the one to cause it. To break her.

The same way he'd broken himself.

"I'm going to pay you back." She lifted her head slightly, her jaw jutting out.

Kris blinked. That wasn't what he'd expected. Though he wasn't sure what he *had* expected either. Certainly not her undying gratitude. He hadn't done it for that. When he'd wired the money over he'd banked on her never finding out.

"You don't need to do that. It's between me and your dad."

"You think I can't do it." Her voice was low. Sultry. "Is that it? You think I'll fail so you're giving me a pass."

"I didn't say that." He took another mouthful of whiskey, enjoying the burn. "I said you don't need to. When your dad dies the debt gets written off."

"What?"

"The tavern returns to you."

"No." She shook her head. "That's not right. You can't do that."

"It's in the agreement. We both signed it."

Kelly stared at him, her lips parted. And he stared back. Neither of them spoke, neither of them breathed. And all he could think about was the way her lips once tasted pressed against his.

The way her body had felt as he held her. Soft against his hard muscles.

His blood heated with the memory of it.

"I can't take the tavern." She lifted her hand to her eyes, brushing her fingers against them. Her mascara smeared on her fingertips.

"It's not your choice. It's what your dad wants." He caught her eye. "And what I want, too."

"But I'd be stealing it from you."

"Kel..." He swallowed hard. "You think I don't know what I stole from you that day I walked away?"

Her bottom lip trembled. Christ he wanted to touch her. Hold her, console her. Like he used to.

How had something that was once so easy become something so impossible?

"Look, I know you don't want to talk about it. But it's there and I don't know how to get around it," he told her. "It's everywhere. It's in the kid I watched play hockey not having his dad there, seeing how he aches for Lyle to watch. It's in the way I could barely bring myself to come back to the town my family lives in because I know how badly I fucked up. And it's in the way I lost the best friend I ever had, because I was too mixed up in my own feelings to give her the support she needed."

A tear ran down Kelly's face and it killed him.

"Can I hug you?" The words came out before he could think them through. But it was all he could think about. "Kelly..."

She was out of her chair and walking around the table before he could finish his sentence. He pushed the chair back in time for her to drop into his lap, her head dipping to his shoulder as a sob finally escaped her mouth.

He put his arms around her as she started shaking, her tears wetting his shirt as she fisted the fabric. He stroked her hair, her back, then her hair again, feeling the pain of her emotions twisting his heart.

"I'm so angry at you." Her voice was muffled by his body. "You stupid ass."

"I know. I know." He slid his fingers through her hair, feeling the gloss of her curls. "And you should be."

"You left me."

"I couldn't stay."

"I had to clean it up. The mess. All on my own." Another sob. Stronger this time.

"I know."

Finally, she looked up. Her eyes were rimmed red but still so beautiful it took his breath away. Tears sparkled like diamonds on her cheeks.

She was close enough for him to feel the heat of her soft breaths on his skin. For him to see the colored flecks in her eyes.

For him to want her more than he wanted anything in his life.

But she was the one thing he couldn't have.

He cupped her cheek, feeling the dampness of her tears on his palm. "I'm so sorry I hurt you," he whispered, pressing his brow against hers. They were so close he could feel the flutter of her eyelashes. Her grip on his shirt tightened, her fingers grazing his nipples.

"I'll talk to you," she said.

"What?"

"If I can't pay you back with money, I'll pay you back with that. I'll talk to you about the past. Do whatever you need."

"No." He didn't want it that way. It felt like a dirty deal. "You don't have to talk to me just because you think you owe me something. Because you don't. You owe me nothing."

She swallowed, her eyes not leaving his. "But that's what you want. To talk."

"Yeah, but not this way."

Kelly shook her head. "I don't understand you."

"That makes two of us." He gave her the softest of smiles. Then leaned forward to press his lips to her brow. "I want you to talk because you're ready. Not because of this." He'd messed up so much, he wasn't going to mess this up, too. She was vulnerable and angry and for once he was going to be the better man.

"What if I'm never ready?"

Then I'll never get over it. He pushed that thought away, because he was right the first time. She owed him nothing. Especially not the forgiveness he longed for.

"I'll live with it."

This time she was the one to cup his face with her palms. He stayed still as a statue as she slowly leaned forward, her lips a breath away from his.

Heat rushed through his body as she closed the distance, softly pressing her lips to the corner of his.

And still he didn't move, even though every part of him wanted to. Wanted to kiss her until she was breathless. Wanted to push all of the papers off her desk, lifting her onto it, and kissing her until she was needy and begging.

But he didn't. Because he was older. Wiser. Knew what an asshole move that would be.

She was upset and wanted comfort, but she hadn't learned that comfort came in different guises.

It came in hot sex and needy kisses. But it also came in hugs. Soft, loving ones that didn't let go until you could breathe again. Ones that made you feel safe and on edge at the same time.

Ones that made you feel alive.

And he was giving her the latter. Even if it killed him.

From the way his dick was pulsing between his thick thighs, he thought it probably would.

Kris, Age 20

"Don't tell Grandma," North warned, passing Kris a bottle of beer.

"Scout's honor." They were sitting outside North's cabin. It was his last night here before he headed back to college. Gabe and his cousins were there, the four of them clustered around Gabe's iPod that he'd plugged into a portable speaker, arguing about what they should play.

Kelly was here, too. Talking to a couple of their friends from school. No Lyle, though. Kris had barely seen him all summer. He seemed to prefer spending time in Marshall's Gap to hanging around in Winterville.

Kris had heard rumors of parties and drugs but when he'd asked Kelly she'd said she'd heard nothing about it. That when she talked to Lyle all was cool.

"You ever gonna tell her how you feel about her?" North asked him.

Kris pulled his gaze from where she was standing and caught his brother's eye. "What do you mean?"

"Kelly. It's obvious how you feel about her."

Fuck. He hadn't meant to make it obvious. "She's a friend. That's all."

"Okay." North shrugged. "I just assumed you two would..." He trailed off.

"We'd what?" Kris frowned.

North glanced at him from the corner of his eye. "I don't know. Forget I said anything."

Gabe walked over to sit on the step with them, as the music started to play. "Party Rocking" by LMFAO. Everley and Alaska were dancing, and they were waving to Kelly and their other friends to join in. Kris lifted his bottle to his lips, watching them.

"Lyle not here?" Gabe asked, his arm brushing Kris' as he sat on the step next to him.

"Nope." Kris swallowed a mouthful of beer.

"Figures. I hear he's been partying hard in Marshall's Gap." Gabe ran his finger over his jaw. "He'd probably find this lame."

"Yeah, I guess."

Kelly met his eye and grinned. Then she pointed at him and curled her finger as though to beckon him over.

He shook his head and she lifted a brow. A second later she was running over to him, grabbing his hand. "Come on, it's your last night. Dance with me."

Her hand felt warm in his as he allowed her to pull him up. She kept hold of him as they walked across the grass to where his cousins were dancing. Kelly put her hands on his shoulders, and he automatically put his palms on her hips, feeling them sway beneath his hold.

Damn, he was in love with this girl.

The music changed. This time it was slower. Adele. Somehow Kelly was in his arms, resting her head against his chest. He tightened his hold on her.

And then over her shoulder he saw a figure winding down the pathway between the cabins. Getting closer. Close enough for Kris to see who it was.

Lyle. Looking sober. His hair cut short, his shorts pressed, his eyes catching Kris.

He immediately let Kelly go.

"Hey." Lyle nodded at him and Kelly. She grinned back at him.

"Hi." Kris nodded back.

"Sorry I'm late. Had to go do something for a friend."

"No problem. Want a beer?" Kris asked.

"Yeah, that'd be good." Lyle leaned down to kiss Kelly's cheek. "Hey, Kel. You're looking terrible as usual."

"Shut up." She rolled her eyes at Lyle and he grabbed her in a headlock, holding her until she squealed for him to stop. As soon as Lyle released his hold on her she started giving him hell for being late.

Leaving them to bicker, Kris walked back to North's cabin and grabbed a bottle from the cooler, turning to watch as his two friends teased each other.

And he sighed.

He was leaving tomorrow. And Lyle had been right all along, now wasn't the time to start something with Kelly and then walk away.

Friendship mattered more. So did the promise he and Lyle had made to each other. Friends didn't hurt friends. He knew that much.

"Who else wants a beer?" he yelled. And when everybody shouted 'me', it made him smile.

Life was good. His friends were happy. Why would he spoil that?

❧ 15 ❧

"There's only one thing left to do," Kelly said to Amber on the phone the next day. "I'm gonna have to set up that OnlyFans account."

"Shut up." Amber laughed softly. "How the hell would you fit that in anyway?"

"I've no idea." Kelly sighed. "All I know is that I now need double the amount I needed before."

"You know I could help…"

"No you can't." Kelly shook her head even though Amber couldn't see her. "I already have your car. I don't need your money, too."

"You know I'd do anything for you and Cole."

Kelly's throat felt tight. "I know you would. And I'd do the same for you and Willow. And the little baby kicking around inside of you." She paused. "And North, too. Though I know he wouldn't let me."

Amber laughed. "He's the only person I know who's more stubborn than you are."

"Hmph."

"So how are you going to repay Kris?" Amber asked,

because that was the whole point of the conversation. She needed a plan. A way to figure it out. "And don't say OnlyFans again, because where would you find the time for that? You're already at the tavern twenty-four-seven."

The truth was, Kelly had no idea. The amount they owed him was massive. Life changing. She'd never seen a sum as big as a hundred thousand dollars in her life.

"He wants to talk to me," she said quickly, then regretted it because she was opening up a whole line of questioning she wasn't sure she was ready for.

"Who does?" Amber asked. "Kris?"

"Yeah."

"What about?"

Kelly took a deep breath. "We were friends back in the day and it all went to shit."

"Yeah, I know that." Amber chuckled. "From the way you were angry when he came back into town."

"He wants to talk about what happened." And she wasn't sure she was ready for it. All those memories she'd pushed down into a little box at the very bottom of her heart. If she opened it up it might overwhelm her.

That was the thing she was scared of the most. She was supposed to be a strong, independent single mom. And she was, most of the time.

When he wasn't around.

"Don't you want to know why our friendship was ruined?" she asked, because the silence was deafening.

"I figure you'll tell me when you're ready. I wasn't planning on forcing it out of you."

Kelly let out a sigh, pulling the last clean plate out of the dishwasher and glancing at the kitchen door. It was closed. No chance of Cole overhearing. "I almost kissed him last night."

"What?"

And that was the reaction she was expecting. She wasn't sure if she felt better or worse after saying it out loud. All she knew was the present was so much easier to talk about than the past. "He didn't kiss me back. Not properly. But I was crying and he was holding me..."

"Hold up. Why was he holding you?"

"To comfort me, I suppose." Though she didn't feel very comforted now. Thinking about it was like touching an electric wire. Sending pulses right through her. "He was holding me and stroking my back and telling me that I didn't have to talk to him until I was ready. He was being so... nice. I guess I'm a sucker for when people are nice to me." She frowned at the truth of that thought.

"Because you've had a lot of experience with people not being nice." Amber sounded sad. "Do you wish he'd kissed you back?"

"Yes. No." She hated how indecisive she was. Every time she got close to him it felt like her world was inside out. "Definitely no. I don't need that kind of complication." Kelly stood, holding the phone to her ear as she rolled her shoulders. She hadn't gotten much sleep last night. Her body ached from tossing and turning while she thought about the way he felt. Strong. Protective.

The Kris Winter she'd once known.

And he was making her feel like the Kelly who'd loved him so much as a kid. Before he broke her heart and walked away.

"Mom, where's my gym bag?" Cole asked, rushing into the kitchen. Kelly looked up, alarmed, worried that he'd overheard the conversation.

But the easy expression on his face told her otherwise, thank goodness.

"I gotta go," Kelly told Amber. And maybe that was a

relief. Because she didn't want to think about last night any more.

"Okay, honey. Talk later. Call me any time."

"Thank you," Kelly said softly. "Love you."

"Love you too."

This was such a bad idea. He knew it as he drove over to Kelly's house. He knew it when he climbed out of the car and knocked on the door.

Hell, he even knew it when Cole opened the door and a grin split his lips when he saw Kris standing there.

"Is your grandpa in?"

"Yeah." Cole nodded. "Come in."

He still needed to have that stranger danger talk with the kid. Though maybe he wasn't a stranger anymore. Kris had spent more time with Cole than he had with his own nieces and nephews since he'd been back in town.

"Hey," Cole said, before he opened the door to the living room. "Do you know what OnlyFans is?"

Kris blinked. How the heck did Cole know about Only-Fans? "Why?"

"Because Mom was talking about joining it. I wondered if it was a sports fan thing."

Kris tipped his head to the side. "Your mom wants to join OnlyFans?" he said slowly.

"Yeah. I heard her on the phone with Amber. Said she's setting up an account. And I'd heard some kids at school talking about it a while ago, too. I just wondered." Cole shrugged.

"Ah... it's probably something you should ask your mom about."

Cole lifted a brow and Kris got the meaning right away.

There was no way Cole was going to ask. Not that he could blame him. There was no way Kris would have asked his own mom if he'd been in the same position.

"Grandpa, Kris is here to see you," Cole yelled, opening the living room door. Kris stepped back at the volume of his voice.

Paul looked up from his seat on the couch. He had his leg propped up, a cane leaning on the arm beside him.

"Hey Kris." He started to push himself up.

"Stay there. It's fine." Kris shot him a smile. "Just want to talk to you."

"I know what this is about." Paul eyed Cole over Kris' shoulder. "Cole, can you go to your room?"

"Can't I stay here? Kris and I are talking about fans."

Kris winced. Kelly's dad really didn't need to hear about that.

"Not this time, son. Go do your homework. I'll call you when it's time for us to start dinner."

Cole frowned. "You won't leave without saying goodbye, will you?" he asked Kris.

"No. I'll let you know when I'm going."

Looking slightly mollified, Cole headed down the hallway. A moment later he slammed his bedroom door.

"Gonna be a scary teenager when he gets there," Paul said. "He takes after his mother."

Kris's mouth twitched. "Lucky kid."

"Can you close the door before we talk?" Paul asked, and Kris walked over and shut it, before taking a seat in the chair opposite the sofa. It was so saggy his knees were almost at his chest level.

But he didn't move.

"I guess Kelly told you she knows, huh?"

Kris nodded. "Yeah. She summoned me to the tavern last night."

"I didn't want to tell her," Paul said, looking serious. "I kept it from her all these years. She was meddling. Trying to find documents she shouldn't want."

Kris leaned forward, resting his elbows on his thighs. "She meant well."

"If you want to call the deal off, I understand. It'll take me some time to get the money together but I'll do it." Paul let out a long breath. "I should never have agreed to it anyway."

"I'm not here to cancel our deal. And I couldn't if I wanted to. The agreement we signed is watertight."

"But you gave me the money on the proviso that Kelly never found out," Paul said, looking confused.

"That part was a verbal agreement. It wasn't on the documents we signed," Kris said. "You've kept to your side, I'm keeping to mine."

Paul looked down at his hands, his brows knitting together. "Kelly's helluva pissed at me. And you."

"I know." Kris nodded. "And she probably should be. I would be in her position."

Paul looked up. "But we didn't have any choice, did we? If you hadn't given me that money we would have lost the Tavern. And if Kelly knew about it, she never would have let me accept it."

"Yeah." Kris gave him a tight smile. "That's about it."

"Is Kelly still angry? I was asleep when she got in last night and she left for work this morning before I got up."

"I don't know. I haven't talked to her since last night."

"And how was she then?"

Your daughter was beautiful. And she kinda kissed me. And I wanted to kiss her back until she couldn't remember her own name.

"Angry," Kris said wryly. "And pretty sad." He swallowed, remembering her tears.

Paul winced. "I prefer angry."

"Yeah, me too."

Paul shook his head. "She's a good woman. The best."

"I know." Kris' voice was thick. "I don't know anybody better."

"She wants to get a loan for my surgery. That's why she was looking for those damn deeds. She'd arranged for a meeting at the bank."

Kris looked at Paul. "For your knee?"

"Yeah. She's insisting I get a replacement but it's not going to happen. But try telling Kelly that."

"She's stubborn." Kris bit down a smile.

"As a damn mule. She tells me she's going to get the money from somewhere."

OnlyFans. Kris blinked at the thought. Would she really do that?

For her dad? Yeah, she would. And he had to admit he admired her tenacity. She never gave up, she never stopped trying. Even when everything was loaded against her, she went down fighting.

The front door rattled. Then a second later a voice filled the hallway.

"Cole? Dad?"

Paul's eyes shot to Kris'. "She's not supposed to be home."

Kris shrugged. "It's okay. We're not doing anything wrong. Just talking about the money."

"Cole's doing his homework," Paul called out as footsteps padded down the hallway. "And I'm in here with Kris."

"Kris?"

It was weird how much he liked hearing his name on her lips.

"Yeah," he answered, his voice low. The door opened and she was there, her eyes wide as she stared at him.

And he stared back. For a moment there was nothing but electricity between them. She swallowed hard and he liked it.

"He came to talk about the Tavern."

Kelly's gaze hadn't moved from him.

"To tell Paul it was fine. Our agreement still stands."

"Until I pay you back." Her voice was low.

He wasn't going to fight her over that. Not now. He liked the peace between them too much. It had been a hard win and it felt good.

Too good.

"It's quiet at the Tavern so I thought I'd come home and have dinner with you," Kelly said, looking from her dad to Kris.

"Sounds good." Paul nodded. "Cole and I were going to make burgers on the grill."

"In winter?" Kris asked.

Paul shrugged. "Best time to grill."

"Kris and I will do it," Kelly said.

Kris lifted a brow. Well that was unexpected.

"You're staying, aren't you?" Kelly asked him.

He smiled, pleased that she'd asked him. "I haven't had a better offer."

"Mom!" Cole ran into Kelly's arms. "Kris is here."

"Yeah, I know." Kelly ruffled his hair and Cole wriggled out of her grasp. Even though Cole was wrinkling his nose, Kris could tell the kid loved it. Heck, he'd love it too if she touched him like that.

"Go finish your homework and I'll call you when dinner's ready," Kelly told her son.

"Does Kris have to go?" Cole asked, a frown in his voice.

Kelly's eyes met Kris'. "Kris is staying."

Cole's smile widened. "Yes." He did a fist pump. "Okay, I only have math left to do. I'll be back soon," he told Kris. "Don't go anywhere."

He ran back out and Kelly inclined her head. "Come with me to the kitchen," she told Kris.

He pushed himself up, his long legs unfurling from the

uncomfortable position after sitting in the easy chair. "I'm right behind you."

It was funny how familiar it felt following her into the kitchen. When they were kids it was the first place they'd head after school. He had the appetite of an elephant back then, his body growing so fast his stomach could barely keep up with it. But now as he watched her hips swing and the way her dark hair tumbled down over her shoulders it was an altogether different kind of hunger he felt.

"Can you close the door?" Kelly asked once he'd followed her inside the kitchen.

"You don't want anybody else to see the way you can stuff three Twinkies in your mouth at the same time?"

Kelly's eyes widened. And damn if the ghost of a smile didn't pass her lips. "I'd forgotten about that."

"It was your party trick."

"And that's why I got all the guys," she joked. And then the smile dissolved from her lips. "Why are you here?"

"I told you, I came to talk to your dad." He leaned back against the counter, running his hand through his hair.

"About the loan? Why? I thought we talked about it last night."

Kris swallowed. "I didn't actually come about the loan. Not entirely, anyway. I wanted to talk to him about something else."

Kelly gave him a searching look. "About what?"

"That's between him and me."

"Oh no you don't." She stepped toward him, her eyes narrowing.

"Kel!" They both stopped talking at the sound of her dad's shout.

"Yeah?"

Kris tried not to smile at the way she shouted back.

"If you can hear me I can hear you. And so can Cole."

Kelly's eyes met Kris'. "Shit."

"I heard that, too," her dad hollered, and Kelly rolled her eyes.

"He didn't," she told Kris, her voice low. "He just knows me too well." She reached for his wrist, circling her fingers around it. The contact of her skin against his made his body heat up. "Come outside," she said, inclining her head to the door.

"Sure." It was stupid how much he was enjoying this. He'd always liked the dynamic between Kelly and her dad. So different to the way he'd spoken to his own parents. And the way they'd treated him.

He slid his wrist out of the bracelet of her fingers and grasped her palm, liking the way her breath had a little stutter at his touch.

Did she feel this too? This stupid yearning? Laura would probably say it was a need to be young again. To be the kids they once were.

The ones who, for just a moment, couldn't keep their hands off each other.

Whatever it was, she didn't let go as she used her other hand to unlatch the back door, pulling Kris out into the cool winter air.

"Where are we going?" he asked her, still amused. "Because if you want me to get naked I'm gonna need more than frozen temperatures."

"Kris!" She shook her head.

"What? You're not dragging me off for my body."

"No, you idiot. I want to talk without people listening." She pulled him to the rundown summer house at the back of her yard, yanking the door open. The smell of old grass and dust assailed his senses as Kelly pulled him inside, kicking the door shut behind him and latching it.

He missed her holding his hand.

The only light came from the holes in the roof. It was enough for him to be able to see some old plant pots and a rusted mower, along with long-forgotten garden tools fixed to the half-slanted walls.

"You've kept the place nice," Kris said, looking around.

Her lips twitched again. "Don't try to make me laugh. I'm mad at you."

She didn't sound it. Didn't look it either. She looked like she was about to laugh out loud.

"What are you mad about?" he asked softly.

"I don't know yet. Whatever you're about to tell me." Her voice was low. Half teasing. Christ, he'd missed this.

Missed everything about this woman.

"What if I was about to tell you that you've won a million dollars?" he asked, lifting a brow.

"I'd be mad."

He chuckled. "Of course you would."

"Because I'd want to know how you knew first? Or if it had anything to do with you." She crossed her arms over her chest and of course it made him look at the swell of her breasts.

Why was he such a damn horndog? Every time she was close he was so aware of her. Wanted to touch her.

Wanted more than that.

"It's a good thing you haven't won then," he said. "And if you want to know, I came to talk to your dad about his surgery."

Kelly's brows knitted. "Why?"

"Why do you think? I want to help."

"No."

His smile didn't waver. "Why did I know you were going to say that?"

"Why did I know you were going to try to save me all over again?" she countered.

"I'm not trying to save you. I'm trying to help your dad. I like him, he's in pain, and I can do something about it."

"Because you have money and we don't." There was a waver to her voice he didn't like.

"No. Because that's just luck, Kel. I got into a business in the right place at the right time and made a lot of money. And you stayed here, doing the right thing, and you didn't."

Her lips parted, her breath escaping in a soft cloud of vapor.

"Remember how you wanted to travel the world and become a millionaire?" he asked her.

"Yeah, well life had other plans." She lifted a brow. "I had to stay here. First for my dad, then for Lyle." Another cloud of breath. "And then for Cole."

"Because you were always the steadfast one. The loyal one. The one who stayed while the rest of us fled. And it fucking sucks that you had to do that while the rest of us thrived."

"Don't worry, Lyle isn't thriving." She lifted a brow.

"Have you heard from him recently?" he asked, trying to ignore the jealousy twisting his gut.

"Only when he remembers he has a son. Which is about twice a year and never on his birthday or Christmas." She ran the tip of her tongue along her lip, and he watched silently. "I guess I'm just easy to run away from."

"Kel..." He reached out, touched her jaw with the tip of his fingers, fully expecting her to pull back. But she didn't. Just stared at him like he had all the answers. "Walking away from you was the hardest thing I've ever done."

She swallowed but still said nothing. He'd never seen her look so vulnerable. Not even last night when she was on his lap and he was as hard as a fucking iron bar.

He ran his thumb along her soft bottom lip and still she didn't pull back. It was like a game. That one where you put all those things on the donkey, pushing your luck until finally it bucked.

He didn't want to lose this time.

"I was a fucking idiot for walking away," he told her, his gaze locked on hers.

"You asked me to go with you." Her voice was low. He felt her lip tremble beneath his touch.

"I knew you wouldn't come. I wanted an excuse to hate you." That was the truth. "You're too good a person to leave somebody who needs you." And so many people needed her back then. Her dad, Lyle. The baby growing inside of her. The one who'd grown up to be the kid sitting inside the house, doing his homework.

"You hated me?" she asked. There was hurt in her voice.

"No. I just wanted to. It would have been easier to walk away like that. Easier to get on with my life. But I could never hate you. You were too good to hate."

"I'm not a good person." She shook her head.

He tipped her chin up, his eyes darkening as he stared down at her. "Stop saying that. You're the best person I know."

Disbelief washed over her. This was what he'd hated. The way she could never give herself credit. "Kelly, you've spent the last twelve years taking care of your dad, of his business. Raising your kid alone. You're the most selfless person I've ever met and if you keep insisting you're not, I'm gonna get pissed."

"I cried every night after you left," she said, and it felt like somebody was squeezing his gut. "I'd hide away so Lyle couldn't see me. Not that he was here much anyway. I was so scared about everything. About the baby, about living in Winterville without you here. I wasn't sure how I was going to keep going."

Kris winced. He didn't want to think of her crying. Didn't want any of this.

"I hate that," he said, his voice soft. "I hate that I made you cry. Hate that I hurt you." He slid his palm around her cheek. She leaned into it, her breath warm against his palm. And somewhere in his head there was a voice telling him that getting this close was a bad idea.

But he couldn't resist her any longer. Couldn't ignore the way his blood heated up just from looking at her. The way his body pulsed in time to hers whenever they were close. This was why he'd walked away. She'd chosen somebody else and he knew he couldn't stay in the same town as her.

Not when her heart always sang to his.

When he kissed her it wasn't soft. It was rough and needy and full of a lifetime of emotions. His mouth pressed hard against hers and she pushed her body against his, her arms circling his neck as she parted her lips and let him in.

Her tongue was soft and reticent. Like silk against his. From the tight bind of his arms as he held her close, to the thick ridge of him pressed against her, it was like he was programmed to respond only to her.

And just like always, she fit against him perfectly. Her body soft against his hard. Her kisses needy against his domination.

Her body arched against him until he slid his hands down her thighs and hitched them, binding her to him as he lifted her up.

He turned, pressed her against something – was it a box? He had no fucking idea. He just needed the solid surface so he could roll his hips against her. She was pulling at his hair, her mouth letting out little mews like a fucking kitten as he slid his hands across her round behind.

"Mom!"

Kelly pulled her head back, her eyes wide as they met his. "Shit."

"Where are you? I finished my homework. Is Kris still here?"

He gently let her down and Kelly stepped back, her hand covering her mouth. He reached down to adjust himself and her eyes followed his movement.

"We're in here," Kris said, his voice even. "Your mom wanted to show me something."

Cole rattled the shed door. "It's stuck."

"You okay?" Kris mouthed to Kelly.

She blinked but didn't answer. So he reached for the latch and opened the door. Cole walked in, grinning. "What are you guys looking at?"

Kelly still didn't seem to have the use of her voice.

"Your mom thought there might be some old photos in here. Of us all when we were kids."

"There aren't any photos in here." Cole gave him a strange look. "Mom keeps them on her phone."

"She must have been mistaken then," Kris said easily, putting his arm around Cole's. "Did you know when we were kids camera phones were crap?"

"That's a bad word."

Yeah, it was. "Shit." Fuck, had he said that out loud? He needed a swear filter. He wasn't used to being around kids.

"So's that," Cole said. "Mom, those are bad words, aren't they?"

Kelly brought her gaze to her son. "Yeah, honey, they are."

"So you should tell Kris off, right? The same way you tell me off."

Her gaze met his again. He smirked at her and she smiled back. "I'm not his mother," she said to Cole. "I'm yours."

"Did your mom used to tell you off?" Cole asked him.

"All the time." Kris nodded. From the corner of his eye he

could see Kelly shivering. "We should go inside," he said. "Before everybody freezes."

"I don't know why you were in here in the first place," Cole grumbled, as the three of them walked back toward the house. "I could have told you there were no photos out here. And you're supposed to be making dinner, remember?"

Kelly pulled the back door opened and they trooped inside, the warmth of the house curling around them like a blanket.

"Okay then," she said, letting out a long breath. "Let's get started on the burgers."

"Can I help?" Kris asked, watching as she washed and dried her hands, before grabbing a tray of ground beef from the refrigerator.

"No. You go watch some television with Cole and Dad. I've got this."

16

K*ris, age 21*

"I didn't mean for it to happen, man. We just..." Lyle shrugged. "She needed somebody. And I was available."

It had felt like a gut punch when Kelly had told him that she and Lyle were dating. But what right did he have to be pissed at his best friends? He should be happy for them. Lyle seemed to have cleaned up his act, and Kelly was smiling as she worked behind the bar.

"Is she happy?" Kris asked.

"Yeah." Lyle nodded. "We both are."

"Then I'm happy for you." He was. Or at least he would be. Just as soon as his stomach stopped twisting. He shouldn't be angry. They made that promise years ago. He was just the sap who'd kept it.

"Thank you." Lyle nodded. "Kelly's been terrified about telling you. If you could just... I don't know, tell her it's okay. That would mean a lot."

"I will." Kris hated the idea of her worrying. "I'll tell her."

Lyle finished his beer and smiled. "Thank you. I know we had that stupid agreement. I'm an asshole for breaking it."

Yeah he was. "We were kids when we made it. It doesn't matter now," Kris said. From the corner of his eye, he could see Kelly looking over at them. Lyle was right, she really did look anxious. He turned around and winked at her, and her shoulders relaxed.

He was happy for his friends. Or he would be. Eventually. As soon as he didn't want to punch something.

"You got somebody at college?" Lyle asked him.

"Kind of." It was a lie. A complete one. "But it's new."

"Can I tell Kelly that?" Lyle asked. "She'll be relieved."

"Sure. Go ahead." Kris shrugged. "Want another beer?"

"Let's have some whiskey instead," Lyle said. "I kind of got a taste for it."

"Sounds good." Mostly because he wanted to get hammered tonight. Forget everything.

Lyle walked over to the bar and leaned across the counter, whispering something in Kelly's ear. She smiled and nodded then looked back over at Kris.

There was a softness to her gaze. Like she was imploring him. He smiled back and nodded but he didn't feel better at all.

As the two of them talked at the bar he grabbed his phone from his pocket, opening up his mail app to see the email he'd received today.

A job offer. For a summer job with an investment bank in New York.

He hadn't planned on taking it, thinking he'd spend the summer with his family and with Kelly. And yeah, maybe with Lyle.

But the thought of watching them together for two months made his stomach twist.

He was going to take the job.

Kelly's mind was a whirl of thoughts as she opened the door of the Tavern. The sound of conversation and laughter hit her ears as she let the solid piece of wood close behind her and headed for the bar.

She'd kissed Kris Winter. No, that wasn't just a kiss. It was a battle. They'd practically eaten each other for dinner like wild animals.

Probably would have done worse if Cole hadn't walked out and broken things up.

And then her cheeks heated again, because what if her son had caught them? How would she have explained the fact she was curled around her ex-friend like a monkey clinging to a tree?

She never should have demanded he talk to her in the summer house.

"Is everything okay?" she asked Will, her voice thick as she hung her coat up and grabbed an apron, wrapping it around her waist.

"All good. Just started to get busy about twenty minutes ago," Will told her. "That's when I messaged you."

Mariah Carey's voice was pumping out of the jukebox, and a group of twenty-something guys were surrounding the pool table, laughing as their friend missed a shot. Kelly turned to the customers lining up at the bar and took the first person's order, thankful for the distraction from thinking about him.

Will's message had come through right as they'd finished dinner. The four of them had been sitting around the table, only two of them aware of the thick atmosphere. And thank God for that. She was glad her dad and Cole were oblivious.

They didn't need to know what an idiot she was being. Just because her past had come striding back into her life, turning everything upside down.

"I asked for a soda, not a glass of beer," the man in front

of her said. Kelly looked down, frowning at the half-filled glass in her hand.

"Sorry. A soda coming right up," she muttered.

She needed to get her head in the game.

"Are you okay?" Will asked her, his brows pinching.

"Yeah, I'm fine," she said tightly.

"You don't look fine. You look kinda peaky." He lifted a brow. "You're not coming down with something, are you?"

Just a case of the stupids. "No, honestly, it's all good."

"I could call Carmen?" he suggested. "If you're not feeling okay."

She opened her mouth to protest, then closed it again. He was right, she really wasn't feeling okay. She was confused and weirded out, and more than a little annoyed at herself. She couldn't even remember who to serve next. "I'll call her," she said.

Will nodded, looking pleased. "Good idea."

It only took Carmen ten minutes to walk through the doors, since she lived right on the other side of the square. But even in that time Kelly managed to mess up two more orders. Will blew out a mouthful of air as the older woman shrugged her jacket off and shot Kelly a concerned look. "You do look a little sick, hon," she said. "You should go home."

Kelly shot her a wan smile. "I will. Thanks for coming in to replace me."

"Any time." Carmen winked and turned to the customer at the front, leaving Kelly to take off her apron and grab her coat.

As soon as the cool night air hit her, she felt another wave of dizziness wash over her. Clicking on the key, she opened Amber's car and sat down heavily on the driver's seat.

She hated feeling so confused. She was supposed to hate Kris Winter, not kiss him. Yet just thinking of him made her body feel like it was on fire.

Grabbing her phone, she pulled up his number, hitting the call button before she could think better of it.

"Hello." He sounded so calm. So serene.

"It's me."

"I know. Your name came up on the phone." And now he sounded amused. Why wasn't he an emotional mess like she was?

"Why do you keep trying to save me and my family?" she asked.

There was a moment of silence. Followed by a chuckle. "Did you make it to the tavern?"

"Yes. Well kind of. I'm now back outside it." She frowned. "Can you answer my question?"

"Why are you outside? It's cold."

"I'm in my car. Well, Amber's car."

Kris cleared his throat. "I just got home. Your dad and Cole said they'd finish the dishes without me."

"Okay. But are you going to answer my question?" She tried not to sound frustrated.

"Are you all right?" His voice was soft. "You sound... I don't know. Worked up."

That's because she was worked up. All messed up and emotional. And it was his fault. "Why do you want to pay for his surgery?"

"Because he's a good guy and he needs help. And maybe I want to give you a break. You're running yourself ragged trying to take care of everybody."

"Oh." She wanted to find the anger again. To tell him no.

"Is that it?" His voice was teasing.

"What do you mean?"

"I was expecting anger. Shouting. Don't you want to tell me I shouldn't interfere and I should get out of town?"

Kelly blinked. "I don't know. Should I?"

"Kel, are you okay?" he asked, his voice low. "Because you don't sound okay."

She opened her mouth to tell him she was fine, but all that came out was the softest of breaths.

No, she wasn't okay. She hadn't been okay since the day he'd walked back into town. Or maybe since the day he'd left it. She was tired and confused but more than anything she was so sick of the fight.

Exhausted by it, truth be told. She could feel it physically seep out of her.

"Where exactly are you?" Kris asked. "I'll come get you."

"No." She took a deep breath. "I'll come to you. At the cabin."

"Do you feel well enough to drive?" he asked, and the concern in his voice made her heart tighten.

"Yeah." She looked at herself in the dark glass of the windshield, taking in the heat of her cheeks, the wildness of her eyes. It was a lie, but it was the truth, too. She wasn't sick, she was emotional. And she never could deal with that. "I'll be there in five minutes."

"I'll be waiting."

She wasn't sure if that was a threat or a promise.

───────

Kris was pacing the porch of his wooden cabin when he saw her car winding along the little lane. The headlamps illuminated him, making him blink, but it didn't stop him from striding toward where she parked. As soon as his eyes accustomed themselves to the dark they focused on her. She was sitting in the driver's seat of Amber's car. Her cheeks pink, her lips open.

He stopped alongside the driver's and pulled it open. Kelly had released her seatbelt but still hadn't moved, and up close he could see the furrows in her brow and the pinch of her lips as she was thinking.

Damn, he knew all her tells. The happy and the sad ones. The thoughtful and the impulsive ones.

Not that she was ever that impulsive. People thought she was because they never got to see this side of her. The one that weighed the options, spent hours thinking about consequences.

She'd spent half of their teenage years warning him and Lyle not to do something because it'd get them thrown off the hockey team or possibly out of school.

"Are you coming inside?" he finally asked her. "It's pretty cold out here."

She looked up at him, her eyes catching his. The vulnerability he saw in them made him ache. It reminded him of the day he'd walked away from her for the last time.

"Are you scared?" he asked, his voice soft.

"Never."

He bit down a smile. Of course she'd never admit to that. "There's no need to be scared. I'm not going to eat you." Unless you want me to. That unsaid part shimmered between them, and she swallowed hard.

"I need to ask you one question," she said. "Before I get out."

He tipped his head to the side. "Shoot."

Kelly swallowed again, that vulnerability still softening her features. It was like she'd shrugged her armor off, just for a moment. So soft. So achingly beautiful.

"Did you ever love me?"

Kris blinked. What kind of question was that? "Of course I did."

"Okay." She nodded. "Okay."

Her hand was trembling on the steering wheel. He

reached inside to touch it. Damn, she was freezing. "Will you come inside now?"

She exhaled, her breath clouding inside the car. "I don't think I can talk anymore. It hurts."

"Then we won't talk. Just come inside."

Kelly nodded and she let him help her out, her suede boots hitting the frozen grass next to where she parked. Kris took the keys from her, closing the door and locking it, before leading her to his cabin and pulling her inside.

She walked over to the fireplace, her fingers touching the garland attached to the mantelpiece.

"You decorated for Christmas," she said, surprised.

"Alaska did." He lifted a brow. "She told me it was looking like the Grinch's hideout. Sent her people in to do their thing."

"It's pretty."

"Yeah." His voice was thick.

"What do you do here?" she asked him. "In the evenings?"

"I help out Alaska at the Inn sometimes. Or I do some work."

"You're still working?" she asked, looking surprised.

"Yeah. Well kind of. I'm on a sabbatical. Leave. Whatever. But I still get emails that need to be handled. And I check in with the people who work for me."

"I bet you're a fun boss," she said, walking back toward him. She tilted her head up to look him in the eye.

"I take care of my people," he said, eyeing her as she came to a stop a few inches from him. He could smell flowers on her, the same aroma he'd inhaled as they kissed each other. It was soft. Pretty.

Kelly.

"You always take care of people," she said softly, lifting her hand to cup his cheek. He put his hand over hers, not willing to break the connection.

"I didn't take care of you."

"You did. All the time. We took care of each other."

He slid his fingers between hers, still holding her palm against his rough cheek.

"Do you ever wonder what would have happened if we'd been brave enough to admit we were attracted to each other?" she asked him. "Back when we were kids?"

"I was a hormonal mess. I would have fucked it up." He smiled softly. "I mean I fucked it up anyway, but it would have been worse..."

"Because you would have fucked me, too." Her eyes were dark. Her voice breathy. And now all he could think about was fucking her. Sliding inside of her, making her gasp like she did in the shed.

He'd been a kid when he'd walked away from her. Now he was a man. He wanted to make her tighten around him, make her groan his name. Wanted to see her skin flush and her body soften and her jaw slacken with the kind of pleasure he knew he could give her.

You're not here for that.

He blinked the voice away. Damn it, he was. He was here for this. Whatever this was.

He'd walked away once. He wasn't going to do it again.

Kelly rolled forward on the balls of her feet – he knew that because she'd never be tall enough to rest her face in the crook between his shoulder and neck otherwise. He felt her breath against his throat, then her lips.

He was as hard as a rock already.

"Kel..." His voice rumbled against her mouth. "Are you sure?"

She kissed him again, sucking his skin in.

"Because if you're not, you need to step away. Or I do."

She kissed his jaw, her tongue trailing along the shadow of his evening beard growth.

"Kel..." His voice was strangled. His restraint hanging on by a string. "Please..."

"I'm sure."

It was like a switch being flicked. He released his hold on her hand and slid his palms down her back, cupping her behind and hitching her against him. She wrapped her thighs around his waist, her body fitting against his perfectly, and he carried her over to the bed in the corner, sitting down so she was straddling his thighs.

Brushing her hair back from her face he could feel the heat of her cheeks. Before he could ask her – again – if she was okay, she smiled and damn if it didn't make him want her more.

"Why are you smiling?"

"Because I can read you like a book. You're wondering if I'm still feeling sick."

He narrowed his eyes. "Are you?"

"No." She shook her head. "I wasn't sick, I was just..." She kissed the corner of his lip and he grabbed her head, centering their mouths to kiss her hard.

"Just what?" he asked when he released her.

Kelly blinked as though dazed. "Just messed up thinking about you."

"And yet here you are. Getting messed up some more."

Her eyes crinkled. "Maybe I like getting messed up," she said. He needed to kiss her again. This time he was soft, teasing, his tongue sliding against hers. She let out a little gasp and he pulled her down hard on his lap.

Letting her know exactly what their kissing was doing to him.

"Mess me up some more," she whispered against his mouth.

"I intend to."

The chemistry had always been there. They'd called it a

friendship once. But now it was different. Mature. Aching. He lifted her again, put her on her back on his bed, climbed over her, and smiled because this woman was everything.

"Are you going to undress me?" she asked.

Yeah, she wasn't sick. Not with an illness anyway. She was comfortable. Teasing. His Kelly.

No, not his. And definitely not Lyle's. She owned herself. That's what he'd always admired about her.

His eyes scanned her face then her body. She was wearing the same clothes she was earlier, but somehow they seemed more figure hugging. Maybe he'd been too busy looking at her face to notice before.

But he was noticing now. Taking in the soft swell of her breasts. The nipped in waist. The hips that he wanted to dig his fingers into as he took her.

"No. I'm not going to undress you."

Kelly's smile disappeared. For the first time she looked unsure.

"I want you to undress yourself. For me." He pushed himself off her, letting her wriggle from underneath him.

"Is that right?" she asked.

"Yep." For some reason he needed her to take the lead. Not just because watching her peel her clothes off would be hot – though that was reason enough. He needed her to be going into this with her eyes wide open. He'd been an asshole to her before. This time he was going to make sure she had the power.

She stepped off the bed, a smile playing at her lips. Then she pulled off her sweater, revealing pale skin and a black lace bra.

"You like?" she asked him.

"I love."

Her lip quirked. She reached behind her back and unclasped her bra, pulling the straps down her arms.

And her breasts. Fucking perfection. Full and yet not too full. His mouth dropped open, his hard-on almost painful as he took them in.

"Come here," he whispered.

"Not yet."

She unbuttoned her jeans, her eyes still on him, shimmying them down her hips and letting them fall to the floor.

He couldn't take his eyes off of her, the woman he'd dreamed of. The woman he'd avoided.

The woman who was always his fucking destiny no matter how hard he'd fought it. Wearing tiny black panties and the smile that always haunted his dreams. Looking at him like he was some kind of god.

He slid from the bed onto his knees, reached for those perfect hips, and curled his palms around them. Pulling her close, he buried his face in her thighs, feeling their warmth, their softness. The damp patch on the scant fabric where they met.

"Kris..."

He yanked at the lace, leaning back as he pulled them down. Kelly's fingers curled into his hair, as though to steady herself as his knuckles met the floor and he pulled her panties off one foot at a time.

"Take your clothes off now."

"Not yet." If he took his clothes off the urge to be inside of her would be too strong. Almost unignorable. And he wanted to ignore it, because she was here and naked in front of him. He needed to savor her. To tease her.

To taste her.

And he did, slicking his tongue along her seam. Kelly let out a gasp, her fingers digging into his scalp as he prised her legs open further, pushing his face into her, tasting the sweet musk of her need. His tongue found the swollen part of her that it needed, playing with her, teasing her until she was calling out his name.

He could do this forever. Lick her and hear her gasps. Touch her and feel her legs tremble. She was still clinging to his head, her breath tight and rapid, her thighs pressed against his cheeks, as he slowly slid his fingers inside of her until her whole body tightened around him.

"Kris..."

Yeah, that's it, beautiful girl. Say my name. Scream it. He wrapped his lips around her, sucking her in. Her body tightened around his fingers, fluttering and pulling him in.

And then everything snapped. Her thighs clamped against him, her body gripped his fingers like they never wanted to let go, as she let out a high, keening cry. He sucked her, curled his fingers inside of her. Did everything he could to prolong the pleasure until she collapsed and he caught her, carrying her to the bed.

"Oh my God." Her eyes were wide. Shocked. "I don't think I've ever come like that."

He half-smiled, still tasting her on his tongue. "In that case, I should warn you. That was just a teaser."

17

If she was being truly honest with herself, the reason she'd driven here was for *this*. For *him*. To let him fill this ache, the one that had been inside of her for the longest time. The one that only he could soothe.

Her body was still pulsing, the pleasure still warming her from the inside out as he leaned over to kiss her, his lips tasting of her need.

"You've got too many clothes on," she whispered, because despite the pleasure there was still some vulnerability there. He'd made her come. It was his turn.

"Then take them off me."

"No. You made me do it myself."

He chuckled against her mouth. "Damn, I'd forgotten how bossy you are."

"No you haven't," she teased.

He pulled back, grinning. "No, I hadn't. Did I tell you how much it turns me on?"

"Then get your clothes off, Winter."

He stood the same way she had, his eyes on hers as he unbuttoned his shirt. Kelly swallowed hard as he shucked it off. Yeah, she'd seen him shirtless before when she'd stormed over to talk to him, but not like this.

Not just for her. She scanned the planes of his chest, taking in the thickness of his pectorals, the ridged ripples of his stomach muscles. His shoulders were thick and broad, his chest hard and defined. Every part of her body pulsed at the sight of him.

Without saying a word, he unfastened his belt then his pants, sliding them down until he was only in a pair of dark shorts. Her eyes traveled down, taking in the hard ridge of him pushing against the jersey fabric. Damn, he was big. And she'd always been tiny.

"You like?" he asked, his voice thick, as he repeated the words she'd said when she was standing before him.

"It's fine." Her eyes crinkled as she said it.

He laughed and she reached for him, fully intending to return the favor. Not that it would be a hardship. She wanted to taste him like she wanted air. Wanted to feel the pulse of him against her tongue, wanted to tease him until he was breathless. She slid down to the floor and pulled at his shorts until his thickness slapped against his stomach.

Leaning forward, she kissed the tip.

"Kel..."

Then she slid her lips around him, feeling the plushness of his head against her tongue.

"Kel, stop. I can't..."

She pulled back from him, her eyes wide.

"Did I hurt you?" she asked. "Did I do something wrong?"

"No. I don't want to come in your mouth. And I'm about thirty seconds away from doing just that."

"It's okay. I want you to." It was weird how much she wanted to know what Kris Winter tasted like. Wanted to know how he felt pulsing between her lips. Did he moan? Did he groan? Was he silent when he came?

So many questions she wanted the answer to.

He reached down for her, pulling her to her feet. His expression was tender as he leaned down to kiss her, his hand cupping the side of her neck.

"You don't have to. It isn't a game of quid pro quo."

"Shut up." She kissed him again then dropped down, taking him back into her mouth before he could protest. God, she loved the feel of him. He was thick and warm, filling her mouth with his hardness. His fingers tangled in her hair as she slid her lips up, her tongue trailing over the plush head, then pushed her mouth down again, as far as she could go.

"Kel, I'm close."

She sucked him hard, her mouth slick, her hands reaching behind him, sliding against his balls.

"You feel so good," he grunted, his movements erratic. "So soft. So fucking soft."

Her eyes flicked up to his. She could see only darkness there. The needy kind that made her body contract with desire.

"You need to pull away now," he whispered.

She lifted a brow and stayed exactly where she was, moving faster over his dick until she felt him swell even more. And then he was calling out her name, his body bucking, as he spilled inside of her. His head was tipped back, his mouth slack, his chest tight, his palm pressed against her head as he gave her his final surrender.

And then he withdrew from her mouth, lifted her up, and put them both onto the bed, his hand cupping her head as he kissed her hard.

"Jesus, woman. Are you okay?"

"Yeah." She nodded. "I'm feeling pretty good right now."

His lips quirked. "Just pretty good? I guess it's better than fine, but it's not exactly life changing. I need to work on my action."

"Shut up. You must know how good you are." She felt the tiredness wash over her and he pulled her against him, her head resting between the crook of his arm and his chest.

"Later then," he whispered, kissing her brow.

"Yeah. Later." It was strange how relaxed she felt. How safe she was in the arms of the man who'd broken her badly.

And how easy it was to fall asleep against his chiseled chest.

Kris slept so well he didn't wake until the light of the day pushed through the thin fabric of the cabin curtains. He rolled his head, his neck tight from sleeping at an awkward angle, then a smile pulled at his lips as he remembered last night. He turned to look at Kelly and it took a moment for him to realize she wasn't there. All that he could see was the empty space beside him.

"Kel?" He rolled onto his side. The door to the bathroom was open and there was no sign of her inside. He slid his feet to the wooden boards and stood, searching the floor for a sign of her clothes.

It was bare. Her clothes were gone.

Not bothering to dress, he walked to the window that looked out over the road to his cabin. Her car was gone, too. His jaw tightened.

Turning on his heel he walked over to where he'd left his pants, grabbing his phone from his pocket. Pulling up her number he pressed the call button, still frowning as it connected.

"This is Kelly. Leave a message."

He let out a breath. "Kel, this is Kris. Where'd you go?

You okay? Please call me and let me know." Frustrated, he ended the call and threw his phone on the bed. She should have woken him before she left.

Yeah, he knew she had a family to get home to. And he also knew she wouldn't want people gossiping about her car being outside his cabin. But dammit, she left without a word.

And that's when he realized he was getting a dose of his own medicine. He let out a low chuckle. He was the one who used to leave, and now he was standing here feeling like a chump.

Do you like that feeling?

Funny how that sounded like Kelly's voice in his head. He walked back to the window, letting his brow rest on the cold glass. His breath misted it as he stared out.

And that's when he saw it. At the end of the road. A car, parked, the engine running, fumes lifting up from the exhaust and dispersing into the cold light of the early morning.

It took him thirty seconds to pull on his jeans and a sweater, not bothering with underwear. He didn't bother with socks either, just shoved his feet into his engineer boots and stomped out of the cabin.

He didn't run but he didn't dawdle. Just strode purposefully toward that car with the idling engine at the end of the path. And when he got to it he could see Kelly sitting in the driver's seat, her back straight as an arrow.

The woman always had poise, even when she pissed him off.

He tapped on the driver's window and she jumped. Rolling the window down, she looked up at him, her face mussed from where she must have slept on the sheets.

"What are you doing?" he asked her.

"Going home."

His lip quirked. "It's gonna take you a long time at this pace. You might want to think about using the gas a little."

She didn't smile and it killed him a bit. "Are you okay?" he asked, his voice lower now.

Kelly exhaled heavily. "I'm always okay."

"No you're not. Nobody's *always* okay." His gaze was soft as he looked down at her. He could see how tired she was. This woman kept a thousand plates spinning every day and she never had time for herself. "Do you regret what we did?"

She pulled her lip between her teeth, then shook her head. "No. Maybe we needed it. To clear the air or something."

"To clear the air." He frowned. "What does that mean?"

"This thing between us. It was messing with my mind. Maybe now everything will come into focus." She reached out to trace the arc of the steering wheel. "I hope it will."

"You sucked my cock to stop your mind from being messed up?" He wasn't sure he had the right to be hurt, but it stung anyway. "Is that what you're trying to say?"

"No!" She shook her head. "You make it sound bad. I just think... I don't want..." She sighed again. "You don't owe me anything just because we made each other come."

He leaned down, his hand resting against the roof of the car, his gaze searching her eyes. Damn, she could be unreadable sometimes.

"I do owe you."

She shook her head again. "No."

"Kelly..."

"I need to go home."

She looked scared. Upset. And he hated that he was the one who'd made her that way. The same way he'd made her have to become strong, hard, unwilling to open herself up in case she got hurt.

"Okay," he said. "Go home. I'll call you later."

"You don't need to."

"But I want to," he said gently. "I want to call you. I want to be your friend." He wanted so much more, but that would scare her. "And I need to talk to your dad. Get the ball rolling on his surgery."

She lifted her eyes to look at him. "Do you think that's why I did it? To make you pay for his knee?"

"No." It was his turn to shake his head. "I think – or maybe I hope – you did it because you have feelings for me and you're attracted to me. The same way I am to you."

He couldn't stand not touching her anymore. "Will you at least get out so I can hug you?"

"You just want to seduce me with your hugs," she muttered, but there was humor there this time. He preferred it to the fear.

"You always said I gave the best ones."

"You did. You do."

"Then get out here and get one." He pulled the handle of the driver's door and opened it, waiting to see what she'd do. A ghost of a smile pulled at her lips as she pushed down on the button to unbuckle her seatbelt.

And then she climbed into his arms. He wrapped them around her, pulling her close, her head resting on his chest, her hands fisting his sweater. Her fingernail inadvertently scraped his nipple through the thin wool layer and he let out a grunt.

"Aren't you wearing anything underneath it?" she asked him.

"I got dressed in a hurry. Underwear wasn't an option."

"So you're not..." Her eyes widened as she looked down at his jeans.

"Wearing underwear there either." He grinned as he completed his sentence. "Now give me another hug, this time without the gashed nipple."

"I didn't gash your nipple. I scraped it."

"It feels like a gash," he said.

"That's because you're a baby." She was finally smiling. He reached down to brush the hair from her face, then kissed her brow.

"You okay now?" he asked, his voice serious. Because he didn't want her driving home if she wasn't.

"Getting there." She nodded. "And I really need to go before my dad and Cole realize I'm not there."

"Okay then." He leaned his head down to brush his lips against hers. Damn, he loved the way she felt in his arms. "We'll talk later."

"Will we?"

"Yep." He grinned. "Now get your ass out of here."

❧ 18 ❧

"You messed around with him again?" Amber said, sounding amused. "What's that supposed to mean?"

"It means we did *stuff*." Kelly widened her eyes. It was almost impossible to have a conversation like this in the coffee shop. She had no idea why she was even trying. Especially when it was full of tourists and Christmas cheer.

But her dad was in the Tavern with a group of his friends playing poker before opening. She could remember when they'd all get together at night, after the tavern was closed.

Now they were getting old and morning poker seemed so much more preferable. Whatever, here she was competing with Bing Crosby to be heard.

"What kind of stuff?" Amber looked like she was enjoying this.

"The kind of stuff your unborn baby shouldn't hear about," Kelly said. At least Willow wasn't here. She was spending time with her cousin and Aunt Everley at the Jingle Bell Theater.

"Wait a minute." Amber leaned down and whispered at the swell of her stomach. "Are you awake, baby?" Then a second later she looked at Kelly. "Completely asleep. Now spill, what's going on between you two?"

"I have no idea," Kelly said honestly. "It's just... I don't know. It doesn't matter. I shouldn't be talking about it without him being in agreement."

"I won't tell anybody."

"You'll tell North," Kelly pointed out. "And North is Kris' brother."

"How about I promise not to tell North if you promise to answer my questions?" Amber sipped at her hot chocolate, whipped cream clinging to her upper lip. And when Kelly didn't answer, Amber lifted a brow at her. "I told you about me and North when it happened. It's only fair you do the same."

"I had to practically prise it from you," Kelly pointed out. "You didn't want to say anything."

"Yeah, but after I did, I felt better. And so will you. Now spill."

"Ugh." Kelly grimaced but she knew her friend was right. She had to get it out before she drove herself up the wall overthinking things. "Okay, but you really promise not to tell?"

"Pinky swear," Amber said solemnly.

Well, here went nothing. Kelly took a long sip of her coffee and then sighed. "Kris and I kind of kissed in my shed yesterday. Then last night I went to his cabin and we, you know..."

"Had sex?" Amber asked. The woman next to her whipped around to stare at them. "Sorry, I meant six. Six coffees."

The woman frowned and turned back to her friends.

"No, we didn't have six coffees," Kelly replied, her voice low. "He just ate... a sandwich. And I had a hotdog."

Amber almost spit her drink out. "A hot dog?" A grin split her face. "As in Kris' hot dog?"

"Can you keep it down?" Kelly pleaded.

"Oh no, I'm getting my payback. And enjoying it." Amber was still grinning. "So how was his hot dog? Did you eat it all?" Her voice lowered. "Was there mustard involved?"

Kelly rolled her eyes. All those times she'd teased Amber about North and now the shoe was on the other foot and she hated it. "Yes."

"And the sandwich? Was that good, too?"

Kelly swallowed. "It was the best."

"Of course it was." Amber nodded. "So what's the problem?"

The woman was still listening, Kelly was sure of it. But she didn't know her. She looked like a tourist, and if she wanted to eavesdrop then let her.

"The problem is, I shouldn't have eaten them. And nor should he."

"Why not?" Amber blinked.

"Because I'm on a diet. And I don't need the calories." Or the consequences.

"You've lost me," Amber admitted. "Tell you what. Want to walk and talk?"

The woman groaned. Ha! Yep, she was listening.

"Sure." Kelly grabbed her coffee and Amber took her hot chocolate. They were already in to-go cups so they waved at Dolores behind the café counter and went outside. The sidewalks were as full of tourists as the café had been. They dodged a group of little kids in winter hats, crossed the road, and walked past the Tavern. The door was closed but she could hear the low hum of jazz coming out of the jukebox. Her dad always did love John Coltrane.

"So..." Amber prompted when it was clear they were

alone. "Let's start again but without the food metaphors. What exactly happened?"

Kelly blew out a mouthful of air and filled Amber in on Kris' visit to her house and then her visit to his cabin.

"Wow. I never realized there were so many unspoken feelings between you two," Amber said.

Yeah, and this was why Kelly had tried not to think about it for so long. Because this was a mess.

"Did you two ever..." Amber trailed off. "Before he left for Europe?"

Kelly knew exactly what she was asking. And the truth was too complicated. "Not really. Maybe. I don't know." All she knew was that she was making an even bigger mess and she had no idea how to stop. "I just wish..."

"What do you wish?" Amber asked.

"That I wasn't such an idiot."

"Oh honey." Amber took Kelly's hand and squeezed it. "You've got a lot going on, don't you?"

Kelly sighed heavily. "Yeah."

"I'm always here. If you want to talk."

"I know." Kelly nodded. But she also knew that Amber wasn't the one she needed to talk to. It was Kris, but she was scared.

More scared than she'd been of anything before.

"It's funny," Amber said, "because North was all worried yesterday. He couldn't get ahold of Kris for a while and started panicking that he'd left."

Kelly nodded. The same fear filled her. Which was silly, because she knew Kris would leave. He was only visiting. Not back for good.

"That's why I don't want Cole becoming attached to him."

It was the truth and a lie. Amber looked at her, full of sympathy, as though she knew Kelly wasn't just talking about Cole.

She was talking about herself. And she was already attached.

It felt like a battle. One she was fighting against her own desires and impulses. But one thing was certain, she'd stay strong for herself and Cole.

And in a few weeks, all of this would be over and things would be back to normal.

"Hey." North looked up from the tree he'd been cutting down, a smile on his face as he saw Kris approaching. "Wanna help me with this?"

"Sure." Kris walked over, grabbing a pair of work gloves from the toolbox next to where North was standing. "What do you need me to do?"

It was the final day of the harvest at the tree farm. Most of the trees had been cut down earlier in the season, ready to be shipped across the Eastern seaboard to North and Amber's loyal customers. But they'd had an unprecedented demand and North had spent the last couple of days cutting down as many trees as he could, working with his helicopter pilot to get them loaded into the truck to be delivered.

"Just hold her up while I finish. Then we'll lay her down gently and wrap her in ropes. The helicopter will lift her into the truck."

There were men working on every row of trees, cutting them down and trussing them up. "Where's the helicopter now?" Kris asked. It sounded distinctly silent.

"Waiting for us to tell him we're ready," North said. "There's no point in it being airborne until there's enough trees to load up." He finished sawing through the trunk, then pointed at the ropes, showing Kris how to truss the tree up for it to be moved. Each tree was wrapped in a net, then the rope was looped around it.

"Remember when we used to come here and play hide and seek as kids?" Kris asked.

"Yeah, I remember. I also remember you falling asleep and us being not able to find you for hours," North said dryly. "Gabe and I were about to call the cops. And we knew we'd get grounded for losing you."

"I'm a heavy sleeper." Kris shrugged. "And it all turned out okay."

"That time." Their eyes met and Kris knew what his brother was thinking about. The way their cousin, Alaska, had disappeared for forty-eight hours when she'd been camping with Gabe. She'd only been eight, Gabe a little older.

And it had torn their family apart.

"So how are things going?" North asked him.

"With what?"

North's eyes crinkled. "I don't know. I assume you're here to get something off your chest. Unless you've developed a new found love of evergreens."

It was strange how well his brother knew him, even though they'd been apart for years. "I think I messed things up with Kelly."

They moved to the next tree. North passed him the net to pull over the branches. "How did you mess things up? Haven't you apologized to her yet?"

"I've tried."

North's gaze flickered to his. "And?"

"And then I messed things up more."

North laughed. "You may have to be more specific if you're looking for advice."

"Who said I'm looking for advice?" Kris asked him.

"Why else are you here?"

Kris blew out a mouthful of air. "Okay, I'm looking for

advice. Kelly came to my cabin last night. We did some stuff. Then she ran away."

"Oh." North started up the chainsaw and touched the blade to the trunk. Kris kept quiet, not wanting to disturb his brother while he was working. And when the tree was down they trussed it together again before moving onto the next.

"What does 'oh' mean?" Kris asked him.

"It means exactly what it says."

Kris frowned. "I thought you were going to give me some advice."

"I thought you were going to act like a grown up."

Annoyance washed over him. Where did North get off telling him to grow up? "Where haven't I acted like a grown up?"

"You two talked yet?"

"Yeah."

"About Lyle?"

His mouth dried. "Not in so many words."

"So you messed around while the elephant danced around the room. And then you wonder why she bolted?"

"It wasn't like that," Kris protested. "She came to me. To my cabin. And I asked her if she wanted to talk and she said no."

North sighed. "Look, I get it, I do. You and Kelly... there was always something there. Before Lyle, after Lyle. During Lyle..."

"We made sure there was nothing there during Lyle."

North shot him an older-brother-knows-better kind of look, then strode to the next tree.

"I just wish I'd done things differently," Kris said.

"Don't we all? I don't know anybody who's got to our age that doesn't have regrets," North said. "I know I do."

"I should have stayed around to help Kelly. Be the friend I thought I was."

"Yeah, well we both know you can't save people from themselves." North gave him a small smile. "Look at Dad."

"I'd rather not."

"Yeah, me either."

North scrunched his face together in concentration, then looked Kris in the eye. "I'm not a big one for talking about feelings. None of us ever were. But the one thing I've learned is that regrets are useless unless you use them for something. For change. Unless you take what you did wrong and turn it around to make it right. That's the only time you should listen to them."

Kris stared at him for a moment. He wasn't sure he'd ever heard his brother talk like that. It touched something inside of him.

Something that knew North was right.

Silently they cut down the next tree, and North's words reverberated around Kris' head. He'd been an idiot. He'd come here to talk to her. To apologize. To make up for the hurt he'd caused all those years ago.

And instead he'd taken the easy way out. Given Kelly what she needed. Taken what he'd needed.

He'd loved it. Loved that she'd come to him to be soothed. That every time he touched her somehow she felt softer in his arms.

But it was too early. Or too late. He wasn't sure which now.

"I need your help," he said when North had finished cutting through the trunk.

"Yeah, that's patently obvious." North lifted a brow.

"I don't mean I need your lectures." God knew he'd given enough of those to himself. "I need your help to talk with Kelly."

"I'm listening."

"I need to talk to her but finding the time to talk is something else altogether," Kris told him. "She's working at the tavern all day and night."

"It's the holiday season. She's busy." North shrugged. "We all are."

"Yeah, she is. But if I want to talk to her during the day, I'm gonna need some help getting her away from the bar and to somewhere quiet."

"Okay, tell me what you need and I'll do it. Or we'll all do it. Just say the word."

And this was why he loved his brother. And his whole family. "Thank you," Kris said, a smile finally pulling at his lips. "I appreciate it."

❧ 19 ❧

K *elly, age 22*

Lyle was drunk again. It was happening more often than it wasn't. His way of coping since he lost his momma five months ago. They'd caught the cancer too late and Kelly and Lyle had been with her as she slowly slipped away. Lyle hadn't been the same since.

And she felt for him, she did. If she lost her dad she didn't know what she'd do. Maybe that's why she was still here. Watching the door as he stumbled in and leaned against the jamb, his face red from the whiskey and whatever else he was on.

"Hey." She looked up from her book. "I thought you'd be home earlier."

"I lost track of time." Okay, he wasn't that drunk. At least he could talk this time.

"You want to head up to bed?" She slid a bookmark between the pages and put her book on the coffee table. "I'm beat."

"Yeah." His eyes weren't focusing properly. "By the way, Kris is back."

Her heart did a little clench. She'd barely heard from him all year. He'd come back for Lyle's mom's funeral but had left right after the service ended. It was like he was avoiding her and she hated it.

"He okay?"

"Why'd you want to know?" Lyle asked, tipping his head to the side.

"I was just wondering." Lyle had started to get jealous when she'd mention another guy. Every time she talked about a guy at the bar he'd grill her until she felt like she was wrung out.

"He's fine."

"Good." She nodded.

Lyle didn't say another word. Just turned and headed down the hallway. A moment later she heard him stumble on the stairs and mutter an oath. With a sigh, she stood and walked to the tiny kitchen and filled up a glass with water, then grabbed the painkillers from the medicine cabinet.

She and Lyle had been living together for six months now, right after his mom got the diagnosis. He'd begged her to move in with him. He'd been so sad about his mom that she'd agreed.

The drinking had started in earnest after his mom had moved into the hospice center in Marshall's Gap. But to be fair, he'd always drunk a little more than anybody else. It had increased slowly, getting worse each day. And by the time she realized he had a problem, she was in too deep.

She heard Lyle crash into something overhead. Their bed, probably. When she got up there she'd have to help him out of his clothes and under the covers. She was tired of it. She needed to stop him. But she was so afraid he'd do something stupid. Because when he wasn't drunk he was sad.

All the time.

Something had to give, though. She pressed her lips together and pulled her phone out, running her finger along the screen until she found Kris' number. The last time she'd sent him a message was after the funeral, just to check that he'd gotten home okay.

. . .

Yes, all good. Take care of him for me. – Kris.

She swallowed hard and pressed her finger on the screen to bring up the keyboard, typing quickly because she needed to get upstairs to help Lyle.

I heard you're back in Winterville. Are you around this week to talk? I need some advice. – Kelly.

If anybody knew what to do about Lyle, Kris would.

It took a minute for his reply to flash up.

Sure, I'm free tomorrow if that works. Everything okay? – Kris.

No. It wasn't. Everything was far from okay. But maybe, just maybe, with Kris' help, they could turn this thing around.

For the first time in a long while she felt some hope.

"What's going on?" Kelly looked at the three Winter brothers standing behind the bar. North was serving a customer, his large hands wrapped around the pump as beer flowed into a glass. Gabe was loading the dishwasher. And

Kris was smiling at her in that soft way that made her stomach do a twist.

He walked out from behind the counter. "I'm taking you out."

She blinked. "What? No. I have to work."

"That's what North and Gabe are here for. I know you're a demon behind the bar, so I figure two of them can equal one of you." It was weird, but he looked almost nervous, an emotion she wasn't sure she'd seen on Kris before. "I'd like us to go out for something to eat and to talk. Just old friends. But if you'd rather not, you can still take the night off, go home, and put your feet up."

She let out a lungful of air. This had been coming for a while, she knew that. And maybe she needed this talk as much as he did.

But there was still that little jolt of anxiety. What came after the talk? Would he feel unburdened and leave?

The thought made her stomach tighten.

You've been through worse, girl. She wanted to laugh at that voice in her head, because it was true. She was surviving. Maybe even thriving.

She let out a long breath. "Okay, let's go talk."

His smile was like the sun coming out after years of rain clouds. He reached for her hand and she let him take it, leading her out of the Tavern and into the cool evening air. It hadn't snowed for a couple of days, but the temperatures had been low enough to cover the sidewalks and trees with a glistening frost.

"Hey!" Dolores called from the café door. Despite it being closing time the tables inside were still half full. "I have your order here."

Kris walked over to take the two brown bags from her, leaning down to kiss her cheek. "Thank you."

"Any time, honey. Now you kids behave."

He chuckled. "We're just going out to talk."

"That's what they all say." Dolores winked and walked back into the café.

"You ready?" Kris asked Kelly, nodding his head at North's truck.

"Aren't we going in your car?"

"I figure if we're gonna freeze our asses off we should do it in a truck bed."

"We're eating outside?" She frowned. "In this weather?"

"I have blankets. And hot coffee." He glanced at the bags he was still holding. "I thought we'd drive up to the mountains and look out over the town. But if you'd rather go somewhere warm we can do that."

"No," she said quickly, because the mountains sounded perfect. The skies were clear and the stars were out and she knew the view of Winterville would be beautiful from there. She couldn't remember the last time she'd seen it from a distance at night. She was too busy working to take a trip like that.

Kris wedged the brown bags behind some boxes in the flatbed, then walked around to open her door. "I don't remember you being such a gentlemen when we were in high school," she said lightly, liking the way he lifted a brow as she teased him.

"Yeah, well I don't remember you being a lady either."

She climbed in and he pushed the door shut behind her, walking around to the driver's side and sliding in behind the wheel.

"I was a perfect lady in high school," she protested.

"Like when you beat up Amelia Day?"

"She was teasing the little kids. She deserved it."

His eyes met hers and his lip twitched. "I know. You were kick ass."

"I just don't like bullies," she told him. Truth was, she'd

tried to stay under the radar at school. It was so much easier to disappear than be the center of attention. That's why she'd naturally gravitated to Kris and Lyle. They were chilled, laid back. All three of them liked an easy life.

Until none of them did.

It took half an hour to drive into the mountains. There were few cars out on this side of town. Only the locals knew the winding roads that led to nowhere but some trekking paths and the lookouts.

"Do you remember the day you got your driver's licence?" Kelly asked.

A half smile pulled at his lips. Lyle had been out of town. She couldn't even remember where he'd been. But Kris had arrived at the tavern with a pair of keys in his hands, a triumphant expression on his face.

"Yeah, North let me borrow his car that day, too."

"I'm surprised he ever let you borrow it again." They'd driven to the lake and swam for hours, but a storm had come in and they'd rushed for the car, not realizing that the beach they'd parked on had already become a river of sandy mud. They'd been stuck there until Charlie Shaw managed to winch them out.

"North was still finding sand in the car four years later." Kris smiled and she grinned back.

"I've never seen anybody look so angry when we finally got the car out." She could still picture the thunder in North's expression.

"Yeah, well he loved that car. It was his first. Important to him, you know?"

Her breath caught. "Yeah," she said softly. "I know."

Silence descended, only broken by the growl of the truck's engine and the sound of the wheels on the gravel road as Kris took a right onto the unmarked road. He was driving slower now, the headlamps on high beam as they passed through a copse of trees that obscured the moon. And then they were out again, high up on the mountainside, Winterville looking like one of those miniature villages Kelly had seen in expensive gift shops as the lights of the town sparkled far below them.

"Here okay?" Kris asked.

Kelly nodded and he climbed out. She followed him around to the back of the truck, and tried not to smile when she saw the blankets and quilts there, along with cushions and pillows to soften the hard metal of the truck bed. "If it gets too cold, tell me," Kris said, helping her climb up over the tailgate. He followed and knelt over to grab the brown bags Dolores had given him, taking out two paper cups, a thermos of coffee, and two still-hot sandwiches that steamed in the cold air.

"Eat, then we talk."

Her stomach growled, reminding her she hadn't eaten any lunch. Hadn't had much of an appetite all day. So she did as she was told, biting into the hot beef sub and chewing it down. Damn, Dolores knew how to make good sandwiches. As she swallowed, her stomach growling with satisfaction, she couldn't stop thinking about another night when she and Kris talked.

When she'd begged him to make everything better. And for a moment she'd really thought he had.

Kris, age 22

She looked tired and upset, but so damn beautiful it made his chest tighten. And this was why he'd been avoiding her for the last year.

Because it hurt too much not to touch her. To know she wasn't his to touch.

"I don't know what to do," she whispered, her eyes full of tears. "He's going to end up hurting himself."

Yeah, but he was already hurting her. Not physically, or at least Kris didn't think so. But emotionally she looked beaten.

"You need to leave him, Kel."

"I can't." She shook her head. "He's always been here for me. I need to be here for him now." He'd forgotten how fiercely loyal she could be. "I thought maybe you could talk to him. Get him to see some sense."

"He won't listen to me. We've barely talked for over a year."

His eyes met Kelly's and he knew what she was thinking. That he'd barely talked to her either. Some of this was his fault. If he'd been there for Lyle when his mom died maybe he wouldn't have spiraled so much.

If he'd talked to Kelly maybe she wouldn't have hung in there for so long.

"Okay, I'll try," he promised and for the first time that night he saw her smile. "But promise me something."

"What?" she asked softly.

"If it doesn't get any better you'll leave. Promise me that."

A tear spilled down her cheek and it killed him. "Kelly..."

He held his arms open and she practically ran into them, her hands on his chest as he hugged her tight. He could smell the sweetness of her shampoo, feel the softness of her body against him, and fuck, he loved her.

He loved her so damn much it hurt to hold her like this. And yet he did it because she needed him.

She inhaled raggedly and looked up at him, and he could see himself reflected in her eyes. Her lips were slightly parted. Swollen.

"Don't leave me again," she muttered.

He wanted to promise her that he wouldn't. Wanted to tell her he'd always be here for her. But the words didn't come out.

"It'll be okay," he promised.

"Will it?" she asked, her eyes still on his.

He stroked the hair from her face and nodded. Because there was one thing he knew more than anything else. Kelly was a survivor. She loved hard and she fought hard and even if there was an apocalypse she'd walk away unscathed.

"Yeah, Kel. It will."

20

The moon was a huge yellow disc in the sky. If you looked hard enough you could see the craters. The sky around it was inky black, not a cloud to be seen.

"The tourists are gonna be pissed if we don't get some snow soon," she murmured.

"Charlie will be happy though," Kris said. The garage owner always complained when he had to get out early to clear the roads before the town opened up. All of Winterville knew it was because he liked spending his nights with Dolores, but neither of them would admit it.

"Yeah, I guess." She finished her sandwich and wiped her lips with one of the napkins Dolores had given them, before taking a sip of the hot sweet coffee. "So..." she looked at Kris.

He gave her the softest of smiles. "So, let me clean this all up and then we can talk."

"You still want to do this?"

"I think we have to." His voice was serious. "Don't you?" He slid the trash from their makeshift dinner into one of the brown bags.

"I guess."

"Will it be easier if we're not looking at each other?" he asked.

"What do you mean?"

"I mean come here." He held his arms out. "If you lay against me I can keep you warm."

It was weird how much she liked that idea. She scuttled across the truck bed and he pulled her against him, her back resting on his chest. His arms curled loosely around her, his chin soft against the crown of her head.

"This all right?" he asked.

"Yeah." She leaned back a little more, until his thighs were caging her in. "You have more muscles than you had when you played hockey."

"I think I just lost the softness of youth."

"Didn't we all?"

He laughed against her cheek. She could feel the warmth of his breath. "I guess we did. You still feel the same though."

"I've put on ten pounds since I was twenty."

"In all the right places," he said. And his words sent a shiver down her spine.

They were facing the view. And he must have been looking at the sparkling lights of Winterville, too, because he murmured, "Beautiful," into her hair.

"Did you miss it while you were away."

"All the time." He slid his hands between her coat and sweater. For a moment she imagined them moving down further. A shot of desire pulsed through her thighs.

"But you built a new life, didn't you? I heard about you getting engaged." It had felt like a knife to the heart back then. Now, it felt like part of the history every grown up seemed to have. Failed relationships, messy feelings about their parents. Fears for their childrens' futures.

She was used to all of those.

"Let's start at the beginning, shall we?" he asked.

"Where is that?"

"I don't know. Maybe the beginning of the end. When I left town the last time."

She stiffened in his hold. It still hurt to think about that.

"I'm so sorry I walked away from you. I never should have done it."

She closed her eyes. Opened them again. Breathed softly. Watched as the vapor disappeared into the inky air.

"You okay with me talking?"

She nodded.

His palms flattened against her stomach, his fingers splayed out. "When you told me you were pregnant it was like a knife to my chest. I knew I'd lost you then. And I knew it was all my fault. If I'd been a better man I would have stayed. Been a friend to you. A support to Lyle. The kind of uncle that Cole deserves."

"But you didn't stay."

"No. Back then I saw everything in black and white. You wanted me or you didn't. I stayed or I went. We were all in or all out. I was a fucking punk."

"You were young. We all were."

"Yeah, but you needed me. More than you had before you were pregnant." His fingers were tracing patterns on her sweater. "I hate that you had to go through it alone." His cheek was resting against hers now. She could feel the roughness of his beard against her. "Can you tell me about it?"

"About Lyle?"

"About all of it. Lyle. The pregnancy. The birth."

Her brows pinched. "Are you sure you want to hear? It was a shit show."

"Yeah, I want to hear. I think I need to. I can't ask for your forgiveness without knowing exactly how much you need to forgive."

A shudder went through her. He must have thought she

was cold because his arms tightened around her waist. She shuffled back an inch, and he let out a soft breath.

"Did I hurt you?" she asked, wondering if she'd pushed against him weirdly.

"No. Not like that."

She wanted to ask what it was like, but she was too busy thinking about his leaving. Her pregnancy, Cole's birth.

The whole shebang.

"Lyle started drinking in earnest almost as soon as you left. But worse, because he knew that I didn't want to be there. It was just the baby that kept me there. This stupid conviction that a child deserves a mom and a dad.

"As the pregnancy continued, he got worse. Started stealing money from my purse for drugs and alcohol. Stayed out nights at a time, sometimes weeks. Those were the good times, when he wasn't there. When I could concentrate on painting the nursery or building the little hope chest for Cole's birth. The bad times were when he was back."

"Fuck. I'm sorry."

"It's not your fault."

"Yeah it is."

She shook her head. "It was Lyle's. He could have gotten help. We tried to get him help." That last summer they'd both pleaded for him to go to rehab. "Neither of us were responsible for his addictions."

"I could have stayed for you. To support you."

She turned to look at him for the first time, twisting in his arms. His gaze was dark and yet soft as cotton. She reached out to cup his cheek. "I think we both know it would have gotten even messier if you'd stayed."

"I didn't even call. Didn't check on you."

She lifted a brow. "So you didn't ask my dad or your brothers how I was?"

"Well, yeah..."

She blew out a mouthful of air. "For the longest time I was mad at you. Even until a few weeks ago."

"Or a few days ago."

She smiled. "Okay, but really, we were kids. I was hurt, you were hurt, neither of us knew what we were doing."

"But you stayed and I left. You carried the burden and I didn't."

"I assume you mean Lyle. Cole was never a burden."

He smiled softly at her. "I know. I wish I'd met Cole as a baby."

Her heart clenched. "I wish you had, too. But you know him now."

"He's a good kid. You did an amazing job with him. And don't think I don't know how hard that must have been. Running a business, taking care of your dad, raising a child alone."

"I had no choice."

"There's always a choice. You just make good ones."

Tears pricked her eyes. "Stop it."

"I mean it. You were always the best of us." He ran his tongue along his bottom lip. "When did Lyle leave?"

"For good? When Cole was one. But even before that he was barely here. Just came around when he had nowhere else to go. And then one day he was drunk and tried to snatch Cole out of my arms and I knew then it had to stop. I could take him being an asshole around me, but not around our son. I threw him out and he didn't come back."

"But he keeps in touch?"

"Barely. A call every now and then. Now that Cole has a phone he calls him occasionally."

"I'm guessing he doesn't pay child support."

"Not really. He'll send money if he has it and it occurs to him. I think he has a girlfriend in California. Not sure how serious it is, and I don't care, except for Cole's sake."

"When was the last time you saw him?"

"A few years ago. His dad died and he came to the funeral. Cole and I saw him there."

Kris nodded, his eyes still on hers. She was sitting so awkwardly that she had to move onto her knees. He helped her, hitching her up until she was resting on his thighs, her legs on either side of him.

It felt natural to loop her arms around him. Natural to touch the soft downy hair on the back of his neck with her fingers. Kris gave her the half smile she always used to love and she felt it down to her little toes.

"Do you ever think what it would have been like if I'd stayed?" he asked softly.

"Only when it was late at night and Cole was asleep and I was curled up in bed alone. I used to pretend you were downstairs, closing up the house before bed. Then pretend you were in Cole's room reading him a story." Her voice wobbled. "Sometimes I used to pretend he was yours."

"That would have been a miracle." They'd both known better than to sleep together when they were trying to support Lyle. That would have been the ultimate betrayal.

"I used to think about that, too," he told her. "When I was in London, alone. I guess that's why I ended up getting engaged."

"You wanted a family."

"I thought I did. Turned out I wanted *my* family. That's another mistake I made. Another load of pain I caused." He brushed his lips against her brow.

"Did she forgive you?" Kelly asked.

"Yeah. She's happy now. Settled with a family." He looked pleased about that, and it warmed her heart. "So now it's just you I need to work on."

"I forgive you."

He chuckled. "You can't go forgiving me that easily."

"I can if I want to." She lifted a brow. "I can do what I like."

His gaze dipped to her lips and then back to her eyes. "I know you can."

"And if I want to forgive you I will."

"I'm not arguing." There was that half smile again. He looked like the kid she'd once loved.

"And if I want to kiss you I will."

He blinked. "Okay."

She leaned forward, her mouth warm against his. His lips were soft, his hands steady as he cupped her hips. She arched into him, their kiss deepening as he parted her mouth with his, their tongues tangling, their breath hot.

And when they parted she was breathless.

"And if I want to do more than that..." she trailed off.

"Then you can. But possibly not in freezing temperatures." He cupped her cheeks. "Let me take you home."

She woke up the next morning feeling antsy, like something was wrong. Her heart was slamming against her ribcage as though a dream had seeped into reality.

Sitting up, Kelly gasped a breath, then frowned, looking around. It was okay, she was at home.

And then she remembered last night.

They hadn't talked much as he drove her home. Kris hadn't turned the radio on either. But the silence hadn't been annoying. It felt like another form of communication with him.

And when he'd pulled up outside of her house, he'd kissed her softly then pulled back, getting out and walking around the car to open her door.

"Don't you want me to come home with you?" she asked

him, feeling confused. Because they'd been kissing and then they'd stopped dead.

"Not tonight." His voice had been soft. "Tonight I want you to go inside and think about what we talked about. I don't want to wake up in my bed and find you've left again."

So here she was waking up in her own bed. Alone. And confused. Because every time she thought about him it felt like her body was on fire. Maybe she felt a little rejected, too, but then she was the one who'd ran away last time.

Maybe he was right. She had a lot to think about. But every time she tried it made her heart hurt.

By some miracle Cole was up and dressed by the time she walked into the kitchen, a bowl of half-eaten cereal in front of him, his cellphone glued to his ear.

"Yeah, that would be great. See you on Saturday." He ended the call and smiled happily at her.

"Morning." She ruffled his hair. "What's put a smile on your face this morning?"

"Kris is coming to the father-son match with me on Saturday."

She stopped mid-ruffle. "He is?"

"Well, he said I had to ask you first." Cole looked up at her imploringly. "But it's okay, right?"

She let out the breath she'd been holding. Kris seemed to have a hold over both of them. "Let me think about it."

"Mom…"

"I'm serious. I need to think."

"I always get teamed up with one of the coaches. I hate that. It's like I'm some kind of social pariah."

"Where did you learn that phrase?" She was pretty impressed that he knew it.

"At school. In Social Studies."

"Good use of it." She smiled at him. Her kid was a smart

one, even if she was the one who paid the price for his learning sometimes.

"Mom! I'm serious. Please let Kris come. I hate being the odd one out."

"You're not the only one without a dad available. And Gramps usually comes."

"But he can't play. And this year he can't even climb in the bleachers to watch."

He was right. And she hated that. "Maybe I can see if I can get someone to cover me at work."

"It's an all guy team," he pointed out. "Please?"

"Okay." She was still going to talk to Kris though. It was one thing for the two of them to find some kind of understanding. Or more than that. She didn't know. Another him making Cole fall for him.

The way she was falling.

"Okay what?"

"Okay, he can come. Now go brush your teeth and get ready or you'll miss the bus."

Cole didn't need asking twice. He jumped up and put his bowl in the dishwasher, a big grin on his face.

Was she doing the right thing? She didn't know anymore. But since Kris had walked back into town it felt like nothing she knew was right anymore.

Maybe Cole felt the same. And maybe this feeling was inevitable.

And that was okay as long as her son didn't get hurt.

21

When he saw her name flash up on his phone, Kris knew what it would be about. He slid his finger across the screen and lifted it to his ear.

"Hi. How are you?"

"I'm good. Tired but good."

Hearing her voice made his chest feel warm.

"You sleep okay last night?" he asked her.

"I must have. Though I woke up this morning in the beginning of a panic attack."

"What?" He frowned. "You get panic attacks?"

"Haven't for a long time, no. And I didn't get one this time. I just kind of felt it coming on so I took a few breaths and it passed."

"Was it me?" he asked, alarmed. "Did I give you the attack?"

"No." She laughed softly. "I used to get them all the time when I was pregnant. After, too. Before Lyle left. Much worse than this morning. I used to think I was having a heart attack or something before I talked to the doctor and he explained what they were."

"And you don't get them anymore?"

"Very rarely. Like maybe every other year. It's not a big thing. I'm fine."

"It's a big thing if you're having panic attacks because we talked about our past," he told her. "Do you think it could be related to that?"

"I think it was the memories. I dreamt about you leaving last night. When I woke up I was in that weird place between waking and sleeping. When I woke I thought I was in the past. In the bad old days. Just for a minute. But I'm fine now."

"You should go to the doctor," he said, because he hated the thought of her panicking all alone.

"I'm fine, Kris. Honestly. It probably won't happen again for years. And anyway, that's not why I'm calling."

"I know why you're calling. And I'm sorry. Cole put me on the spot. I wasn't sure what to say."

"It's okay. I told him I'm good with you going to the game with him. I just want to talk to you first." She took a breath. "He's getting attached to you and it worries me."

A weird mix of pleasure and annoyance washed through him. "Why does it worry you?"

"Because you'll be leaving soon. And he'll be upset. He doesn't understand that people have different priorities. Plus his dad... Lyle..."

"I'm not Lyle."

"I know you're not. But you're only here for a while. Then you'll go back to your home and I'll have to deal with the heartbreak."

Again. She didn't say it, but he heard it anyway.

"If I leave I'll stay in touch with him. And be back to visit." He shifted his feet. "And I may not go back anyway."

"What?"

She sounded shocked. He'd have preferred happy. And

wasn't that a crock of shit? He hadn't cared about her opinion when he left, but now he cared too much.

"I've kind of taken a break. The company I work for got taken over this year. All the partners got a huge payout. And the choice of whether we want to stay or go. That's one of the reasons I'm here. To think about it."

"Why didn't you say anything?" she asked him.

"I guess because I wasn't sure what I'd be doing. At first I thought I'd come here for the winter and then go back. And now..."

"And now?"

"I guess I'd forgotten how much I love it here."

"Oh."

"But either way, whatever I decide I won't hurt Cole. I know I have no track record on this, but I love the kid."

"You do?" Her voice sounded strange. And he realized what he'd just said.

"Yeah. He's a good kid."

"Thank you. I think he's a bit in love with you, too."

"And that's why I'll be careful. I promise you."

Kelly put the phone down as her dad walked into the kitchen, one hand curled around his cane, the other holding a large white envelope.

"What's that?" she asked him.

"Got my date for my consultation with the new doc. And the surgery won't be until the end of January at the earliest." He flashed her a smile. "That's good, right? I'll be here to take care of Cole during the busiest time at the Tavern."

"Yeah, that's good." She nodded, still thinking about Kris' words. That he might stay around. He might be here after the holidays were over. It confused her and warmed her and it was all too much.

And maybe not enough.

"We'll need to figure out who'll watch Cole while I'm in the hospital," her dad said.

"And afterward. You won't be able to take care of him while you're recovering." Yeah, it was another thing she needed to think about, among all the other competing priorities in her head. Sometimes she felt like she was a walking scheduler, trying to juggle who was supposed to be where and when at any given time.

"You think you'll be able to get a sitter?"

Truth was, they were hard to come by. But after the holidays it would be easier. "I'll find somebody. Let's not worry about it now. What else is in that letter?"

"All kinds of information about the surgery. A few forms. And what I'll need to do for rehab."

"It's exciting."

"Yeah, it is." Her dad's eyes were warm. "I owe Kris a lot. I need to buy him a bellyful of beers some time."

She lifted a brow. "That makes two of us."

"I heard you were out with him last night," her dad said slyly. Kelly blinked, surprised.

"You did?"

"Yep. Charlie saw Dolores who told him that North and Gabe were covering the tavern while you and Kris went out somewhere."

"We just went to talk," she told him. And it was mostly the truth. She'd wanted more. She'd wanted to go home with him.

And he'd rejected her. Kind of.

"I'm glad." Her dad gave her a pat on the arm. "And I wouldn't have minded if you were doing more."

"Dad!" She was shocked.

He chuckled. "I may be old but I'm not decrepit. And you're in your prime. You deserve to have a bit of fun. A bit of kindness, too. And Kris is a good man."

"Yeah he is." There was a lump in her throat.

"It's funny, because I can remember you being so upset when he left," her dad said, sitting down heavily on one of the kitchen chairs. She should be heading to the tavern, but her dad obviously wanted to talk, so she sat down on the chair opposite his.

"You do?"

"Yeah. And the funnier thing is I don't remember you being half as upset when Lyle left. Even though he's Cole's dad and you two were together."

"I guess the relationship ended long before he left."

"Yeah, I guess it did. But you and Kris always seemed... like your friendship was unfinished business. For him as well as you." He gave her a pointed look.

"Why for him?" she asked, tipping her head to the side.

"I don't think he saved the tavern for me, that's why. It was for you."

She let out a long breath. "He said he might not be going back to England when the holidays are over."

Her dad quirked an eyebrow. "Really?"

"Yeah. Apparently they had a huge payout and he's thinking through his options."

"How about you?" her dad asked. "Are you thinking through your options?"

"What options?" she asked, confused.

"The man is in love with you. I can see it now and I saw it back then. Back when you and Lyle were together."

Her mouth turned dry. "We never..."

"I know you didn't. You're an honorable woman. And he's a good man. But you two were so close for so long. Closer than you and Lyle." He gave a little chuckle. "Remember when Kris came home from college and carried you out of the bar?"

She smiled. "Yeah, I remember."

"I thought that was it. He was going to declare himself."

"It was just a bit of fun, that's all."

"Was it?" her dad asked. "I still wonder about that. I wonder if Lyle hadn't been here what would have happened."

Her chest tightened. She and her dad never had conversations like this. She sometimes wondered if he even noticed what was going outside of his friends and their poker games.

"Like what?" she asked, curious. And maybe needing to hear what she hoped he'd say.

"I don't know. I guess it's old history. I just hated what Lyle did to you. He was never good enough for you. I was glad when he left, for yours and Cole's sake." Her dad looked down at the envelope he'd placed on the table, as though he couldn't meet her eye. "And he's gone, and that's good. But you're a young woman. You have the rest of your life in front of you. Don't let fear stop you from taking a leap forward."

"I'm not afraid."

"Aren't you?" he asked. "Because I'd be in your position."

That was unexpected. He looked up and nodded. "I was afraid, Kel. After your mom died. For so long. And I thought if I waited until I wasn't afraid anymore it would be okay. But the fear doesn't go away as you get older. It just changes. Maybe even gets bigger."

"So what should I do?" she asked him.

He smiled. "I can't remember the last time you asked me for advice. And I hate to tell you, but I'm not the one to give it." He cleared his throat. "But if I was in your position, still young, still beautiful, with a woman looking at me the way that Kris looks at you, I'd push away that fear and take the leap. Because life flashes by like a damn bolt of lightning. You think you've got forever, then suddenly it's gone. I love you, and I love Cole, but part of me wishes that I hadn't pushed away happiness after your mom died."

He reached out and took her hand, squeezing it gently and she squeezed back. She felt wrung out and she hadn't even finished her morning coffee. Between talking to Kris last night and her dad this morning it felt like she was so full of words she didn't know what to do with them.

But she felt lighter. Like she'd lost ten pounds and gained a helium balloon. One that contained the most important emotion of all.

Hope.

She'd forgotten it existed for a long time. Been too busy surviving to think about what would happen in the future.

But her dad was right. What happened next was up to her – or at least some of it was. She was afraid of her feelings. She wanted Kris, and the way he held her last night made her think he wanted her, too. But was it enough to push the fear away?

❦ 22 ❦

"You're doing what?" North asked him. Kris had taken a bottle of wine to his house to thank him for holding down the fort at the tavern last night. And now he was regretting only bringing one because his brother looked tired and Kris felt guilty. North worked so hard all day at the tree farm – harder than ever this year because Amber was pregnant.

"I'm playing in the father-son hockey game," Kris told him. "Cole asked me."

"I bet he did." Amber bit down a smile. She was sitting by the fire, sorting through baby clothes. They looked so tiny he could hardly believe a human could fit in them – even a baby human.

"Are you sure your kid is gonna be that small?" he asked her. "Because North is a tall guy."

She laughed. "At the moment, they think he's going to be smaller than Willow was. The birth size is usually related to the mom. How big they grow after that, well that's genetics."

"Remember when you had that growth spurt?" North asked, looking as amused as his wife. "You went to bed talking like the chipmunk, Alvin, and woke up sounding like Barry White." He looked at Amber. "Mom thought we had intruders. She was about to call the police."

"Shut up. You don't have room to talk." Kris lifted a brow and smiled at Amber. "When North hit puberty Mom couldn't figure out why all the packs of tissues kept disappearing."

North gave him a death stare. "Let's not talk about tissues disappearing. But I'm happy to talk about those long ass showers you used to take. We all knew what you were doing in there."

"Oh my God, can you both stop?" Amber was laughing, but she also looked appalled. "My baby doesn't need to hear about such depravity." She lifted up a onesie. "Oh this was my favorite on Willow."

North walked over, his expression soft. "I remember. She looked so cute in it."

"I guess we can't use it for this baby. It's too pink."

"Boys can wear pink," North said. "If we want him to wear it, he'll wear it."

"I think I'll put it in Willow's memory box."

As though she could hear her name being said, a cry came out from the nursery. North was still knelt next to Amber, one hand on the baby outfit, the other on his wife's stomach.

"Want me to go?" Kris asked them.

They both looked up, surprised.

"What?" he asked.

"Nothing." Amber shook her head. "And yes, please. Bring her in here if you need to."

He walked along the hallway to the nursery, the sound of North and Amber's soft voices becoming distant, overpowered by Willow's yells. She was on her knees in her crib, her eyes red and her mouth open.

"Hey." Kris smiled at her. She cocked her head as he

walked toward her, as if she was as surprised as her parents that he was here to take care of her.

When he lifted her up she was still looking at him, her soft eyelashes sweeping down as she blinked.

"I know. I'm the scary uncle," he said, smiling. "The one with no kids. But I'm a lot of fun."

Willow grabbed hold of his shirt. And then she opened her mouth again and wailed. It took him a minute to work it out, but then the aroma of something really bad wafted up.

"Ah." He nodded. "I think this is a daddy kind of job."

She was still sniffling as he carried her back into the living room. North was still next to Amber, but he stood as soon as he saw Willow in Kris' arms.

"She okay?" North asked.

"She needs her diaper changed. I would have done it, but I figure you like her nursery walls cream colored."

Amber laughed. "I'll do it." Putting the onesie she was holding onto the pile, she stood up and reached for Willow, taking her from Kris' arms. "You two want a drink when I'm done?"

"I'll get them," North told her. "You sure I can't change the diaper?"

"Nope. I got this." Amber winked at them. "I'll see you after Poopmageddon."

It was funny how North followed his wife with his eyes wherever she went. It wasn't until she'd closed the door behind her that North finally bought his gaze back to Kris.

"So, last night with Kelly..."

"It went fine." Kris smiled, because he was stealing Kelly's phrase. But that was about as much as he was willing to share. Because it had been more than fine and he'd been walking around with a smile for most of the day.

North lifted a brow. "I'm real glad it went fine. But I've got a woman whose gonna be pushing me for all the details and I'm not planning on making her push me too hard, if you know what I mean. So give me them and we'll speak no more about it."

"Hasn't she spoken to Kelly? They're supposed to be friends."

"And apparently Kelly's keeping her lips sealed." North sighed. "And normally I'd be more than happy if you did the same. But my wife is pregnant and what she wants, she gets. So spill."

"There's nothing to spill. We talked. We kissed. I drove her home, we said good night."

North gave him one of those looks. An older brother I-know-you're-shitting-me kind of look. Kris tried not to laugh.

And failed.

"I'm serious. Nothing happened. I wouldn't have let it anyway."

"Why?" North asked. "I thought you like her."

"I do. But we had things to talk about. Painful things. And it might sound stupid, but I didn't want her to do something in the heat of that emotion and regret it after. And I guess I needed to breathe, too. There's a lot going on. Kelly comes as a package, I need to think about both of them."

"Her and Cole?" North asked.

"Yeah. And I guess her dad, too." Kris shrugged. "They come as a package." And he was okay with that. "Then this morning, Cole asked me to go to his father-son game next week. Kelly's worried Cole's getting attached to me."

"Yeah. I noticed that."

"So did I." Amber walked in, curling back onto the sofa. "What did I miss?"

"Everything okay?" North murmured.

"Yeah, she's clean and dandy." Amber nodded then looked back at Kris. "So?"

"So nothing happened. Kelly told you the truth."

Wait. What? "You spoke to Kelly?" He glanced at North who looked sheepishly away. He was hustling for information, the asshole.

It was a good thing Kris loved him.

"Yeah. She said nothing happened. You talked then took her home."

"Well she's right." Kris shrugged. "I can't believe you tried to catch me out," he told North.

"We were just checking." North winked.

"But something happened before, didn't it?" Amber said to Kris.

"She tell you that?"

"Yes." Amber grinned. "Not all the sordid details. But I know you guys fooled around in your cabin."

Jesus. Luckily, North looked as horrified as he did. "Enough," North said. "Let's not get into details."

"Why don't guys want the details?" Amber asked. "They're always the best."

"Firstly, because imagining my brother doing anything like that makes me want to hurl." North grimaced.

Kris nodded. "Case in point, when North caught Gabe slapping the salami in the living room when we were kids."

"You never told me about that," Amber said, turning to look at him. "Seriously?"

"Yes." North looked pained. "But can we never speak of it again?"

Kris watched them, amused, because for once they weren't grilling him. "Well, I've gotta go. It's been a good time."

"Wait." Amber tore her gaze from North's. "What are you going to do?"

"Nothing I'm willing to tell either of you about."

"He's worried about Cole," North said. "That he's getting attached."

"I didn't say that. I said Kelly's worried about it," Kris corrected.

"I know." Amber nodded. "But she shouldn't be."

"Why not?" Kris wasn't expecting that. Of all people he thought Amber would be the one to agree with Kelly. They were friends. She'd known Kelly for years.

"Because you're a Winter," she said. "And if there's something I know about you and your brothers, it's that you fall hard. And if you're willing to step up for Cole, that means you've fallen for him too." She reached out to squeeze North's hand. "A father isn't the one who created a kid. He's the one who'd do anything for him."

Kris' stomach twisted. Because he'd had a chance at this before and he'd messed it up. But that time Cole wasn't born. Now he was a kid with real feelings, hopes, and dreams.

He nodded at Amber and she smiled back.

"Good night, Kris."

"Yeah. I hope it is."

Kelly, Age 22

"I'm sorry. I'm sorry." Lyle was weeping as she tried to carry him upstairs. His legs were wobbling and his whole weight was on her, making her shoulder muscles scream as they made it to the top rung.

"Come on, just a few more steps," she muttered. It was getting worse. So much worse. And this time he'd been arrested. A huge fight at a bar in Marshall's Gap – because everybody in the Winterville Tavern knew not to serve him. She stumbled across the landing and into the bedroom, her arms wrapped around his waist because he kept trying to slide down to the floor.

When she managed to get him onto the bed she let out a long sigh.

"I love you, Kel."

"I know."

"I'm going to stop. I'm sorry. You don't deserve this."

She pulled his shoes off, putting them neatly on the floor, then unbuttoned his shirt. "You need some sleep."

"I'd be dead without you. You know that? You've saved my life."

"Sit up, let me take your shirt off."

He was asleep before she'd put his clothes into the laundry basket. And for a moment she stared at him. Taking in the familiar flop of his brown hair over his face. His lips were pressed together, his arms splayed out. He looked so young.

They were young. Too young to be dealing with this. In the morning he wouldn't remember anything. He never did.

When his breaths were coming evenly, she tiptoed out of the bedroom, pulling the door closed gently. And when she made it to the small living room Kris was still there.

"He's asleep."

"I could have carried him up for you," Kris said. "You didn't have to do it on your own."

Yeah, she did. This was her mess. "It's practice. For when you leave." Again. She didn't say it but the word hung in the air.

She and Kris were Lyle's only friends now. Since the drinking had pushed away everybody else. And of course his mom was gone – the reason he'd started drowning his sorrows in the bottom of a whiskey glass.

"You can't stay with him," Kris told her. "He's going to end up hurting you."

"If I leave he'll hurt himself. This is Lyle. He took care of us at school. We promised we'd all take care of each other."

The accusation hung in the air as they stared at each other. Kris was leaving for London on Monday. He'd been offered a job at an investment firm there, and she couldn't blame him for taking it.

He'd be able to forget about Lyle. Forget about her. Move on and not be involved in this mess anymore.

"Come with me." His voice was soft. He was staring at her intently.

"What?"

"Come to London with me." He wasn't joking. There was no smile on his face, no twinkle in his eye. He walked toward her, only stopping when he was close enough that she had to stare up to look at him. His palms cupped her cheeks as he lowered his brow to touch hers. "You can't save him. You know that somewhere deep inside. You can only save yourself."

She let out a breath of ragged air. For a moment she pictured herself in London with Kris. Eating cakes and drinking tea in a small café by the river. Exploring another country together. And in her mind they were always laughing, because that's what they did.

Until now. Here. Lyle.

"I can't."

He kissed the tip of her nose. And every part of her lit up like she was the tree in the town square. "I don't want to leave without you."

"Lyle..."

"Is gonna kill himself or get into rehab. We know that. I want you to come with me. I'm in love with you, Kel."

Tears itched at her eyes. How many times had she longed to hear him say that over the years?

And now it was too late.

"I'm pregnant."

It was the first time she'd uttered the words since she'd taken the test that morning. It sounded like a bomb going off in the room. Kris stared at her, his thick eyelashes sweeping down as he blinked.

"Are you going to keep it?"

A sob pulled through her. "Yes."

Kris said nothing for a moment. Just held her face in his strong, sure palms. He stared down at her, his breath warm against her skin.

"Then you both come with me." He kissed her brow, her cheek, and then his lips brushed against hers.

She should pull away. But she couldn't. Instead she kissed him *back, that sob still in the back of her throat. His mouth was soft, sure, his fingers trailing down her cheeks to her neck, sending a shiver down her spine. How could a kiss make her feel so desired yet so safe at the same time?*

"What the fuck?"

Lyle staggered into the living room, looking almost ludicrous in just his boxers, his hair askew, his eyes not quite focused.

"Lyle..." Panicked, she looked from him to Kris. "It's not what it looks like."

"You're cheating on me? With him?"

"No." She shook her head. "I'm not. It was a mistake. I'm sorry."

But Lyle wasn't looking at her. He was looking at Kris. And Kris was staring right back at him.

She felt her hands start to shake.

"She's leaving with me."

"What?" Lyle's voice was tremulous.

She felt mortified. Like she'd betrayed him. Oh God, she had.

"You're leaving me, Kel?" Lyle asked her. His eyes were full of tears. And she hated that.

"I..." She tried to breathe.

"Don't go. Please don't go." A tear ran down his face. And it was worse than anger. So much worse. "I'll go to rehab, I promise. I'll make it better. Don't leave me."

There was a twinge in her stomach. And logically she knew it was way too early to be the baby. But it was a reminder still. A little life was growing inside of her. A little person who one day would want to know their father.

She looked from Kris to Lyle, and it felt like her heart was breaking.

"You won't do it," Kris said, his voice low. "You won't do it for her. And you won't do it for your kid."

She gasped. But luckily Lyle didn't take those words in.

And then Kris turned to her, his gaze still soft. "Come with me now."

But she couldn't. She needed to be able to look this child she was carrying in the eye someday and tell them that she tried. That she did her best to make sure they had a dad who was alive, sober, who loved them.

What other choice did she have?

"I'm sorry."

Kris winced. He reached out to touch her cheek and she heard Lyle slide to the ground.

"If I go I'm not coming back," Kris told her.

And she knew it was the truth. "Goodbye," she whispered.

And it felt like her heart had cracked in two.

23

Had he been wrong to take her straight home last night? He wasn't sure. He'd known from the way she'd been so soft in his arms that if he'd taken her to the cabin she would have gone inside willingly.

Starting up the car, he turned right instead of left, heading toward town. The Tavern's lights were still on and he parked outside, walking into the warm bar, the sound of laughter and music immediately assailing him.

"Is Kelly around?" he asked the man behind the bar.

"She left early," he said, drying a glass and putting it on the rack.

Again? That wasn't like her. He pulled out his phone to call her. Then he put it back into his pocket. If she'd gone home it was for a good reason. Either she was sick or maybe Cole was. Fuck it, he'd drive there and check on them, then head home.

"She's at the tavern," Paul said, giving Kris a weird stare five minutes later as he stood on Kelly's doorstep. "It's a weeknight. She's always there. Except for when she's with you."

"Was that the door?" Cole shouted out as he ran down the hallway, skidding to a stop behind his grandpa. "Oh, hey Kris."

"Hey kid." He smiled at him. "Isn't it past your bedtime?"

"He's just heading there," Paul said gruffly.

"Can't I talk to Kris?" Cole asked. "I want to tell him about the movie we watched. Have you heard of *Slapshot*?"

"You let him watch *Slapshot*?" Kris asked, his voice low. "Isn't that kind of adult?"

"It wasn't *Slapshot*. It was a movie like it. I'm an idiot but I don't have a death wish. Kelly would definitely kill me."

"I'll tell you what, why don't we talk about it on Saturday on our way to the game?" Kris suggested. He wanted to get out of there. Call Kelly. Find out where she was.

Paul winked at him. "Want me to tell Kelly you came over?"

"No, it's fine. I'll call her."

Paul looked back at Cole. "Go brush your teeth and I'll let you stay up an extra five minutes."

Cole grinned. "Okay. Night, Kris."

"Night, Cole."

When he was sure Cole was out of earshot, Paul turned back to Kris. "Go easy on her when you talk to her."

"Why? Is something wrong?"

"Nah." Paul wrinkled his nose. "She was just a little sensitive this morning. Said she had a lot to think about." He ran his finger along his jaw. "She's a lot more vulnerable than most people think she is."

"I know." Kris' voice was low. Thick.

"Yeah, I know you do. And that's why I trust you with her."

Paul caught his eye and Kris felt the older man's words hit a nerve in his body. "I've hurt her before."

"You have. But you're grown. I can see it. And I'm not just

saying that because you paid for my tavern and you're gonna pay for my knee."

Kris nodded, saying nothing.

"She's the best of all of us. I know you're going to take care of her."

"I will." Kris nodded.

"Good." Paul shifted his feet, reminding Kris he shouldn't be standing for this long. But he was too intent on talking to hear any urges to go sit down. "She's not at the tavern, is she?"

"No, sir. I don't know where she is."

"I do."

Kris blinked. "Where?"

"She'll be at your place. Waiting for you. She's had all day to think about things. I'm guessing she's done thinking."

"My place?"

Paul nodded. "Go find her. Please."

"Okay."

"And Kris?"

"Yes, sir?"

"I've got things under control here. Say if Kelly needs to work all night at the tavern or something, I can get Cole ready for school tomorrow."

Kris would have laughed, but Paul looked deadly serious. And maybe he should, too. It felt like his life was balanced on a fulcrum, teetering only one way.

Toward her. The way it should have been years ago.

He lifted his hand out to Paul and the older man shook it.

"Take good care of my girl."

She'd been sitting inside his cabin for half an hour. At first she'd stayed in the car, letting the heating warm her skin. But she'd needed to get out and move, so she'd walked up to his porch, a weird sensation pulling at her neck.

When they were kids he used to hide a key beneath a plant pot in case she or Lyle got here first. Mostly her, because she'd catch the bus home while he and Lyle would go to hockey practice. She'd let herself in, do her homework, and put on loud music because it wouldn't disturb anybody like it would have at home.

And when her two best guys walked through the door it always felt like she'd finally come home.

Hunkering down, she tipped the empty plant pot next to his door on its side. And smiled, because there it was. His spare key. Had he left it there knowing she might come? It was in the same place it had been when they were kids, but the cabin had been remodeled since then.

His room was neat and tidy when she walked inside. His bed made, his shoes lined up carefully against the wall, and when she pulled his closet open his clothes were perfectly hung up. She was closing the door when she heard the rumble of an engine cutting through the night air.

When she peeped through the window she could see the glare of his headlights sweep across the drive.

Kelly pressed her face against the glass, watching as he climbed out and strode toward the cabin, his stride not faltering when he glanced to his left and saw Amber's car parked there. He pushed the handle down and as the door opened her breath caught in her throat.

But there was a smile on his face when he stepped inside. "Hey you."

"I let myself in."

"So I see." He kicked his shoes off, and removed his coat. He was wearing a black Henley and a pair of jeans that hugged his thick thighs. "You doing okay?"

"Aren't you wondering how I got in?"

"The key under the pot."

"Yeah."

"I put it there for you. Figured if you ever needed to disappear you could use it."

Weird how much that affected her. She felt her face flush. "You don't mind that I'm here?"

He looked at her, his gaze warm. "I love that you're here." Then he smiled. "I always did. Escaping with you was always a blast.

"It was?"

He nodded. "Yeah." He inclined his head at the kitchen. "Want me to make you something to drink?"

She shook her head.

"Want me to kiss you?"

She nodded. And his smile widened. Covering the small distance between them, he cupped her cheeks in his hands, tipping her face toward him, until she could see her reflection in his dilated pupils. For a moment she felt dizzy, like she was going to fall over. Curling her fingers into his shirt, she steadied herself.

"Okay?" he murmured, his strong fingers keeping her chin steady.

"Yes," she breathed. She was more than okay. She was sure. This was what she wanted. What she'd possibly always wanted. The one thing she couldn't have.

She'd been a kid then. Thought in black and white and wrong and right.

Maybe she still did. But this was right, she was sure of it.

They'd kissed before. But this felt so much more meaningful. Like a first kiss should. Warm lips curled into a smile. Breath feathering across skin. Then he tipped her head, his nose sliding against hers, his tongue slowly drawing a line across her lips. Begging for an entrance she was all too willing to give.

He slid his tongue against hers and she let out the softest of moans. She had to steady herself, hold him tighter, closer. Close enough to feel the effect this kiss was having on him.

His mouth was moving slowly against hers, making her skin heat and crackle with electricity. His fingers moved up, into her hair, as she pushed herself against his body.

Sliding one hand down her side, he curved it over the swell of her behind, digging his fingers into the back of her thigh. Then he was hitching it up, around his waist, and she could feel him there. Thick and hard.

"Kris."

"Still okay?" he asked her.

"More than okay. I need you."

His other hand slid down her side, pulling her up against him. Then she was clinging onto him like a monkey as he carried her the three short strides to his bed.

They were a frenzy of kisses and fingers, taking each others clothes off. His Henley first, her sweater next. His eyes darkened as he took in her bra, her breasts, the way her mouth was already swollen from kissing him.

When was the last time anybody looked at her like this? Like she was some kind of goddess made just for him? She liked it. No, she *loved* it.

Loved the way his fingers felt as he traced her bra.

"Please."

He nodded, his mouth unsmiling, as he reached behind her and unfastened her bra. Then he dipped his head, his lips pulling at her nipple, and oh god, she wasn't ready for every nerve ending to feel like it was on fire.

"Kris..."

"What do you need?" He looked up from his adoration of her breasts, his expression serious.

"I need you. Inside me. I just..."

"You just what?" There was the ghost of a smile on his

face. He traced his finger around her breast, making her arch her back.

"It's been a while."

He kissed her temple, her cheek, the corner of her lip. "How long?"

She felt the fear again. Then remembered that she shouldn't. She was brave, she was strong. This felt right. "Since Lyle left."

"All that time?" He frowned. "Kel..."

"And you?" She needed to know.

"A while. At least a year."

She waited to feel a pang in her chest at knowing he was so much more experienced than she was. But it wasn't there. Because she was brave.

And he was here with her now. That's what mattered.

"Any time you want to stop, you tell me."

"I don't want to stop. Not at all." She reached up for him, a smile playing at her lips. "Now shut up and kiss me."

He didn't need telling twice. He kissed her again, this time with intent. His fingers unbuttoned her jeans, and she wriggled to help him slide them down her legs. And then his jeans were gone, too.

Two thin pieces of fabric separated them, and as he smiled at her she could feel just how hard he was. She rolled her hips against him and he groaned. She liked that she had that effect on him.

His eyes caught hers, and butterflies exploded in her stomach. He gave her that soft, half smile that she loved so much and kissed her again, before trailing his lips down her throat.

This time when he pulled her nipple into his mouth she arched her back and let out a cry. He sucked again, his fingers feathering down her stomach, tracing the line of her panties before he slid his hand beneath the fabric.

She was wet, she knew it. He did, too, as soon as he found the nub of her, his finger tracing circles around it. And when she started to feel the electricity fizzle inside of her, he kissed his way down her stomach, then slid her panties down her hips, his lips joining his fingers.

Oh god, his tongue. Her head tipped back, her breath caught, and she could feel the pleasure start to radiate. Against his mouth, around his fingers, making her slick and hot and needy.

"Kris!" Her fingers dug into his hair as she convulsed around him, pleasure making her buck off the bed. And still he carried on kissing and licking, until she couldn't take anymore.

When he moved to kiss her lips she could taste herself on him. He cradled her head, whispered how perfect she was, then reached for his wallet, pulling a foil packet out.

"You don't need to."

"I don't?" A confused smile played at his lips.

"I'm on the pill."

One of his brows lifted and she smiled, the pleasure still making her feel giddy. "I have heavy periods. It regulates them."

"And you're sure you're okay with me..."

"I'm clean."

"So am I."

She nodded and he grinned. "You're perfect.

The smile slid from his face as he pushed into her. Replaced by a groan and a roll of his eyes. "Jesus. You feel amazing."

Every hitch of his hips felt exquisite. Every slick of his tongue against hers. He kissed her and slid inside of her, grinding exactly where she needed him, one hand cupping her behind to angle her perfectly as he hit her deeper than she ever thought possible.

And she could feel it. That quickening. Before she could even call out his name, she was coming again. And when he felt her tighten around him, he let out a groan, following her into oblivion as he spilled inside of her, his eyes never leaving hers.

For a long minute neither of them moved. The only sound in the room was their rapid breaths, as they slowly came down from their high. Then he smiled at her again, rolling over to pull her against him.

"Just so you know," she said, letting her face fall against his chest. "We'll be doing that again."

24

The shower was running in the cabin's tiny bathroom when she woke up. Panic washed over her – not an attack this time, thank goodness – as she picked up Kris's phone to check the time.

It was seven a.m.. Cole would be awake, wondering where she was. Why the hell did Kris let her sleep in when he knew that. She went to put the phone back down on the table next to his bed when she saw a message flash up, white on green.

Are you still okay to talk today? – Laura.

The shower had stopped. She quickly put the phone back where she'd found it and grabbed her clothes. She was buttoning up her jeans when Kris walked out of the bathroom, a towel wrapped around his slim waist.

"You're awake." He smiled at her.

"It's seven. I should be home." She pulled her sweater over

her head and caught a glimpse of her hair in the mirror over the dresser. Damn, she looked rough.

"Your dad has it all under control." He had another towel in his hands and used it to rub his dripping hair. "He said he'd get Cole off to school this morning."

"You spoke to my dad?" Her voice lifted. Oh this was worse than she thought. "My dad knows I stayed here? Did you tell him we had sex?"

"Three times?" Kris grinned. "No I didn't. I spoke to him before I came home last night, not after. And I didn't tell him I was going to fuck you until you were dazed. He just suggested you needed a break, that's all."

"But my dad." She felt so weird. What would he tell Cole? Damn, she wished she'd woken up earlier.

Kris walked over and put his hands on her face. They were warm and damp. "Stop overthinking."

"I can't help it. It's literally my job." She was a mom, a daughter, she had a business to run. Her brain ran at a high speed whenever she was awake.

"It's not your job here," he said softly, brushing his lips against hers. "Here you don't have to think."

"I'm thinking I need to get into my car before my kid finds out I've spent the night with his new bestie," she muttered.

Kris's lips curled. "Your dad won't tell him. And nor will we. I get it, you need to protect him."

Her breath caught. "He's the most important thing in my life."

"And he should be. But you're important, too. Do you regret coming here?" he asked, his hands still cupping her face.

"No."

"Do you regret what we did?"

She exhaled softly. "No, I don't."

"Good. Because neither do I." He kissed her again, more deeply this time. And damn this man knew how to kiss. Her legs were like jelly as he slid his hands down her back, his tongue sliding against hers until those thoughts in her head disappeared.

"Let's make a deal," he murmured when the need to breathe overrode the need to kiss.

"What kind of deal?"

"When you're here you don't have to think. You leave it all outside the door. This is the one place you can be Kelly and nothing else."

"I don't understand..."

"Don't you get sick of having to think all the time?" he asked her. "It looks like hard work."

She smiled because he was teasing her. "Of course I do."

"Then let me take the worries off you. Just for a few hours whenever you're here. Leave them behind."

Damn that sounded enticing. She'd been mom and daughter and boss for so long she wasn't quite sure who she was without those titles. "It wouldn't work."

"Why not?"

"Because my brain is a bitch," she said and he chuckled.

"How about if I tamed your bitch of a brain," he murmured, kissing the side of her mouth. His breath was soft against her skin and it made every part of her feel needy. "If I demanded that every time you came in here you forgot about everything but this?" He kissed her jaw, her neck, then pushed her sweater up to kiss the swell of her breasts. Then his lips closed around her nipple, sucking her through the lace of her bra.

She let out an achy sigh and she could feel him smiling against her taut skin.

"What are you thinking?" he asked, his voice gritty.

"That you're going to kill me."

He looked up at her, his gaze warm. "Anything else."

"I want you to touch me."

"Good." He winked. "But now you have to go home."

"What?" Her mouth dropped open. "But you..."

"Don't worry, we'll do this soon." He pulled her sweater down, still grinning. "And when we do, I'm going to make you forget your own name."

"You're an asshole." She wrinkled her nose at him, because her body was still buzzing.

"Yeah. And you're beautiful. Now go home and shower. I'll call you later."

"It's Kris, right?"

Kris looked to his left at the guy standing next to him in the line for coffee. The Cold Fingers Café was overrun right now. Dolores had three people working the counter with her and they still couldn't get the line down fast enough.

"Yeah, that's right."

"I'm Greg. Reece's dad. He plays hockey with Cole. I saw you at the last game."

"Oh yeah, I remember." Kris shook his hand.

"I was planning to call you. Cole told Reece you're playing in the father-son game. I'm the dad's captain." Greg lifted a brow. "Have you played much hockey?"

"Not recently. Played a lot in high school and college."

Greg grinned. "Excellent. What was your position?"

"Center, but I'm happy to go anywhere. It's just some fun, right? We're not gonna try to beat the kids or anything, are we?"

Dolores called his name and Kris gave her a smile.

"Your usual, honey?"

"Yes, please." It was funny that he already had a usual.

"Can you make a cappuccino, too? I'll drop it off at the tavern for Kelly."

Dolores winked at him. "Of course."

Kris tried not to roll his eyes. For starters, he knew Kelly would hate any gossip about them. They were doing well keeping things on the downlow. But damn, he just wanted to buy the woman he liked a coffee.

"Is Kelly your sister?" Greg asked. From the corner of his eye Kris could see Dolores chuckle.

"No." Kris shook his head, shooting Dolores a dirty look.

"Oh. He said you were his uncle. You on his dad's side?"

"Just a good friend," Kris told him.

"Okay." The guy shrugged. "I was just wondering. I know Melissa, that's my wife, wanted to invite Kelly and Cole for dinner. Her brother's coming to town for Christmas. She thought they might hit it off. He's newly divorced. A doctor. Thinking of moving closer to here so he can spend more time with us."

"No." Kris shook his head.

"I'm sorry." Greg frowned. "No, as in they won't hit it off? Or no as in he isn't moving here. Because I think he is."

Annoyance rushed through Kris. "No, as in Kelly won't be able to come to dinner. She's busy."

"I didn't tell you the day," Greg said. "Hell, we haven't even thought of a day yet."

"She's running the tavern. No nights off."

"The Tavern is closed Sunday afternoons though, right?"

"Your coffees are ready," Dolores said, passing the two Styrofoam cups over to him. There was a smile on her face so big that it ramped his annoyance up even more.

"Thanks," he said, taking them. "I gotta go," he told Greg. Because there was no way Kelly was going for dinner with this man's brother-in-law. He turned on his heel and headed for the door.

"Hey, I'll call you about the game," Greg shouted.

"Sure," Kris said through gritted teeth, squeezing past the line of people that spilled out of the door onto the sidewalk. "You do that."

———

She was laughing like he'd just told her the most hilarious joke, not that she needed to let Greg know she wasn't available to date his brother-in-law. Kris narrowed his eyes as she leaned against the bar, the coffee he'd brought her on the counter in front of her.

"It's not funny."

"It's hilarious." Her eyes crinkled and damn she looked pretty when she was happy. "Do you know the last time anybody propositioned me? Now I'm getting two in one day. Do you think I'll get a third?"

"You better not," he muttered.

She wiped her eyes and leaned over to kiss him softly. "You're all possessive. I never thought I'd see the day."

"You came on my cock three times last night. Damn right I'm possessive."

"You forgot about the one on your tongue," she told him, her voice low.

"No, baby, I didn't. I thought about that one this morning in the shower. For as long as it took."

"You jacked off in the shower while I was asleep in your bed?" Her cheeks pinked up as she asked him.

"It was that or wake you up. And you looked like you needed some sleep."

"That's sweet, I think." Her brows knitted. "Sweet or dirty. I'm not sure."

"Can I be both?" He gave her a crooked smile.

"Yeah, I think you can." She lifted the coffee cup to her

lips, taking a sip. "And by the way, you didn't have to bring me a coffee. I'm not expecting you to shower me with gifts just because we had sex."

For some reason that rankled him. "I'll bring you a coffee if I want to bring you a damn coffee."

Her eyes crinkled. "Well okay then. I'm just telling you I don't have any expectations. We had fun last night, we'll have fun the next time. That's enough."

"Jesus, Kelly." He raked his hands through his hair. "That's not enough. Not anywhere near enough."

She looked at him, confused. "I don't understand, isn't that what you want?"

"No." He shook his head. "It isn't."

"Then what do you want?" she asked him. Her cheeks were still pink from her laughter and he reached out to touch them. So warm and soft.

"I want you to stop settling for something less than what you deserve," he told her, his voice tight.

"How do you know what I deserve?" She looked at him carefully, like she was trying to work him out.

"I know you deserve more than to have sex with someone then think them bringing you a damn coffee is too much," he told her. "It cost me three dollars. Jesus." He shook his head.

"I've annoyed you and I don't know why."

Kris let out a mouthful of air. "It's not you. It's me. And Lyle. And every other asshole whose made you think you deserve less than the best."

"I don't think I deserve less. I'm just pragmatic. If you don't have expectations they can't get dashed. You're the one who told me to stop overthinking. So here I am, not thinking about it at all."

Damn it, she was right and he hated that. "I just wanted you not to worry."

"And I took it to heart. I'm not worrying."

He pressed his lips together, his eyes scanning her face. He could always read it like a book. She was being honest, and he hated that.

"Yeah, well I'm worrying now. For both of us."

"That's one for the books. Kris Winter worrying."

"I worry all the time," he told her.

"No you don't. You were always the one who lived in the moment." She could remember how free he'd always been. Unafraid of the future. So different than her.

"That's what I wanted you to think." His eyes dipped to her mouth. She had a little froth on her bottom lip and he reached out to wipe it. "Do you think I would have left if I was unafraid?"

"I don't know." She shook her head.

"I left because I was deadly afraid," he told her, his voice low. "Of seeing Lyle drink himself into oblivion. Of watching you tear yourself apart trying to stop it."

"Well those things still happened. Then he left."

"I know. And I can't imagine how horrific it was. And I'll always be sorry I wasn't here for you both." He swallowed. "But I'm here now. And I need you to promise me one thing."

"Okay," she breathed. And the tightness in his chest loosened.

"If Greg and his wife ask you over for dinner, tell them to fuck off."

25

I t was later in the afternoon when Amber walked into the tavern wearing one of North's coats that seemed to swamp her despite the swell of her stomach. "Don't ask," she muttered. "Nothing fits. He knocked me up, he can lend me some clothes."

Kelly laughed. "Sit down. Let me get you something to drink." She looked around. "Where's Willow?"

"With North. He's taken her shopping to choose a gift for the baby. Said he wants more daughter time with her so she doesn't feel pushed out when the baby comes." Amber cupped her stomach.

"That's so sweet."

"I know." Amber caught her eye. "And I never thought I'd say North and sweet in the same sentence." She coughed. "Anyway, talking of sweet."

"Not here." There were three of them behind the bar. And she liked her staff but she didn't want them knowing about her intimate relationships. Especially when she was trying like hell not to panic about her night with Kris.

"Where then?" Amber mock-whispered.

"I'll take a break. I'm overdue anyway." She whipped her apron off and hung it on the hook. "You guys okay if I head out for twenty minutes?" she asked them.

"Sure." It was busy but steady in here. The lunchtime rush had finished and the evening rush had yet to begin. She didn't feel too guilty about taking her first – and possibly only – break of the day.

She walked around the counter to where Amber was standing. "Come on, let's go for a walk."

As they stepped outside into the cool winter air, Kelly inhaled deeply. It was one of those winter days without a cloud in the sky, the sun beating down like a promise of better weather to come. Amber slipped her arm through Kelly's and in silent agreement they headed to the town square to join the line at the hot dog stand that opened up earlier that year .

"So," Amber said, a smile playing on her lips. "Something you want to tell me?"

Kelly grinned and shook her head. "Sounds like you already know."

"I don't. Not really. I mean I can guess that something happened between you and Kris. He came to see me and North last night."

"He did? Why?"

"Oh, I think he needed to talk. Plus North had some skates he's lending him. They're the same size."

"For the father-son game?" Kelly asked.

"Yeah." Amber nodded. "He said you're worried about Cole getting too attached to him."

Kelly exhaled heavily. "I guess I am." Truth was, she never wanted her son to hurt the way she once had. She could stand to hurt herself, she knew she was resilient, but Cole? He already had a dad who barely contacted him, and only when it suited Lyle.

She couldn't let Kris hurt him, too.

"So what are you going to do?" Amber asked her. "Because from where I'm standing Cole is already getting attached."

"I don't know." That was the honest answer. Since Kris had come home it was like her whole life had become a roller-coaster after trundling along on old straight tracks for the longest of times.

It was exhilarating. And scary.

"Maybe you should trust him," Amber said.

And wasn't that the scariest thought of all? Because what if he broke her again?

Kelly, age 23

The screaming pushed through her dreams, pulling her out of them, making her sit up fast as she looked around.

The action made her stitches pull so tight she audibly groaned, even though the baby was the only one to hear her.

Cole, she reminded herself. She'd spent the whole time he was growing inside of her calling him 'the baby'. It was a bad habit she needed to break.

As though he could sense her thoughts, Cole screamed again, and she reached across the bed to pull him out of the crib.

And something tore.

"Shit!" A tear rolled down her face. Smelling the milk on her, Cole started to scream louder, his face red and angry.

"Lyle?"

No answer. Of course there wasn't. Since she'd come home with Cole last week he'd barely been here. Her dad had been by to help, and people had left casseroles and gifts at the door, but it was just her and the baby.

And she had no idea what she was doing.

Lifting her nightgown, she put Cole to her breast, wincing, because that hurt, too. His tears dried up as hers continued to roll down her face.

She had no idea what she was doing. She had no right to bring a baby into the world. No wonder Cole hated her.

Cole's sucking slowed as he finally got his fill, his eyes drooping until they were closed. Kelly let out a long breath, still holding him with one hand, using her other to lift the covers to check her abdomen.

The skin around her incision had gotten infected. She'd had to make an urgent visit with the doctor which had cost even more money. Money she didn't have.

Cole let out a long sigh and she tried to push the fear away.

She had to be strong for him. He was all she had. Her and her dad, and maybe the few friends she had left.

But not the one you need.

She tried to blink that thought away, too. Because this one cut like a knife. Felt worse than any pulled stitch she could have.

And because she was a masochist she looked at her phone. There it was, his last message. Unanswered like the rest.

I hear you had a son. Congratulations. You'll make the best mom. – Kris.

Above it were other unanswered texts. One telling her he'd found somewhere to live in England. One telling her he missed her. And more asking about her pregnancy, about Lyle, about stupid stuff that made her feel so wistful it hurt.

But she hadn't replied. She couldn't. She'd chosen Lyle.

And Kris had chosen to leave.

Cole let out a soft cry, his eyes still shut.

"Hey," she whispered softly. "It's just a dream. I won't let anything hurt you."

She wouldn't. Not ever. She'd made a mess of her life so far, but it stopped right now. This little baby in her arms didn't deserve her tears or her fears. He deserved to grow up happy. To know he was loved more than anything.

He deserved the world.

"It's just you and me, kid," she whispered, and Cole's lips curled. It was too soon to be a smile, she knew that, but it still looked so much like one.

Her heart filled with love for the vulnerable curled up baby in her arms.

It was just her and him. And that was okay.

Being inside of the woman he adored felt like he'd ripped off a little bit of heaven and hid it in his heart. She was looking up at him, her swollen lips parted, her eyes never leaving his. Her skin was pink from coming once already, her hands digging into his behind as he moved in and out of her.

He leaned down to kiss her and he felt himself tighten.

"Kris, it's too much. I'm gonna..."

"I know." He could feel her tighten around him again. He was gritting his teeth trying not to come too soon, not to end this moment. It was too much. Too perfect.

Too everything.

"But don't stop," she added quickly.

"Not planning on it." He kissed the corner of her mouth, her throat, the swell of her breast. And then he pulled her nipple between his lips, sucking on her as she called out his name again. This time higher, needier, as she convulsed around him.

And he was coming, too. Surging inside of her, every part

of him buzzing with electricity as she raked her nails down his back. They were kissing, their mouths moving as their bodies stilled, and he felt the emotion pull at his chest.

When he pulled out she was smiling at him, her face shining.

And he grinned back, because she made everything feel good. "Come here," he rolled over, pulling her with him, loving the way she fit perfectly into the crook of his arm.

"Twice in two hours. That's pretty impressive," she teased.

"Yeah, well, until I can persuade you to stay over again I have to make sure you leave sated."

"I'm definitely sated." She sighed against his skin. "And I can't stay tonight. Cole has a dentist appointment in the morning and then I'll need to drive him to school."

"I know." He kissed her temple. "You sure you don't want me to go with you?"

"No. I remember how much you hate the dentist."

He grimaced. "I don't hate the dentist. I hate needles."

She laughed, wriggling her fingers. "I swear my hand is still deformed from the way you held onto it so tight when you had to get that filling."

"Yeah, well it was your fault. You always brought candy wherever we went."

"I also brushed my teeth religiously."

He lifted a brow. "So did I." He ran his fingers down her side and she nestled closer into him. "Can I take Cole out to dinner on Saturday?" he asked her. "After the father son match? Apparently everybody's heading to the diner at Marshall's Gap. Reece's dad called me to ask if I wanted him to save us seats." He gave her a lopsided smile. "If you can get off work maybe you can come, too?"

"I can't. It's the last weekend before Christmas. All hands on deck at the tavern." She reached out to trace the line of his jaw. "Thank you for being so kind to Cole."

"I feel like I have a lot of time to make up for."

"You don't have to make up for anything."

He turned his head to kiss her fingertips. "I shouldn't have left. That's the long and short of it. I should have stayed and helped you with Lyle."

"It would have made things worse. He..." She sighed. "When I told him I was pregnant he thought it was yours. I don't know if he ever truly believed me that Cole is his."

"I wish Cole had been mine."

Her breath caught. How many times had she wished that back when her life was falling apart?

"Then he wouldn't have been Cole."

He smiled at her. "I guess not."

"I think I needed you to leave," she said, her eyes full of honesty. "I think I needed to learn how to stand on my own two feet. I was so afraid of losing you and then Lyle that I pushed all my needs away to make sure you were both happy."

"I never wanted you to do that."

"I know." She nodded. "And that's why I needed to be on my own. I'd relied on you two for so long."

"We'd relied on each other."

"Until we didn't," she said.

"Yeah, until then." He exhaled and kissed her again. Needing the connection. A reminder that this was real. "And I like the way you are now."

"Me too." She smiled. "I like who you are now."

"Good."

"Can I ask you something?" She turned on her side to look at him, propping her face on her hand.

"Sure."

"Who's Laura?"

He wasn't expecting that. And for a moment no words came out.

"I saw her name on your phone. I wasn't snooping or

anything, just checking the time the other morning. And her message came up."

Kris swallowed. He wasn't sure if he was ready for this conversation yet. But here it was and he'd promised himself he'd always be honest with her. "Laura is my therapist."

Kelly blinked. She didn't look shocked, just interested.

"We were all offered therapy at work. Part of our health-care plan. And I went to a session with her because the CEO wanted our whole team to. I thought I was just ticking boxes but then all this stuff came out. Things I'd been ignoring for years. I've never been one big for talking but..." He trailed off. "I dunno. What she said made sense."

"What did she say?" Kelly asked him.

He ran the pad of his thumb across his shadowed jaw. "I guess she made me see things differently. For the longest time I thought circumstances were a bitch. But she made me realize that I made bad decisions."

"What kind of bad decisions?"

"Leaving you." He gave her a lopsided smile. "Messing things up with Lyle. And later, having bad relationships because I wasn't willing to give them anything of myself."

"Like your ex?"

"Yeah. That was the bad one. I was in danger of becoming an asshole. I wanted to be a better person. Make things right. Since coming back to Winterville, I've kept in touch with Laura. Let her know I was here, talking to you."

"Is she happy about that?"

He caught her eye, a half-smile on his face. "She thinks I'm making progress."

Kelly nodded but said nothing.

"I'm not asking for you to believe in me. Not yet."

Her lips parted and a soft sigh escaped. "It's not you. I just... I've spent a long time depending on myself."

"I know that. And you've done a great job." He reached

out for her hand, taking it in his own. "And I know you're worried about Cole."

"I'm always worried about Cole. That's a mom's job."

"And you do it well." It made him think of his own mom. The one who barely gave him or his brothers any attention. "Cole's lucky to have you."

"I'm the lucky one," she whispered. "Even if I do have permanent scars."

It was like she was finished with the conversation, as she rolled on top of him, her legs straddling his. She looked magnificent, her breasts high and tight, her stomach curved and smooth. And there was that scar, right above her pelvis. He reached out to slide his finger along it.

"Ugh. I hate this thing." She looked down at her stomach, grimacing.

"I like it. A reminder of just how amazing medical intervention can be. Somebody cut into you and brought out a baby."

"Yeah, and then I got an infection and for six weeks I couldn't bend over without crying out in pain."

He frowned. "Did Lyle help after Cole was born?"

"The first day or two, yeah. And then he got upset because every time he went near Cole he cried."

"Lyle or Cole?"

She grinned. "Cole. And Lyle thought it was because he hated him. I told him babies can't hate anybody but he walked out in a huff."

"I wish I'd been there to help you." He propped himself up on his elbows, capturing her lips with his.

"You're here now," she said, her voice thick.

He felt himself stir again, the need for her as strong as ever. And she must have felt it too, because she rocked against him, her body slick.

"You need to go home," he murmured.

"I know." She rocked again, leaning down until her breasts were pressed against his chest, her lips against his. "So let's make this fast." She reached down to curl her fingers around him, putting him right where she needed him.

And when he slid inside of her again he groaned.

He'd never get bored of this. Never get sick of watching her face as she slowly rode him to the sweetest oblivion he'd ever tasted.

Curling his hands around her hips, he moved her faster, harder, until they were both breathless and on the edge.

And when they tipped over the edge for the last time that night he wasn't sure he'd ever recover.

26

"Everything okay?" Carmen asked as Kelly walked into the tavern the following afternoon.

"All good. Thanks for holding the fort while I dropped Cole off at school."

"No problem. I've been amusing myself watching the guys over there try to repair the tree."

Kelly followed the direction of Carmen's gaze. Sure enough, North was halfway up the huge tree that stood in the center of the town square, a harness around his waist as he tried to fix something in his hands. Was it the lights? She knew they'd been temperamental this year, mostly thanks to a huge storm they'd had the week after the tree had gone up. The water had caused problems and North was constantly trying to sort the lights out.

He was shouting down to somebody. And then her heart did a little dance in her chest when she saw Kris standing at the bottom of the tree, wearing jeans and a hoodie, with a sleeveless padded jacket over the top, shouting back at his brother.

She hadn't spoken to him since last night. And she

wouldn't be able to see him tonight either, since it was Friday and they were short staffed. She'd be stuck at the tavern until the early hours of tomorrow.

He was nodding at something North was saying, then he crouched down to get something out of the box in front of him. Her stomach did a little flip as she watched him languorously stand up, then clip something onto his belt.

He was climbing up with North. Oh.

"That family knows how to make fine men," Carmen whispered. Kelly swallowed, watching Kris as he easily climbed from branch to branch, before he reached up to where North was, handing him something she couldn't see.

What she could see was North saying something that made Kris grin. And then he was laughing, and so was North.

God, he was handsome. Especially when he smiled. She felt herself yearning for him, shocked by her attraction toward this man.

If he leaves this time it will kill me.

She wasn't sure where that thought came from. It hit her straight in the chest though, like a cannon ball, making her feel winded.

She inhaled raggedly. *Stop it.* She didn't need to be thinking like that.

A minute later, Kris was climbing back down again. He jumped the last six feet or so, and she felt her cheeks heat up. And then he looked over toward the tavern, his gaze falling on her car.

He knew she was here. It made her skin tingle.

Then he turned away and she couldn't see him any more. She should probably get some work done now. But then her phone buzzed in her pocket.

You back? Cole okay? Would you like a coffee? – Kris.

She smiled, because he was sexy and sweet in equal measure.

I am. And he is. And no – I drank a vat of it before we went to the dentist. You okay, Monkey Man? I was starting to wonder if you were auditioning for the circus. – Kelly.

You been watching me? – Kris

Might have been. – Kelly.

Excellent. I'm here for your entertainment. And the only circus I plan to be joining is the one in my bed. With you. – Kris.

Yeah, that doesn't work. As a pun I mean. As an image I'm all good with it. – Kelly.

It doesn't, does it? Still planning on getting you back in my bed soon. – Kris.

Looking forward to it. – Kelly x

"Mom, is he here yet?" Cole asked, his face flushed with excitement as he stuffed his change of clothes for after the game in his bag.

"Not yet. It's still early." She glanced out of the window, but all she could see was the soft white of the snow that had fallen overnight.

Thank goodness Charlie Shaw had been around in his plow to clear the roads before the sun had even risen over the mountains. Today and tomorrow were the busiest days of the year for Winterville.

Cole joined her next to the window, and she realized he'd grown again. His head was past her shoulders, and when she looked at the sleeves of his hoodie she could see they ended right where his bony wrist jutted out.

Thank God she'd planned ahead and bought him some clothes a size up for Christmas. In only a year or two he'd almost certainly be taller than her.

"There he is." Cole's eyes lit up as Kris' car pulled into the driveway. "I'll see you later, Mom!"

"Wait up." She reached for his hand. "Give me a hug before you go."

"Okay." He rolled his eyes and put his arms around her. His hug was cursory at best. But she'd take it.

"Be good for Kris."

"I will." His eyes were on the hallway. In his head he was almost certainly already out of the door.

"And good luck. Give them hell."

He laughed. "Thanks, Mom."

"I'm sorry I can't be there." She'd looked at the schedules over and over again. But this weekend was impossible. Every table in the tavern was booked from lunch until close. And there'd be more customers to come in to stand or play pool or just hang around in the hopes that one of their reservations would be a no show.

"It's fine." Cole shrugged. "Kris will be there. And we're heading out for dinner after, did he tell you?"

"He did. But when he says it's time to leave, you have to go, okay?"

Cole gave her one of his 'what are you talking about' looks. She knew it well. She'd used it herself a few times as a teenager.

"I'm serious," she said.

"Okay, okay."

From the corner of her eye she could see Kris tramping up the path. She hadn't had time to clear it yet, and his dark brown boots were making perfect imprints in the thick white snow. He looked up and saw her looking at him through the window and his mouth split into a grin.

Damn, her heart needed to stay cool.

"Hey." Cole's voice was further away. She hadn't heard him run out to the hallway to open the front door.

"Hey." Kris' low voice echoed through the hall. "You ready?"

"Yep."

There was a slap of hands – a high five, she presumed.

"Great." There was so much warmth in his voice it made her smile. "Go throw your gear in the car. I'll just say hi to your mom."

"Bye, Mom!"

"Bye, honey." She walked out of the kitchen to where Kris was standing and Cole was already halfway out of the door. "Hi," she said softly.

"Hey you."

"Thank you for this. It means so much to him." She was fighting a losing battle, she knew that. Cole hadn't stopped talking about Kris all morning.

His gaze drifted over her face. "It means a lot to me, too." He ran his thumb over his jaw. "You sure you don't want to go watch? We can switch, and I'll cover the tavern?"

"You can't." They'd already talked about this. But he had a thing about her not being able to see Cole play. "I'm terrible at hockey. And anyway, Cole would kill me if you didn't play against him."

"I'm looking forward to it, too."

"Are you coming?" Cole yelled from the car. Kris lifted a brow.

"I guess that's my cue. I'll let you know how it goes. And call you later."

"Thank you. If there are any problems and I don't reply immediately, just call the tavern. Somebody will pick up." She knew from past experience that she'd barely have time to breathe, let alone check her phone for messages.

But she'd definitely be checking to see how Cole was doing.

"I told Cole you're in charge. When you want to leave you

tell him. Don't take any sass from him or he'll make you stay there all night."

Kris laughed. "I don't mind."

"Yeah, well I don't want him to take advantage, that's all."

"Kris!" Cole's shout was louder this time. "Come on!"

His eyes flickered to hers. "I'll see you later, beautiful." Then he walked toward her, leaning down to brush his lips against hers. And she felt his kiss — as soft as it was — all the way down to her toes.

And she was still smiling when he walked out of the door, covering the distance between her house and his car in a few easy strides, pulling the driver's door open before he climbed inside.

And as the engine started up, she realized that most of her heart was in that car. The child she adored and the man she'd loved since she'd been a child herself.

"Good luck!" she shouted and Kris put his arm out of the driver's window, giving her a thumb's up.

And as they drove away she felt her chest tighten. Her son was growing up and she couldn't stop it. She shouldn't want to.

But it was getting harder and harder to protect him the way she wanted to.

❧ 27 ❧

"**O**kay, this is your locker room," Cole said, pointing at the away team room. "All the dads are in there."

Kris shifted his rucksack from his arm to his hand, curling his fingers around the handle. "I'll wait here until you're in your locker room."

Cole shot him a strange look. "You don't need to do that."

"I know. But your mom will kill me if I don't keep an eye on you." He shrugged. "I promised." And he'd learned from experience that if he promised Kelly something, then she was damn sure going to get it. Not because he was scared of her but because he had something to prove.

A lot of things.

"Okay then. But don't follow me. We'll be talking tactics and the dads can't know our plans."

Kris bit down a smile. Cole had been so excited on the drive over here. Not just because Kelly had allowed him to go in Kris' car alone, but because they'd be on the ice together for an hour. He'd made Kris promise not to take it easy on him, and yeah, Kris may have curled one finger over the other for that.

Cole's team was full of kids. There was no way he was going in like he used to when he played in school.

Once Cole had disappeared inside his own locker room, Kris pushed the dads' door open. Inside, there were at least fifteen dads, all in various states of undress. Some of them looked less than enthusiastic about climbing into their compression shorts and jockstraps.

"You made it."

Kris looked up to see the guy he'd met in the coffee shop walking toward him. "Hey, Greg."

"Let me introduce you to my brother–in–law," he said. "The one I told you about. He's stepping in for Daniel's dad. He had to drop out, some kind of work emergency. Ian, this is Kris. He's just arrived in town, too."

Ian reached his hand out. And Kris shook it, but he wasn't exactly feeling ecstatic about it. The man was well built, smooth, with one of those jaw lines he could remember his GI Joe toy having back when he was a kid.

"Good to meet you," Ian said. "I hear you're a center. Me too."

Excellent. They wouldn't be playing at the same time then. "I was. Once. Now I'm just going to try to keep upright on the ice."

Ian laughed. "Yeah, I feel that. I pull a muscle getting the milk out of the refrigerator."

"I was telling Ian about Kelly," Greg continued. "I know she's busy all the way up through Christmas, but Ian's staying until the new year so hopefully we can all get together then." Greg smiled at Kris. "You're invited, too, of course." He glanced at Ian. "Kris is kind of like Cole's uncle."

"I hear he and Reece are good friends," Ian said.

"I've no idea." Kris lifted his bag. "I gotta get ready. I'll catch up with you later."

"We're on in ten minutes," Greg reminded him. "And

don't worry, you and Ian can catch up at the diner. He's coming, too."

"Great." Kris nodded, even though he felt anything but great.

He felt jealous. And annoyed. And like hitting the puck at the groin of the grinning man in front of him.

Christ, he was out of practice. Sure he'd hit the gym three days a week when he was living in London, and since he'd been here in Winterville he'd kept fit by helping North at the farm. But hockey required a whole new level of fitness, one he'd found so easy as a teenager with all the energy and loose muscles that came with it.

But now, five minutes into the second period and he was feeling every single slide of his skates as he raced after the damn puck.

Worse, most of the kids were smaller than Cole and he had to make sure to look out for the little ones in case he slammed into them, or tripped over them, or – horror of horrors – sent a kid flying.

"Ah shi—I mean crapola," Greg shouted as he hit the puck and it went straight toward Cole's stick. Cole looked like he couldn't believe his luck, scooping the puck up and skating away at what looked like some kind of break neck speed.

The crowd roared, Greg groaned, and Cole grinned as he maintained control of the puck. His skates lit up the ice as he flew past the defense for the dad's team, an expression of sheer joy on his face and a determined gleam in his eyes.

Kris turned on the ice, a smile pulling at his lips as Cole weaved through players both big and small, somehow still keeping control of the puck. The kid was good, no doubt about it – or maybe it was just that determination that kept him ahead of the pack.

As Cole raced toward the net Kris found himself watching intently, rooting for him, not giving a flying fuck that this would put the kids ahead of the dad's team. He held his breath as Cole hesitated a second too long, enough for Greg to almost catch him.

"Shoot!" Kris yelled.

A second later Cole was pushing his stick, the puck gliding across the ice. Kris' lungs were tight as the goalkeeper lunged toward it, his stick just missing the puck before it slammed into the back of the net.

The crowd erupted in cheers and Kris let out a whoop of his own, pumping his fist in the air. Cole skated back to his team, his teammates patting him on the back and congratulating him. Kris couldn't help but feel a swell of pride in his chest as he watched Cole skate by, still grinning from ear to ear.

"Did you see it?" Cole asked, his eyes shining behind the helmet guard.

"Yeah." Kris fist bumped him. "You were amazing."

The referee blew his whistle and Cole skated away, still looking like the cat that got the cream.

Kris felt his chest tighten with pride. The kid wasn't his but he didn't care. He loved seeing him happy. That was the truth of it.

And yeah, Kelly still didn't completely trust him. But he'd do whatever to make sure Cole stayed happy. That they both did.

He was still smiling as he skated over to the boards. It was time for the dads on the ice to take a break. Even seeing Ian take his place didn't annoy him like it should.

"That was my fault," Greg said, sounding breathless as he

joined Kris on the bench. "I shouldn't have sent the puck Cole's way."

"Doesn't matter." Kris shrugged. "You made a kid very happy."

"Yeah, but my kid won't let me hear the last of it," Greg muttered. "Nor will my wife."

"You'll get over it," Kris assured him, leaning forward to rest his elbows on his knees as he watched Ian, the brother-in-law he already loved to hate, fall over his skates after a failed attempt at hooking the puck from a ten year old.

He chuckled to himself. All in all this game was going pretty well. Maybe dinner at the diner would, too.

The ten-year-olds won. Four-two. Your kid got chosen Most Valuable Player. He was pretty awesome, just like you. – Kris

He slid his phone back into his pocket and opened the car door so Cole could climb in. He hadn't stopped grinning since the end of the game.

"Did Mom reply?" he asked, almost bouncing in his seat as Kris pulled his own seatbelt on.

"Not yet. She's busy, remember? But she'll check her phone as soon as she can. You can always call her when we get to the diner."

"I'll probably forget at the diner." Cole wrinkled his nose. "Everybody wants to sit next to me because I'm MVP and I'll have to decide who I want next to me the most." He sighed. "It's hard being popular."

Kris bit down a grin and started the engine up. "Who do you want to sit next to you?"

"I don't know. I mean Reece is my best friend, so he probably should. And Noah is popular, everybody loves him. If he sits next to me everyone will think I'm cool." He pressed his lips together, his brow furrowing like he was thinking hard. "But Daniel's dad didn't come and I feel kind of sorry for him because his dad is always letting him down. He promised to take him to Disney World in the summer but then he got married instead. So I don't know. I guess I'll have Reece and Daniel."

There was a lump in Kris' throat that he couldn't swallow away. "You're a good kid, you know that?"

"It's hard on Daniel. His dad left home last year. His mom keeps crying all the time and Daniel hates that. He keeps asking me if he'll get over it but I don't know. I can't remember a time when Dad lived with us."

"Do you miss him anyway?" Kris asked.

"No, not really." Cole shrugged. "Can you miss what you've never had?"

"Yeah, I think you can." Kris turned left, following the long line of cars toward Marshall's Gap. The roads were thick with traffic, but most of it was heading the other way, to Winterville. "I wish I'd known you when you were little."

"You do?" Cole asked. From the corner of his eye, Kris could see him grinning.

"Yeah. I do. I regret not keeping in touch with your mom and you."

Cole was silent for a moment, the only sound in the car was the tapping of his fingers against his denim-clad legs. "Will you be leaving again?" he asked.

Kris took a deep breath. He wasn't used to the candidness of kids. They didn't skate around a subject like adults. Just wham and you were there.

"I'm not sure."

"I wish you'd stay. I like you coming to my games."

They'd reached a red light. Kris pressed the brakes, pulling the car to a stop. "I like coming to your games, too."

"And Mom's been happier since you've been here."

He bit down a smile. "Your mom deserves some happiness."

"Yeah, she does. So will you stay?"

Kris turned to look at him. Cole was staring right back at him, his eyes wide and honest.

"I'd like to."

"Then do it."

He made it sound so easy. And maybe it was. But the kid didn't know what was going on between him and Kelly. And it sure as hell wasn't Kris' right to tell him. It was up to Kelly when and where they talked to Cole about their relationship.

Or if. That thought made his throat feel tight.

"I think my mom likes you," Cole said right as the light turned green.

"What?" Kris almost forgot to put his foot on the gas.

"Like girls like boys, I mean. Would you stay if she liked you?"

Damn his perceptiveness. "I... yeah... I guess."

"Then tell her that. I don't mind if you become girlfriend and boyfriend. As long as you promise not to do that kissy stuff in front of me. Daniel had a girlfriend last summer. They kept holding hands and running off together. It was kind of gross."

Kris laughed. "Isn't Daniel a little young to have a girlfriend?"

Cole shrugged. "I dunno. But he'd liked her for the longest time. And then she broke his heart." Cole sighed. "It took him two days before he wanted to play Pokemon Go again."

"That's a long time," Kris agreed, trying not to laugh

again. He felt on steadier ground now that they'd stopped talking about him and Kelly.

"It was. We missed a rare Pokemon because he was too busy being sad."

"You missed a Pokemon for your friend?" Kris asked.

"Yeah. I couldn't go get it without him. We play that game together, you know?"

"I know." Kris nodded. He could remember the way he and Lyle were the same. Best buddies. His chest felt tight. Because that felt like a hundred years ago yet it had completely changed his life.

They'd made an agreement and only one of them had kept it. But he didn't blame Lyle anymore. He owned his decisions. Even the bad ones.

It took another ten minutes to finally get into Marshall's Gap, and Cole kept up a steady monologue about the game, Christmas, and friends. By the time they pulled into a space at the diner, he was so excited he'd opened the door before Kris had even cut the engine.

"Thank you for driving me."

"Anytime, kid. Go on in and have fun. I'll just check if your mom's messaged back."

"Sure. Tell her I love her." All thoughts of talking to her seemed forgotten, just like Cole had predicted. "Oh, and she told me that I have to leave when you want to. So just tell me when."

He was a good kid. Kelly had made sure of that. "I'm happy to be here as long as you want," he told Cole. "Now go enjoy yourself. You deserve it."

❧ 28 ❧

Winterville was dark and silent as she drove home from the tavern, turning off her headlamps as she pulled onto the driveway so they didn't shine into the house. Snow still lay on the ground – it was too cold for any thaw – and it seemed to deaden all the noises she made as she climbed out of the car and softly closed the door.

"Hey."

She jumped at the sound of his voice. And then she smiled because it was *him*. Sure, she was exhausted and every muscle in her body felt like it was on fire after running around the tavern all day, but seeing him made everything feel better.

"How long have you been waiting outside?" she whispered.

"Not long. I brought Cole home around ten and then sat with your dad for a while. I just wanted to see you before I head back to the cabin and crash."

She lifted her head up to look at him. "I'm glad you did."

"Me, too." There was a half-smile on his face. The only light came from the porch lamp outside her house, but it was enough for her to see the sharp line of his jaw and the warmth of his gaze.

"Thank you for taking Cole today."

"It was my pleasure. Seriously. He's a good kid, and I'm glad I got to play against him."

"Even if you lost."

His smile widened. "It kind of felt like winning." He shrugged. "Anyway, he's absolutely exhausted, so he should sleep well tonight. Although I think he ate a little too much. He was complaining of a stomach ache."

"How much did he eat?" she asked, grimacing.

"A lot. They all did. And a lot of sodas were drunk. I think your dad gave him some Pepto Bismol or something. He went straight to sleep after that."

"Thank God for dad. And being able to sleep in." She tipped her head to the side. "So are you going to kiss me or not?"

"I don't know." He gave her a teasing smile. "Am I?"

"You'd better, buddy."

He laughed and pulled her close, smelling of cold air and the pine shampoo he used. Up close she could see the shadow of his evening beard growth against the sharpness of his jaw as he lowered his head to brush his lips against hers.

Though she felt the tug inside of her, the need to press her body to his, it was secondary to the hammer of her heart against her chest. What was it that Amber had said to her when she and North had gotten engaged.

"I thought I knew what love was, until I watched him fall for a child that wasn't his. If somebody loves your baby that hard, it's impossible not to love him back."

And yeah, she understood that. Understood how impossible it was not to fall for a man who loved your child. Who showed him kindness, who took care of him, would do anything to make him happy.

But it was more than that. She'd always been in love with Kris Winter. First as friends, then as more. And now?

It was like a tidal wave. Impossible to ignore. Impossible to run away from.

The perfect way to drown. If only she'd let herself.

Kris slid his hand down her back, to the swell of her behind, pulling her against him as he kissed her neck. Damn she loved that. Too much. It was impossible not to let out a loud sigh as her body responded to his touch.

And then she yawned.

It wasn't deliberate. More the result of a fourteen hour shift that had left her almost broken. "Oh Lord, I'm sorry."

He started to laugh. "Am I boring you?"

"No. I'm just... gah. I'm an idiot."

He cupped her face with his hands. They felt warm against her chilled skin. How did that happen? Did he have some kind of internal heater? "You're not an idiot. You're exhausted. Now go inside and I'll call you tomorrow."

"I wish you could come inside with me. I sleep better when you're around."

He looked pleased at that. "I wish I could, too. And maybe soon I will."

"You sound sure of yourself." She liked that a bit too much.

"Yeah, well I apparently have a second in command." He pressed his lips together. "Cole wants me to be your boyfriend."

"What?" Her mouth dropped open. "How did that come up?"

"I don't know. He was just saying that he wanted me to stay around. And that I make you happy. Apparently, he doesn't mind if we're boyfriend and girlfriend as long as we don't do – and I quote – 'kissy stuff' in front of him."

"Eek." She grimaced. "I'm sorry. I didn't ask him to say anything."

"I know you didn't." He pressed his lips against the tip of her nose. "I know you, sweetheart. You'd do anything for him not to say anything."

She yawned again, this time it was so big it was embarrassing. He smiled and pulled her scarf back around her. "Go inside," he said. "I'll call you tomorrow."

"I have another all day shift."

"I know. This time I can come help."

"What?"

"I'll come work with you. I figure it's a win-win, I get to spend some time with you and you get some free labor."

Her eyes met his and she felt every muscle inside of her soften. This man was going to kill her.

"Thank you," she whispered. "I'd like that a lot."

"Me, too." He grinned and kissed her again then walked to his car.

"Mom, I feel sick."

Kelly blinked, trying to push the sleep from her eyes and focus on her son standing in her bedroom doorway. She'd fallen asleep as soon as her head hit the pillow, and though it was still dark she had no idea what the time was.

"Okay honey, let's head for the bathroom." Her voice was groggy but she'd already jumped out of bed. Damn the diner and the soda and too much food. She put her hand on Cole's back and led him down the hallway to the bathroom at the back.

They both knew the drill by now. She'd lost count of how many times he'd brought home a bug since he'd started kindergarten. He knelt down on the bathroom floor as she stroked his head and he emptied his guts.

She hated this. Watching him turn green and look so awful. Whenever he was sick she wanted to take whatever illness he had from him, suffer it herself.

All moms did, she figured. Who liked seeing their child suffer?

"Ooohh." Cole lifted his head and she wiped his mouth, then gave him a glass of water.

"I can't."

"You'll feel better if you do," she told him. "Just swish some around and spit it out again."

He did as she told him but he didn't look like he felt any better.

"You think you're done?" she asked him.

Cole nodded.

"Okay. I'll grab a bowl from the kitchen just in case. You want to sleep with me tonight?"

"No. I'll stay in my room."

She blinked, surprised. He'd always curled up with her whenever he was sick. And though she hated that he was unwell she kind of loved taking care of him. "Are you sure?"

"Yeah." He was growing up. Didn't even need her when he was sick. That was a good thing, what she wanted for him.

And yet a tiny part of her felt sad that she couldn't make everything better.

So he headed back to bed and she brought him the bowl, sitting next to him until he drifted off to sleep. When his breathing was steady and his face was peaceful, she tiptoed back to her bedroom and glanced at her phone by the side of her bed.

It was three in the morning. In another four hours she'd need to be up and heading to the tavern.

If Cole was feeling better.

But what if he wasn't? She couldn't leave him sick while she worked. But she couldn't not work, either. There wasn't enough staff and those that would be working were too green to open and close, let alone to troubleshoot any problems that came their way.

It wasn't often that she worried about being a single mom, but right now she felt it right to her bones. Her dad wasn't well enough himself to look after a sick child.

"Maybe he'll be better in the morning," she murmured to herself. Especially if it was just the effects of overeating.

That was the only thought that calmed her enough to go back to sleep.

At least until she heard the sound of her son being sick again an hour later. From the light shining in the bathroom, she knew he'd at least made it there. "I'm coming," she whisper-shouted, because her dad was asleep and she wanted him to stay that way. "Hold on, honey."

When she got to the bathroom this time Cole was hunched on the floor, his skin so pale he looked like a ghost. His hair was plastered to his face and his lips looked almost blue. "It hurts."

"I know. I hate being sick, too." She brushed the hair off his face. "It's going to be okay, sweetie. I'm here, I'll take care of you."

Then he let out a groan, touching his stomach. "Mom, it really hurts."

"Where?" she asked him, trying not to panic as he clutched at his belly. "Show me where."

"Here." He pressed his hand to the center of his stomach, his fingers on his belly button. "Right here."

"Okay. Let me see." She lifted his pajama top gently, but his skin looked normal. No rashes or discoloration. "Do you think it hurts because you've eaten too much?" she asked him.

"I don't know," he grunted. A sheen of sweat covered his

face.

"Okay, okay." She pulled her lip between her teeth. "Let's see how you feel come morning. If you feel worse in a couple of hours we'll call the doctor."

"We can't afford the doctor," he said.

It was her turn to pale. Had he been listening to her money woes? "Of course we can. It's fine. We just need to make you better, that's all, honey."

"No doctor. I'll be fine."

She felt her heart crack a little. She was so careful not to talk about her fears with him. "Listen to me, we're absolutely fine. We have a roof over our head and food in the house and I have a job that keeps us going. And if we need to pay for a doctor, that's not a problem. You're the most important thing in my life."

"But you're going to do OnlyFans. And Matty says that's a porn site. That you'll be a porn star."

"I'm not." She shook her head vehemently. "I promise I'm not."

"I don't want you to." He reached out for her. "Please."

She was racking her brain to figure out where this was coming from, and then she remembered joking about it with Amber. Had he overheard the conversation all those weeks ago? Poor Cole. She was a damn idiot.

She took a deep breath, ready to reassure him again, but then he let out a cry so close to a scream that it chilled her blood. "Mom..."

Oh God, oh God. This wasn't just overeating. She could tell that from the fear and pain in his eyes.

"Dad!" she screamed, all thoughts of disturbing him forgotten. "Dad!" And then she leaned forward to hold onto her son, because he was clutching at his stomach in agony. "Honey, hold on, okay? I'm going to call an ambulance."

Grabbing her phone, she dialed 911.

29

Kelly hadn't replied to his message, but Kris figured she was either sleeping or busy trying to get ready for her second busiest day of the year, so he headed straight to the tavern to meet her.

When he saw three of her staff standing outside, one of them smoking, the other two on their phones, he frowned.

"Where's Kelly?" he asked them.

"No idea." Will shrugged, looking up from his screen. "She asked us to arrive early, too."

Kris pulled his phone out and tried calling her again, but it went straight to voicemail. "Kel, it's me. We're at the tavern and I'm hoping to hell you're not still asleep."

Dammit, he'd just drive to her place to check.

It only took him a couple of minutes before he was pulling in her driveway. Most of the tourists hadn't awoken or arrived in town yet, so the drive was fast. Her car was still parked outside, the curtains were still closed, and he bit down a smile.

What a day to sleep in. He'd grab the keys from her and get the staff going as best he could before she got herself ready. He hated to do it but he knocked on the door, knowing phoning her again was pointless.

After a minute of no replies, he walked around to Kelly's backyard, checking the door. But it was locked and everything looked dark.

"Hey."

Kelly's neighbor was standing out on his porch.

"Hi. I was just trying to wake Kelly up."

"She's not there." The man was drinking a coffee and smoking a cigarette at the same time. It was a pretty impressive feat.

"Her car's here," he said, looking at it.

"Yeah, but they were taken by the ambulance really early. The sirens woke my wife up. Not me, though. I'd sleep through a hurricane."

Blood rushed to his head, making him feel dizzy. "Are they in the hospital?"

"No idea. My wife just tried to call Kelly but there was no answer."

Shit. "Okay." He pulled his phone out and found Amber's number, pressing the dial button even though he hated to wake her.

"Hello?" Amber sounded groggy.

"Hey, I'm sorry to wake you. I was just wondering if Kelly called you this morning?" God he hoped she had.

"No. Why? Is something wrong?"

"I'm at her house. Her neighbor said an ambulance took her and Cole early this morning. I'm guessing her dad, too. I've no idea who's hurt or where they've gone." He had no idea how much Amber knew about his relationship with Kelly. Right then, he didn't care. He just needed to know she was okay.

"Have you called her?"

"It's going straight to voicemail. I'm going to call some hospitals, see if they're at one."

"Does it look like there was an accident?" she asked him.

"No. The curtains are closed. It looks peaceful." In an absolutely gut wrenching way. "I just need to find her."

"They'll be at the Gordon Memorial Hospital. That's the closest one. Let me call and see if they'll give any information."

Kris was already pulling his car door open. "I'm driving there now. Call me if you find anything out."

"I will. And you do the same." Amber sounded as panicked as he felt. "I hope she's okay."

"Yeah, I do, too."

The first person he saw when he rushed into the hospital waiting room was Paul, sitting heavily on one of those uncomfortable chairs that seemed to be made especially for hospitals, his cane propped up against the wall beside him. He had his head resting on his hand, and from the way he was slumped he looked half asleep.

"Paul?" Kris touched his shoulder gently but the older man still jumped. "Sorry."

"S'okay." Paul looked around, as though working out where he was. "Any news?"

"I was about to ask you that. Nobody would tell me anything at the desk." Kris took a deep breath, ready to voice his worst fear. "Is it Cole or Kelly?"

He'd had enough time to think about that on his drive over here. He was an asshole because Paul was his safest bet. If it was his knees, they could get it sorted. He'd pay whatever it took.

But Cole or Kelly? The thought of something happening to one – or both – of them made him want to vomit.

"It's Cole. He was real sick last night. In a lot of pain."

Okay, this was definitely the worst. Kris' throat tightened. "Where is he now?"

"I don't know. They took him and Kelly back. Made me stay out here."

"When?" Kris was trying to keep his voice even, but it was a losing battle.

"I'm not sure. I don't know." Paul was starting to panic and Kris needed to calm him down. "It's fine. I'll get someone to come and talk to us." And that would work because Paul was a relative. Sure, Kris was going to listen in, but he needed Paul to do the asking.

It took twenty minutes for a doctor to come out. Her eyes were shadowed as she walked over to where Kris and Paul were sitting. He'd called Amber and suggested she stay home until there was more news, even though she wanted to come sit with them. But she was too pregnant and this place was too uncomfortable.

"Mr. Fraser?" The doctor looked at Kris.

"That's me," Paul said, trying to straighten himself up in his chair. "I'm the grandpa."

"Okay. Good." The doctor nodded. "First of all, we've made Cole as comfortable as we can. We're still running a couple of tests but we're pretty certain he has appendicitis."

"Appendicitis?" Kris frowned. "Isn't that dangerous?"

"It can be, yes." The doctor nodded. "If the appendix is allowed to rupture it can cause a bad infection. But from what we can tell Cole's appendix is distended but hasn't ruptured yet."

"So what happens?" Paul asked, his voice thick with worry. "Can you give him some medicine to make it better?"

"I'm afraid not. We're recommending emergency surgery

to remove Cole's appendix. There's a big risk that if we do nothing it will end up rupturing and we don't want that."

"Do you know what caused it?" Paul asked, and Kris immediately felt guilty. He'd let Cole eat and drink whatever he wanted last night. "He played hockey yesterday," Paul continued. "Could that have done it?"

"No." The doctor shook her head. "We're not certain what caused it but it wouldn't be from activity. It's more likely to be a blockage in the appendix or an infection. Either way it's important to remove it as soon as possible, so we're prepping Cole for surgery now."

"Like *right* now?" Paul frowned. "Can I see him?"

"I'm afraid not. We have infection control procedures and only his parents can be with him right now." She checked her chart. "I believe his father is on his way."

"Lyle?" Paul asked, his voice raising. "He's coming here?"

Kris blew out a mouthful of air.

"I believe so." The doctor nodded. "I need to get back to my patients now. Do you have any other questions I can help you with?"

Paul shook his head, and Kris did the same.

"Okay, then. We'll keep you posted with any updates."

Kelly stood and watched them wheel Cole out of the pre-op room and into surgery, her heart breaking because she couldn't go with him. They'd allowed her to sit with him while they prepared him for surgery, double checking his medical notes, his allergies, and giving her the consent forms to sign. She'd called Lyle again before they went in, but he hadn't answered. She assumed he was on his way – he'd said as much when she'd spoken to him right after they arrived at the hospital.

Though she assumed it would be over by the time he got here. It was a long way from L.A. to Winterville, after all.

"He's going to be fine," the nurse who stayed behind told her.

Tears sprung at Kelly's eyes. "I hope so."

"Let me walk you to the waiting room. Your dad is there, right?"

Kelly nodded, her throat tight, as she followed the nurse down the hallway. When she got to her dad she'd ask him to call Kris because she wasn't sure she'd be able to talk without crying. Seeing Cole laying on the gurney, his body looking so small in the hospital gown they'd put him in, had made her want to sob out loud.

But she'd kept it in somehow. Smiled for him. Squeezed his hand and told him it was going to be okay. "Come on," the nurse said, opening the door to the waiting room for her. "Go give your dad a hug."

As soon as she stepped into the room she saw Kris. He stood and walked over to her, enveloping her in his arms and for the first time in hours she let herself go, her body feeling weak as he held her.

Her breath was short, her eyes wet, and dammit she was snotty. Kris stroked her hair, his face resting against her hair, and she cried against his shoulder because she'd been strong for too long.

"Is he okay?" Kris murmured.

"They took him away. The surgery should take about an hour or so, they said. They'll let me see him once he's in recovery."

Kris nodded, then took her face in his hands, his eyes taking in her wet eyes. "He's going to be okay. Cole's a fighter."

"I know." She nodded, pressing her lips together. "He is."

"And you're an amazing mom. You got him here quickly. That's the important thing."

She looked up at him, her face crumpling. "I'm not amazing. I spend too much time working. If I didn't I would have known there was something wrong."

"I was with him all day and I didn't realize it either." He brushed her tears away with his thumbs. "I just plied him with fucking sugar and meat. If anybody's to blame it's me."

"When the doctor asked him, he said he'd been having stomach aches on and off for weeks. But he hadn't wanted to say something because I had enough to worry about."

Kris winced. "That's not your fault. You're just trying to keep a roof over your heads."

She shook her head, feeling miserable. "I'm his mom. He's just a little kid. It's my job to know what's happening."

"You're the best mom." Paul had walked over to them and patted her on the arm. "No kid could ask for better."

"See?" Kris smiled at her and she tried to smile back. "Let's just get through the next hour or so and then you'll feel better."

She nodded and he smiled at her again, and it was funny how warm he made her. How safe she felt with this man. How much she wanted to believe in him.

"Thank you," she whispered.

"Any time." He leaned forward to brush his lips against her.

And then the door opened and it felt like everything went to hell.

30

Kris hadn't seen Lyle in more than a decade. Since that night he'd asked Kelly to leave for London with him and she'd told him she was pregnant. He'd cleaned himself up, that much was clear. His hair was cut, his face tan, and he was wearing clothes that looked like they must have cost him more than a few bucks.

It was weird because behind the face of the man, Kris could still see traces of the boy. The one he'd been friends with since kindergarten. The one he'd got up to no good with, the one who was always by his side.

Until he wasn't.

Kelly stepped out of Kris' embrace, reaching up to wipe her fresh tears away with the back of her hand.

"Where is he?" Lyle asked Kelly, ignoring Kris completely. Had he even recognized him? Probably not.

"In surgery."

Lyle nodded. "How long will it take?"

"About an hour. Then we can go see him." She blew out a long breath. "I didn't think you'd get here this fast. Aren't you living in L.A.?"

"I've been working in Virginia."

Kelly frowned and Kris knew exactly what she was thinking. Lyle had been in the next state over and hadn't bothered to let her or Cole know. Hell, he could have made it to Cole's father/son hockey game, or arranged to see him at Christmas.

A wave of fury washed over Kris. Lyle had cleaned up physically, but emotionally he was still an ass.

Lyle still hadn't looked at Kris. He was too busy looking at Kelly. "I.. ah.. you have health insurance, right?" he asked her.

She shook her head.

"Fuck. I can't afford to help with this," Lyle said, wrinkling his nose as if it was Kelly's fault. "My girlfriend's pregnant. We're trying to save for a house."

"I've already taken care of it," Kris said, because this asshole needed putting in his place. "I'm paying for it." Lyle still hadn't looked at him. He was too busy glaring at Kelly.

Had he really left her behind all those years ago to deal with this?

Kelly frowned. "No, you can't."

"I told him you'd say that." Paul chuckled and shook his head. Kris had spoken to the front desk and the billing department would call him tomorrow. It was the least he could do while Kelly bore the brunt of the pain.

"I'm sorry, who the fuck..." Lyle finally looked at him. Recognition swept over his face. "Winter? Why are you here?"

"I'm here for Kelly. And Cole."

Lyle looked from him to Kelly, his brows pinching as he took in their closeness, the way Kris was looking at her. The way he was still holding her back.

"You two? *Again*?" He laughed but there was no humor in it. "Fucking hell, you do love sloppy seconds."

Kris' jaw tightened. "I'd suggest you shut the hell up in front of the mother of your child."

"Yeah, well I've wondered about that, too."

Kelly stiffened. "Shut the hell up."

Kris knew exactly what he meant. And he wanted to beat the smirk off his ex-friend's face.

"Come on now," Paul said, clearing his throat. "Cole is sick. Let's keep calm."

"It's just all too convenient, isn't it?" Lyle said, looking at Kris. "You always did have the hots for her, even when she was my girl. Especially when she was mine. Typical rich kid, always wanting what's not his."

"There wasn't anything between us," Kelly said, her voice low. "Apart from us both trying to save you from killing yourself."

"That's why he asked you to leave with him, right?" Lyle's voice was loud enough for the other people in the waiting room to turn and look at them.

Kris glanced at Kelly. Her face was red, her cheeks stained with tears. He hated seeing her like this. Hated hearing her being treated like this by Lyle even more. When she was at her lowest, scared for Cole, and beating herself up over it.

He had no idea how he and Lyle had ever been friends.

"This isn't the time," Kris said, his voice low.

"Who are you to tell me what to do?" Lyle asked him. "Haven't you done enough already?"

The waiting room door opened and a nurse strode in, glancing at the four of them standing in the corner.

"Is there a problem here?" he asked. "Because we can't have shouting in the waiting room."

"My only problem is him," Lyle said, pointing at Kris. "He's not a relative, he shouldn't be here."

The nurse turned to Kris. "Are you the stepfather?"

He shook his head. "I'm a family friend."

Lyle snorted. "The fuck he is."

The nurse ignored Lyle. "Could I ask you to wait outside

in the main hospital waiting area? Just for the comfort of the rest of our visitors."

Kelly caught his gaze. There was fear in her eyes. He hated that so much. He'd left her looking that way before, and it was going to kill him to do it again.

"You okay with that?" he asked, his voice low. Because if she wasn't he'd do whatever it took to stay with her.

She nodded. And yeah, it hurt a little. But he wasn't the one whose kid was in surgery right now. "I'll be right outside. Call me if you need me."

"Thank you," Kelly whispered, and he walked toward the door, the nurse following behind him.

It was weird how much it felt like he was walking away again. From the woman who needed him.

He hated it. And he fucking hated Lyle.

And yeah, maybe he was jealous of him, too.

Mortification washed over Kelly as she watched Kris being practically escorted out of the surgical waiting room. She felt furious, too. Wanted to scream at Lyle, but then that would just cause more problems.

So she sank down into an empty chair facing the doorway where the doctor would come out once Cole's surgery was over. Her cheeks blazed as the people in the waiting room watched her every move, as though they wanted a repeat of the drama earlier.

Her dad sat next to her, grabbing her hand in his, his fingers cool and rubbery. "You okay?" he asked.

She nodded, saying nothing.

Lyle pulled his phone out and leaned against the wall, not looking their way.

Each minute felt like an hour as it ticked by. Her dad

offered to get her a coffee but she shook her head. Then a man dressed as Santa bustled into the room, looking around before walking out again.

"Wrong room you think?" her dad asked.

"Probably."

It was strange to think Christmas was right around the corner.

"Dear Lord, the tavern." Her eyes widened. "I was supposed to open up hours ago."

Her dad patted her hand. "It doesn't matter. Kris arranged for North to pick up the second key from Dolores. Amber's going over there to supervise the staff."

"But Amber's pregnant." Her eyes widened. She loved her friend but she didn't need to do this.

"She's fine. And she's under strict instructions from Kris not to move from her stool. He's called everybody he knows. They're all going over to help, even Charlie Shaw."

He'd done so much for her. Her heart clenched at the thought of him calling around to make sure her business kept going. And then she remembered the other thing he said. She quickly pulled her phone out and turned it on – she'd kept it off while she was with Cole to try to save the battery. Once she'd unlocked it with her thumbprint she sent Kris a message.

Thank you for all you've done. Dad told me about the Tavern. But I can't let you pay for Cole's surgery. That's mine and Lyle's job to do. – Kelly x

And yes, she had no idea how they'd pay it, but they would. From the corner of her eye she saw Lyle shaking his head at something on his phone.

She sighed heavily. Okay, she'd pay for it.

Can we talk about it later? I don't want you worrying about anything but Cole right now, okay? – Kris x

Her dad let out a yawn, shifting in the uncomfortable chair.

"You should go home," Kelly told him. "Get some sleep. I'll call a cab for you." Or ask Kris to take him. But she didn't want to say that out loud. Not when Lyle was here and he'd already made a scene.

"I'm waiting right here with you," her dad replied. He shot a wary look at Lyle and she realized he was worried about leaving them alone.

"I'm good, Dad. Honestly." She gave him a reassuring smile. She wasn't scared of Lyle. She just hated scenes. Hated people noticing their family and making judgments.

She'd had enough of those to last a lifetime.

"I'll stay until he's out of surgery," he conceded. "And then I'll go."

Kelly nodded and he took her hand again, squeezing it tight. And that's how they sat for the next thirty minutes until the doctor finally walked through the door, his eyes landing on hers.

"Cole Fraser's family?"

She hadn't realized how much tension was building up inside of her until he said her name. She stood but her legs felt boneless beneath her. Her body swayed until she could get her balance.

"Is he okay?" she whispered.

"He's doing good."

Relief rushed through her.

"It looks like we did the surgery just in time. His appendix was about to rupture. If you'd left it any longer we'd be talking about a whole different scenario."

But she should have gotten him there earlier still. If only she'd listened.

"Can I see him now?"

"Yes. He's in recovery. Slowly coming out of sedation so he's a little groggy. We'll monitor him for a little while in post-op before we take him up to his room. Why don't you come with me."

She looked at her dad and he nodded, a smile on his face. "Give Cole a big hug from me."

"I will."

"I'll be coming, too," Lyle said. The doctor looked at him with a raised brow.

"You're the father?"

"That's right."

There was something in his tone that made the doctor look at Kelly again. She shrugged, because Lyle had every right to be with Cole as he recovered. At least in the eyes of the law.

Giving her dad a hug, she urged him to go home again, then followed the doctor through the door, Lyle trailing behind. She still hadn't gotten over how he'd arrived so fast. How he'd been close and hadn't said a damn thing to Cole.

But this wasn't the time or place to get into that.

When they reached Cole, he was laying on the hospital bed, his head elevated, a sheet covering him, an oxygen mask on his face. He was hooked up to an IV drip, and his eyes were closed like he was asleep.

"Hey, bud." She touched his shoulder. Cole murmured but didn't open his eyes.

The nurse next to him looked up. "He opened his eyes a few minutes ago, but he's very groggy. It'll take him a while to wake up fully. I'm just monitoring his vitals and waiting for his room to be ready, then we'll arrange for you to be taken up.

"How long will he be in here for?" Kelly asked.

"Not long. If all goes well we should be able to release him tomorrow."

"So soon?" She was happy to hear that but scared as well. She wasn't exactly the world's best nurse.

"Yes. He'll recover faster than you can believe. He's young and the surgery wasn't that invasive. He'll be up and walking around in the next few hours."

Tears stung at her eyes. Happy ones this time. "Will he be in any pain?"

"No. We'll take him off the IV pain meds in a while and then transition him to normal painkillers. Don't worry, we'll give you everything you need to make sure he's comfortable before you take him home."

"Mom."

The sound of Cole's voice – no matter how soft his whisper was – made her lip wobble.

"Yes, honey?"

The nurse lifted the oxygen mask from Cole's face so he could speak easier.

"I'm hungry."

She wanted to laugh. And wasn't that a miracle, because less than an hour ago it felt like her world was collapsing. "I bet you are, honey. You've been through it. But everything is good now. They took your appendix out and now you can get better."

"Once you're in your room we'll arrange for some food," the nurse promised him. "Hang in there."

"I'm here, bud." Lyle walked forward. "Dad's here. I'll take care of you." He stepped between Kelly and Cole.

"Dad?"

"Yeah, son. It's me."

"Why are you here?"

Well, that gave Kelly some satisfaction. Out of the mouths of babes.

"To see you. I came as soon as I heard you were sick. I was planning on seeing you for Christmas anyway."

Kelly said nothing.

"Okay." Cole sounded tired again. "That's nice."

Realizing she hadn't told Kris that Cole was in recovery, Kelly pulled out her phone. "Can I use this in here?" she asked the nurse.

"Yes of course. No problem."

"Who are you calling?" Lyle asked, turning around to look at her.

"I'm messaging Kris." She wasn't going to hide it.

"Is Kris here?" Cole asked, his eyes opening wider. He sounded a mixture of groggy and excited.

"He came as soon as he heard you were sick."

Lyle shifted his feet and lifted a brow at her, as though he was angry she'd even mentioned his ex-friend.

"Can I see him?" Cole whispered.

"Of course, honey. When you're allowed visitors." She nodded. "I know he wants to see you. He was so worried when he heard you were in the hospital."

This time Lyle let out a huff. It would have been funny if it wasn't sad. But she wasn't going to apologize for Kris becoming close to Cole. Lyle could have that same relationship with his son if he'd wanted.

He just always seemed to put himself first instead.

The phone next to the bed rang and the nurse picked it up, murmuring some answers down the line. When she disconnected the call she smiled at them. "Okay, we have a room available for Cole. We'll get him wheeled up and settled in."

"Can we come, too?" Kelly asked.

"Of course. I'm just going to hook Cole up to the mobile monitors and we'll be on our way."

31

He's out of surgery. Awake and talking. We're just waiting for him to be taken up to a room. Thank you for being you. And for coming here to support us. I couldn't do it without you. – Kelly x

Kris' throat tightened as he read the message. Cole was going to be okay.

You're the hero here. I'm so proud of you. And I know Cole is, too. Let me know if there's anything I can do. – Kris x

She didn't respond to his message, but that was okay. Cole was her priority right now. He pulled up Amber's number and sent her a message to let her know the situation in case Kelly hadn't had a chance.

Cole is out of surgery. Doing well. Just waiting to be taken to his room. Thanks for your help this morning. – Kris

Almost immediately, Amber replied. Which he hoped meant she was doing as she was told and sitting down at the tavern, supervising.

That's wonderful news. I'm so happy. Are you with

Kelly? If so you can tell her that everything at the tavern is fine. We've worked out a schedule through the new year so she can concentrate on Cole. – Amber

I'm not with her yet. Cole's only allowed two people with him at the moment and Lyle's here. – Kris

LYLE'S HERE? ARE YOU KIDDING ME? GOOD THING I'M BUSY HERE OTHERWISE I'D BE WRINGING HIS DAMN NECK. – Amber

The all-caps reply was a treat. He tried not to smile because he knew how much Amber resented Lyle for the way he treated Kelly and Cole. And yeah, he pretty much felt the same way. And if he was being really honest, he hated the way that Lyle had swanned into the hospital and asserted his rights.

Being doubly honest, there was a hint of jealousy mixed in with the anger, too.

But he needed to hide it. Kelly didn't deserve any of that.

"You heard from Kelly?"

Kris looked up to see Paul standing there, leaning on his cane. "Yeah, she just messaged me. Good news."

"Damn right. You know what would be even better news?" He had an idea. "What?"

"If that asshole ex of hers disappeared from all our lives." Paul shook his head. "The way he talks to her."

"Everybody's a little heated right now. But the important thing is Cole," Kris said.

"You're right. Still hate the guy." Paul sighed. "I'm going to call a cab and head home. That way I can make sure I'm ready to split caring duties with Kelly later."

"I'll drive you home. No need to call a cab." He'd probably be waiting for hours anyway. There were so few taxis in this part of West Virginia, and today they'd be busy picking up tourist fares.

"You sure?"

"Of course. Can you message Kelly and let her know I'll be driving for a while? I'll drop you off and come right back here."

"No problem." Paul touched Kris' arm. "And thank you. It's a relief to know there's at least one good man in Cole's life."

His words touched Kris. He nodded at Kelly's dad. "Two. Between you and me there are two of us."

Cole was asleep again. They'd settled him into his room on the children's floor – a sunny corner room that overlooked the parking garage. The floor was decorated for the holidays, with a little tree on a dais near the nurses' station.

Lyle was sitting in the chair on the other side of Cole's bed, his feet resting on the rungs beneath Cole's bed, his phone in his hand. Kelly was holding Cole's palm in hers, watching for any signs of pain or distress. The pediatric nurse had taken his vitals when they'd arrived in the room and told them to call her once Cole was awake and wanted some food.

Her phone buzzed and she could see Kris' name flash up. He was calling her, not messaging. She answered right away, lifting her phone to her ear.

"Hi." Her voice was soft because she didn't want to wake Cole. Lyle heard her, though. He looked up from his phone and frowned at her.

"Hey. How are you doing?"

It was so good to hear his voice. She swallowed and nodded. "Yeah, holding up I think. How about you?"

"I'm fine. You don't need to worry about me. I just wanted to let you know that your dad's settled at home. I cleaned up the bathroom. And then I checked in on the tavern. Everything's fine, you don't need to worry about anything."

She exhaled raggedly. This man was just... God, when was the last time somebody took care of her like this?

The last time you were friends with Kris.

Yeah, maybe then. Whenever it was, it felt good until it didn't.

"Thank you. I appreciate you so much."

"I just want to take care of you, Kel. You're not alone in this. Anything you want you just message me, okay?"

"Thank you." She could feel herself choking up. Lyle narrowed his eyes, still watching her as though she was some kind of show put on for his entertainment. And then, because her brain was stupid and it was the most inappropriate moment, the three words she'd been hiding from her heart slipped out. "I love you."

Her heart hammered against her chest. Had she really just said that out loud? She looked at Lyle who was staring back at her, his eyes narrow.

Yes, she had. She held her breath because it was so stupid and she felt so vulnerable. But she'd finally stopped lying to herself and to Kris.

Thankfully Cole was still asleep. And she was already regretting it, because that was not how you told somebody you loved them for the first time.

Or perhaps ever. In front of your ex and your child while he was recovering from surgery.

Kris chuckled and the panic slowed. "I love you too."

Oh. *OH*. Her heart felt like it was about to burst. Her chest actually hurt but in a good way. "Good," she whispered. Oh so good.

"I'll hang around the waiting room," he told her. "If you need anything just holler."

"You don't have to. You should go home, get some rest. There's nothing you can do here."

"You just told me you love me. I wasn't going anywhere before and I'm definitely not now."

Okay then. So this was what support felt like.

She could get used to this. And maybe she'd let herself. This fear had been holding her back for too long.

Maybe it was time to stop letting it dictate her reactions.

A few hours later, Cole was more awake. He'd eaten half a bowl of plain pasta and was sitting up in the bed. They'd taken him off the drip, though the catheter in his hand would be there until discharge. He'd even managed to get out of bed and walk to the bathroom with her assistance.

And now the doctor was in, checking on his wound.

"It's all looking good for discharge tomorrow," she told them. "I'm about to go off shift, but I'll be here in the morning to make sure all is well before we let you leave." She gave Cole a wink. "You're one of my favorite kind of patients."

"I am?" Cole asked, looking pleased.

"Yep. You're recovering fast and doing everything we ask of you. If you can keep doing that for your mom and dad when you get home I think you'll be able to have a great Christmas."

"Dad's coming home with us?" Cole asked.

Kelly glanced at Lyle. He wouldn't meet her eye. "I'll be around," Lyle muttered.

The doctor looked at Kelly and mouthed 'sorry', as though she realized she'd messed up.

Kelly gave her a reassuring smile. It was fine. Cole was

used to Lyle not being around. And if he decided to spend more time with his son this holiday season, well she was fine with that, too.

She just wanted Cole home, healthy and happy.

An hour later Lyle left, saying he'd be back the next morning to help get Cole home. And if she was being honest she wasn't sure if he was going to come back or not, but that was okay. She had this covered. Although Cole would love to spend time with his dad.

Either way it was good. She wasn't going to let anything spoil her happiness now that her boy was okay and recovering from a horrible day.

At six, the nurse came back in and Kelly asked her a question. "Is it okay for Cole to have visitors?"

"Of course. Two at a time including you. Or if you want a break, two people can come in while you're gone."

Kelly wasn't going anywhere. But she wanted Kris to come in now that Lyle was gone, so she sent him a message and five minutes later he was walking through the door. At the sight of him her heart started doing some kind of workout against her ribcage.

His first glance was at Cole. And she liked that a lot. Because Cole was the most important thing in her life and Kris knew that.

When he saw that Cole was dozing, Kris walked over to her and pulled her into his arms. She hugged him back so tightly she was surprised he could still breathe.

And yet he could. He could kiss her, too, his lips brushing against hers in the sweetest possible way.

"He still doing okay?" he asked when he let her go.

"Great. We're going home tomorrow." She lifted a brow. "Apparently Lyle is coming back for that."

"And how do you feel about it?"

She shrugged. "He's Cole's dad. He has the right." Her eyes caught his. "How about you?"

"It's not about me, it's about you and Cole. And he's Cole's dad," Kris repeated. "So if he wants to be here and Cole wants him here, then it's right that he comes back." He looked thoughtful, not annoyed. And she appreciated that.

"Mom?" Cole's voice was clearer than earlier. Less laden down with the painkillers and the after effects of surgery.

"Yes, honey?" She walked back over to him, stroking his hair from his face. "You doing okay?"

"Is that Kris?"

"It is." She smiled at him. "He's come to check on you."

"Hey, Cole." Kris walked over to the bedside. "How are you feeling?"

"I'm good." Cole looked so happy to see him, and it made her throat feel tight. "Did you hear I had surgery?"

"I did." Kris grinned at him. "And I hear you got through it like a champ. No wonder you're the MVP."

"I forgot about that." Cole's cheeks pinked up with pride. "Hey. Do my teammates know about my surgery?"

"Not yet," Kelly told him. "But I can tell them if you want."

"Yeah." Cole nodded. "I want them to know I won the game while I was sick."

Kelly laughed, because it was so good to see him feeling better. "Then I'll tell them."

"And then can I have more food?"

"Sure, honey. What would you like?"

"I really want a burger."

"I'm not sure they have those here."

Kris caught her eye. "I'll go get him one from the burger place down the street. If the nurses are okay with it."

Damn this man was going to kill her.

"And you'll come back, right?" Cole asked. "You'll eat with us?"

"If you'd like that, yeah." Kris nodded.

From the look on his face it felt like Cole would like that very much.

32

To Kelly's surprise, Lyle actually turned up at the hospital the next morning right as Cole was getting ready to be discharged. He strode into Cole's room like he owned the place, his gait only faltering when he saw Kris standing with Kelly.

Kris had come because he was worried Lyle wouldn't, and somebody needed to drive Kelly and Cole home. He'd gone home last night after they'd eaten dinner together around Cole's bed, and then been up at the crack of dawn to make sure the tavern was ready to open before heading back to the hospital.

"Okay," the nurse said, handing the discharge pack to Kelly. "I think you're all ready to go. Any problems, our number is in here. It's monitored twenty-four hours a day. And Cole's check up appointment card is in there, too."

"Thank you." Kelly took the pack. "I appreciate it so much."

"Let's go," Lyle said, jangling his keys. "I'll take you back."

"Kris is happy to take us," Kelly said, her voice mild. She

was trying to keep everything civil for Cole, after all he was the reason they were all here.

Ignoring her, Lyle looked at Cole and asked him, "Who do you want to take you?"

And Kris knew that couldn't happen. There was no way Cole should be made to choose between them. "It's fine," he told Kelly. "I'll follow."

"Don't you have anything better to do?" Lyle asked him.

"Not really." Kris shrugged.

The nurse arrived with a wheelchair, and Cole grimaced when she insisted on him sitting in it until they got to the car.

"It's cool," Kelly promised. "Not everybody gets to ride in a wheelchair. You can tell your friends all about it when you see them."

The nurse wheeled him down to the elevator, Kelly walking beside her, and Kris found himself walking next to Lyle. His ex-friend looked so much better than Kris remembered, even though he was a decade older than the last time they'd seen one another. He was freshly shaven, his hair was cut. His cheeks still had that hollow look but he didn't look wasted on drugs anymore.

He looked like any other man their age.

There were already people in the elevator when it arrived, and it was a squeeze to get the nurse, Kelly, and Cole in his wheelchair inside.

"Are you all right to take the stairs?" the nurse asked Kris and Lyle. "The elevators are always busy at this time of day. We have a lot of discharges."

"Sure." Kris nodded. The two of them walked through the door next to the bank of elevators into the stairwell.

Neither of them spoke as their footsteps echoed in the stairwell. And for a minute it reminded Kris of the year they both bought Doc Marten boots and stomped everywhere they could. Eventually they'd been pulled into the principal's office, and told they couldn't wear them again.

Lyle's shoulder brushed his and he pulled it away again, as though Kris had cooties or something. He started walking faster, as though it was a race to be the first one down.

Kris let him. This was childish. Didn't Lyle know he'd already won? Back when it mattered.

And he'd walked away, the same way Kris had. But instead of one broken heart behind he'd left two.

They reached the bottom of the stairs and Lyle slammed the door to the parking lot open, then strode over to where Kelly, Cole, and the nurse were waiting.

"Are you okay getting Cole into the car, or do you need some help?" Kris asked Kelly.

"I can do it," Lyle muttered. "You're not needed."

Ignoring him, Kris walked over to Kelly. "What do you want me to do?" he asked, his voice low. Because he wasn't going to make this harder on her or Cole. He'd do whatever was needed to make sure they were okay.

"Let him take Cole and me home. I'll call you later when he's gone." Her eyes met his and he could see the love in them. It made every part of him warm. She'd told him she loved him on the phone and it was all he'd wanted.

But he also needed to hear it again. When they were together. Alone.

"Okay." He reached for her hand and squeezed it, all too aware that Cole was here and they hadn't had a chance to speak to him about their relationship yet. "I'll head over to the tavern to help out. Call me if you need anything."

"Thank you," Kelly whispered. "For everything."

"Always." He brushed his lips against her temple. "I'll call you later."

They'd gotten Cole comfortable on the sofa. His head was resting on the pillows she'd brought in from his bedroom, his body covered with a blanket she'd crocheted when he was a baby. There was a Christmas movie on the television that Cole and her dad were half watching between dozes.

She wished Kris was here. They could have had a giggle about how her dad and Cole were turning into old men.

Instead Lyle was hovering about, looking uncomfortable, mostly scrolling through his phone. She'd never seen a man so attached to a screen. It was like he'd exchanged one addiction for another.

Cole let out a snore and she bit down a smile.

"I'm going to make some coffee," she whispered to Lyle. "Would you like one?"

"Sure."

He followed her to the kitchen, that damn phone still in his hand.

"You don't have to stay if you have something better to do," she said. "Cole is fine. He'll be sleeping for a while."

"You desperate to get me out of here so Kris can come over?" Lyle asked. "I guess I should be thankful that you're not kissing him when I'm in the same house like last time."

She frowned. "That was a long time ago. And I apologized so many times. I was upset, scared. And you were not in a good place."

"Because you were pregnant with my kid and you were kissing someone else. Probably sleeping with him, too."

She opened her mouth to protest but stopped. He'd never let it go. She knew that now. She'd probably known it then when he'd punished her over and over again. "I never slept with anybody but you when we were together."

Lyle looked away, shaking his head. "He's not going to stay around for you. You know that, right?"

Kelly swallowed, even though her mouth was dry. "It's

none of your business if he stays or not." She grabbed the coffee from the cupboard, scooping it into the machine. She wasn't going to let Lyle upset her.

"Remember how you felt when he left for college?" Lyle continued. "He was fucking his way across campus and you were crying in my arms. You were always the second choice, Kel. The small town girl he came to when he wanted to get his dick wet."

Her stomach turned. Why was Lyle such an asshole?

"You know how I know he never wanted you?" Lyle asked.

God, she was sick of this. She looked over at Lyle who was leaning against the counter. She wanted him out of her house. One more minute and she'd be kicking him out.

"Because we made a pact, that's how. He threw you away with the shake of a hand, you know that? Said he wasn't interested in you."

She blinked, her brows furrowed.

"That surprise you?" Lyle asked. "I guess he never told you about that when you two were fucking."

She wasn't going to give him the satisfaction of asking, but somehow the words crept out. "What kind of pact?"

"That neither of us would touch you. You were seventeen then. Pretty as a fucking peach. All the guys wanted to be your first."

She stared at him, trying to comprehend. "So why did you break the pact?" she asked him.

"Because I was in love with you, believe it or not. And if Kris had been in love with you he would have broken it too. But he wasn't. He didn't care. Until he came home and his options were limited so he decided to try to take my girl. Nearly did, too. Don't you think I know how much you cried when he left? How my kid heard those tears while he was in your belly? You never knew what loyalty meant, I know that now."

She felt weirdly cold, despite the heat blowing full blast in the house. Why had Kris agreed to that? And why had he not told her?

They'd agreed to something behind her back when all three of them were supposed to be friends. Like she was a piece of meat to be bargained over.

The coffee machine started to sputter. She turned to look at it, mostly so Lyle couldn't see her tears.

All those years. All that waste. And Kris had never said a word about his agreement with Lyle.

It hurt. She hurt.

"You can have this coffee and then you can leave," she said, her voice low. "If you want to see Cole tomorrow, that's fine. Just call first."

"I'm heading back to California tomorrow."

She wasn't sure whether to be relieved or annoyed. "I thought you said you'd visit Cole over Christmas."

"I changed my mind."

Of course he did. But right now she couldn't bring herself to care.

She wanted to talk to Kris. Find out if what Lyle had told her was true.

And then she wanted to cry. For the girl who'd been totally oblivious to their agreement.

Kris' phone buzzed in his pocket as he was loading the dishwasher behind the bar for the third time that day. There were eight of them working at the tavern, and all of them had been run off their feet. He was glad, in a way, because it kept him from thinking about what was happening at Kelly's house.

Standing, he pulled his phone from his pocket, and saw Kelly's name on the screen.

"I just need to take this call," he said to Will. "I'll be right back."

"Can you bring some bottles back with you?" Will asked him. "We're getting low."

"Sure."

Walking into the back room, he swiped to accept the call, using his shoulder to wedge the phone against his ear as he kicked the door shut behind him. "Hey."

"Hi." She sounded so far away. "How's the tavern?"

"Busy. Making lots of money. Nothing you need to worry about. More importantly, how's Cole?" he asked her.

"He's good. He had a long nap but he's awake now and playing some car chase game against Dad."

"On the playstation rather than real life I hope?" Kris smiled.

"I think so."

"And Lyle? Is he behaving."

"Lyle left," she said abruptly.

"When?"

"An hour ago. He woke Cole up to say goodbye. He won't be staying. He's heading back to Virginia tonight, California tomorrow."

Kris blinked. It would be a lie to say he wasn't relieved, but he hated that Cole might be hurt. "How did Cole take that?"

"He barely noticed. He's so used to Lyle being absent." She let out a long breath. "Lyle said something to me before he left."

Of course he fucking did. Lyle never left anywhere without a scorched earth policy. "What did he say?"

"That you and he..." She swallowed, or that's what it

sounded like. "That you both agreed not to touch me. When we were younger."

He pinched the bridge of his nose. What a little shit Lyle really was. "Yeah, that was the biggest mistake of my life."

"I was wondering why you didn't tell me about it."

The honest answer was, he'd forgotten about it. The longer one was that he'd regretted it from the moment he came home and she and Lyle were together. "I..."

"I'm so sorry," Will said, bursting into the room. "We're all out of Coronas. I just need to get some."

The sound of laughter and loud discussion rushed into the room. From his vantage point he could see a line halfway down the tavern. "Kelly, I gotta go help. Can we talk about this later?"

"Sure."

"I'm going to close up." He couldn't ask any of the staff to do it. Most of them had families and it would be late as hell. "You'll be asleep when I'm done. How about I come over tomorrow?"

He hated not seeing her. Hated even more that he'd forgotten about that damn pact. Fuck, he'd been a dumb shit in those days.

"Come tonight. If you're awake enough."

"What about Cole and your dad?" he asked.

"They'll be in bed. And I think Dad knows exactly what's going on, don't you?"

A smile pulled at his lips. "Yeah, I think he probably does. I'll see you tonight." He glanced at Will, kneeling down in front of the crates, filling up a tray with bottles.

"See you later."

❦ 33 ❦

Kris parked in her driveway and sent Kelly a message that he was here, fully expecting her to have fallen asleep already. It was just after two in the morning. The whole damn town was sleeping, and most of them hadn't spent the night before full of anxiety about their sick son in the hospital.

But within moments of him sending her the message she'd opened the front door. He walked over to her, and damn she looked tired.

Silently he pulled her into his arms and kissed her, half afraid she wouldn't kiss him back. But she did. Hard. Her arms wrapping around his neck, her fingers sliding into his hair.

Christ, she tasted sweet. Despite the cold air around him and the tiredness in his muscles, he lifted her up and held her against him, her legs wrapping around his waist.

And then he carried her inside because it really was fucking freezing outside and she was only in a pair of fleece pajamas. Walking into the hallway, he gently closed the door behind him.

"Nice welcome." He was still smiling.

"I've been thinking about you."

"I've been thinking about you, too. Have you gotten any sleep tonight?"

"A little." She shrugged. "More than you."

"But I wasn't in the hospital all night." He cupped her face with his hand. "How's Cole doing?"

"He's good. Ate a bit of dinner, had a shower, and managed to keep his wound dry. So I'm counting it all as a win."

"I'd like to come over to see him tomorrow, if that's okay."

She nodded. "Yeah, I know he'd like that. I told him you were holding the fort at the tavern." She threaded her fingers into his, as though she didn't want to let him go. "Let's go talk in my bedroom. We won't disturb anybody there."

He lifted a brow but followed her to her room anyway, all too aware that he'd never been in there before. It was small but neat. The bed was unmade but he guessed she'd been laying in it. By the side of the bed on a little table was a box. He could see something sticking out of it. Something familiar. He leaned forward to check.

"Is that the hat I bought you?" It was suede with a fur trim. It looked like something from an old Russian town. He'd bought it for her for Christmas when he was in college, thinking she'd like it.

"Yeah."

"You kept it."

"I kept a lot of things." She reached beside him and pulled out an old photograph and passed it to him. It was of the two of them when they were thirteen or fourteen. They were covered in mud from head to toe, the only white he could see was in their eyeballs and their teeth.

"I don't remember this," he said. "When was it taken?"

"North took it, I think. We went with him and Gabe to

the lake for the day. It started raining and you dared me to roll in the mud. Then you laughed so much I pulled you in with me."

He chuckled, looking at the picture again. Damn they were so young. So fucking happy.

"Why did you make that pact with Lyle?" she asked him.

He pulled his gaze from the photo he was holding and looked at the woman he loved. Her expression was confused. Hurt. He hated it.

"It was a long time ago. You were just... I don't know. One day we were all kids and then you became a woman. You were beautiful." It happened over night. Or at least it felt like it did. The hormones rushed in and he'd started seeing her differently.

"I told Lyle that I wanted to ask you to prom."

"You did?"

He nodded. "And he said I couldn't. Not if we all wanted to be friends. And I got that. He would have been left out. I would have hated that. So we shook on it. Neither of us would see you as anything other than a friend."

"But I would have said yes."

His eyes caught hers.

"I was in love with you. Didn't you know that?" she asked him. "I used to follow you around like a damn puppy dog."

"I didn't know. I thought..." He shook his head. "I came home from college and I'd missed you so damn much. I'd decided I needed to talk to Lyle and tell him enough was enough. We were grown ups, we could all stay friends and you and I..."

"You and I..." she prompted.

"Could have gotten together. But when I came back everything had changed. You and Lyle were an item. I was too late."

Her eyes didn't leave his. "When you left I felt so alone.

And Lyle kept telling me about all the girls you were seeing. What a great time you were having. I was so lonely and sad and Lyle... he told me he was in love with me. I was an idiot. I was afraid of losing him like I lost you."

"I don't blame you. I was the one who should have said something earlier."

"And Lyle broke your pact," she said, frowning, as though she was realizing what a betrayal that was.

"Yeah. He did."

"Why didn't you say anything then?" she asked. "If he'd broken it, you could have too."

"Because I thought you were happy. That you loved him. I wouldn't have come between you. I loved you both."

She ran her tongue over her dry lip. "What a waste. All that time." She looked so sad and he hated it. Hated knowing what they'd lost. And yes, they had now. That was wonderful.

But if he'd been a braver kid, things would have been so different.

He breathed out. "I thought about telling you. I came close that night when I asked you to leave with me."

"But then I told you I was pregnant."

"Yeah. And that wasn't the time to admit anything to you. You had enough to deal with. You didn't need my emo bull-shit. I knew that much, at least."

She reached up to trace his jaw with her finger. Her touch felt so good it made him sigh.

"But I don't understand why you didn't tell me once we were together. Now?"

"Honestly?" He trapped her hand under his, pressing it against his face. "I didn't think about it. I barely thought about Lyle. These past few weeks have just been about us. And Cole, nobody else."

"I feel..." She pressed her lips together, as though trying to find the right words. "Sad. For the girl I was. Wistful."

"Yeah, I get that. I feel sad, too."

"And I don't know what to do with those feelings," she told him. "I want to shout at somebody. Blame somebody. Lyle maybe. Or you. You made a decision about me that I wasn't part of."

"I know. And we shouldn't have done that. I'm sorry."

"I can't help but think of what if..."

He let go of her hand, reaching for her. Sitting on the end of her bed, he pulled her toward him, pressing his face into her stomach.

"I'm glad it didn't happen then," he told her.

Her fingers tangled into his hair. She scraped her nails against his scalp and he let out a low groan. "Why are you glad?" she asked him.

"Because I didn't deserve you then. Any guy who makes a pact like that doesn't deserve a woman like you." He looked up at her, his eyes shining. "But there's something much more important than that. If I'd have told you, you wouldn't have Cole. And I'm so damn glad you have him. I love that kid."

It was like the final piece of armor she'd fastened around her heart disintegrated. This man loved her son, and she loved him. Why had she spent so long fighting this? She only had to look into his eyes to know he was telling the truth.

He was a good man. The best. He'd saved her from hunger that first day of school and he was still trying to save her.

Maybe it was time to let him.

A tear rolled down her cheek. He pulled her closer until she was straddling his legs, and reached up to wipe it away. His hands were on her hips. Their faces were close, enough for him to feel the warmth of her breath on his skin. He was smiling at her, a soft, goofy kind of smile.

An I'm-in-love-with-you smile that he never wanted to go away.

Leaning forward, he brushed his lips against hers. Needing the connection. To wipe the past away.

And then they were kissing, his mouth moving against hers, her fingers in his hair again, his digging into her hips. She moved against him as their tongues touched, making him hard, making him needy.

"Mom?"

Cole's voice was like a bucket of cold water on them both. Kelly jumped off of him, touching her hair. And he stood too, adjusting himself.

"Give me a minute," she whispered, running out of her bedroom. "Don't move an inch."

He sat back down and lifted that photo up again, taking in their smiling faces, their muddy skin, the way they were holding hands. Damn, he'd been happy then. But he felt happier now.

Fucking ecstatic, in case anybody was wondering. He'd spent most of his life messing things up. Making decisions that hurt people.

But now? He was older. Wiser. And more importantly he was ready for love.

"Hi." She pulled the door closed. "Sorry about that."

"You never have to say sorry for putting Cole first."

Her gaze softened. "Thank you."

"Just telling you the truth." He reached for her and she joined him back on the bed, this time beside him, their hips touching as she took the photograph from his hand.

"One day I'm going to make you recreate this," he told her.

"Can we wait until summer? I don't want to catch hypothermia."

He grinned again.

"What?" she asked, smiling back at him. "What did I say this time?"

"You said the summer. Like you're happy for me to stay with you. Like you're mine for more than just the winter."

She leaned forward to wrap her hands around his neck resting her head against his shoulder. "I've always been yours. It just took us a while to realize."

And what a damn journey it had been. They'd walked through dark shadows and bright sunshine and all the things in between. But they'd got here, and it was perfect.

Even better, their journey was only just beginning.

"I love you," he told her, pulling her close. "So damn much it hurts."

"But why can't I go to school?" Cole asked, his hair mussed and his pajama pants half-twisted around his waist. Kelly tried not to smile because she couldn't remember him ever begging to go to school before.

Kris had left early that morning. They'd talked and nothing more. But it had felt good. Cathartic.

Like they were back to where they should have been all along.

"The doctor says you need to rest for a few days. You can go back after Christmas break. You'll only be missing two days." She poured some milk into a glass and passed it to him, ruffling his hair before picking up her coffee cup.

"But I won't be able to show anybody my wound then." He huffed. "It'll be all healed by then."

Thank God for that. "And that's why you're not going to school, honey. You expose your wound and it gets infected and then we'll end up back in the hospital again. Anyway, you'll almost certainly have a scar. You can show it off to your heart's content once you're healed."

It made her chest hurt to know that his body would bear a

permanent mark from his illness. He was so young and his skin was so perfect.

But then she had scars, too. Visible and invisible ones. They were the building bricks to her life. The only way to avoid them was to hide yourself away until the day you died.

And she didn't want to do that.

"I will?" He grinned. "Scars are cool. Danny has one on his eyebrow. It cuts right through the hair. Makes him look badass."

"Badass?" she repeated. "Really?"

"Yep. He got it from skiing into a tree last winter. His dad says he'll get all the girls with it when he's older."

"I bet." She heard a rap at the front door and her heart did a little skip. Kris had arranged to come over early to see Cole, before heading to the tavern to open up. "I'll get that, you stay here and finish your milk."

It was impossible not to be the mother hen, at least for a few more days. She didn't sleep last night after Kris left, going in to check on Cole every twenty minutes just to make sure he was breathing. She knew she'd have to chill it, not least because Cole hated it when she fussed.

But for a few days she was going to make a fuss of him regardless.

"Hey." Kris was standing on the stoop when she opened the door, a warm smile on his face. Next to him was a huge cooler, the plastic kind with wheels that people took on picnics in the summer.

"What's that?" she asked him.

He hunkered down to pop the lid off, revealing at least a dozen dishes topped with silver foil stacked on top of each other. "It's your dinner for the next three months."

"You made all of this."

He put the lid back on and stood back up, grinning. "Nope. Half the town did. There's more in the freezer at the tavern. I spent most of last night at the tavern taking them in from the townsfolk because I didn't want them to disturb you by leaving them at the front door."

"People cooked for us?" Her throat felt tight.

"That's what people do." He shrugged. "Around here at least. I don't remember anybody bringing me food in London when I was released from the hospital."

She tipped her head to the side. "You had surgery in London?"

"Had to have my tonsils removed. The surgeon told me I was the only person over fifteen who had them done that week. I felt like a loser." He gave her a lopsided grin. "Now are you going to ask me inside or am I going to stay out here and freeze my balls off?"

Her dad was shuffling out of his bedroom when the two of them stepped into the hallway, Kris pulling the cooler along behind him.

"Morning," her dad said. He didn't look at all surprised to see Kris.

"Morning, Paul." Kris put his hand on the dip of Kelly's back, his palm firm against her sweater. "Want to come with me to the tavern today? We could use your guidance."

Her dad's face lit up. "Yeah, I'd like that." He glanced at Kelly. "If it's okay with you."

"It's fine with me." She nodded. "I'll be here taking care of Cole."

"I'll go get myself ready." Her dad turned back to his room, leaning heavily on his cane. He glanced back at Kris. "You're a good man."

She heard Kris' sharp breath. Her dad's words meant a lot to him. For too long he'd seen himself as the bad guy in a situation where nothing turned out well.

When they got to the kitchen, Cole was eating a huge

bowl of cornflakes. A grin split his face when he saw Kris standing there.

"Hey, bud. How you feeling?" Kris asked him, grabbing a bowl and filling it with cornflakes.

Kelly lingered in the door, watching as Kris sat down beside her son, and Cole leaned in to show him what he'd been watching on his iPad.

"You think they'll make the playoffs this year?" Cole asked.

"They'll need to amp up their defense to make it anywhere close. Jackson is weak as hell." They were leaning in so close their heads were touching. Kris' dark against Cole's blonde.

"Yeah but their offense is whack. Nobody can hit a puck like Goran." Cole paused as they continued to watch. "See? He's amazing."

Kelly picked up the cereal box and put it back in the cupboard, trying to figure out why there was such a big lump in her throat.

"I'm ready." Her dad walked into the kitchen, wearing a sports jacket over his crisp shirt. "What are you watching?"

"The Boston Razors. They won last night, again."

Her dad leaned over between the two of them, leaning on Kris' chair. And for a moment the sight of the three of them overwhelmed her.

Three generations all watching sports together. Her past, her present, and her future. She hadn't known how much she needed this. To watch the three men she loved the most enjoy each other's company, bonding over hockey.

Tears pricked at her eyes as they laughed at something on the screen.

And then Cole turned to look at her.

"Why are you crying?" He sounded concerned. "Did I do something wrong?"

She tried to blink them back. "No, honey. Not at all."

Cole turned back to Kris. "You'd better go kiss her before she sobs all over the floor."

Kris looked over at her, lifting a brow. She shrugged back.

"You are her boyfriend, aren't you?" Cole continued. "Isn't that what boyfriend's do?"

A smile pulled at the corner of Kris' mouth. "Would you be okay with that?"

"Yeah, as long as you promise to keep taking me to hockey." Cole turned back to his iPad as though it wasn't a big deal.

And maybe it wasn't. Not to Cole. He hadn't been through the emotion and the pain and the years of yearning. But to her it was huge.

The biggest.

It was Kris' turn to shrug as he stood and walked over to her, a wry smile still playing on his lips.

"You okay?" he murmured, wiping a tear from her cheek.

She nodded. "Happy tears."

He leaned in closer, his hands on the counter on either side of her hips. Her dad and Cole weren't even looking at them, too busy watching the final play on Cole's iPad.

"I'd like to see more of those." He leaned in, brushing her lips with his. The smallest of kisses but it sent a shiver down her spine anyway.

"And I'd like more of those," she whispered, her heart so full it could burst any minute.

"Okay, one more," Cole yelled out. "And then enough of the kissy kissy. I know I said it was okay, but still..."

Kris caught her eye and laughed, then kissed her softly once more. It felt like a promise. And she liked that very much.

"I think he's feeling better," Kris murmured.

"Yeah, I think he is, too."

And wasn't that the best news in the world? A wave of happiness washed over her, and this time she didn't fight it. Didn't try to tell herself not to be too happy, or have too much hope.

"Well that was a good game," Cole said.

"Yep," her dad gruffed out. "Be good for your mom today while I'm at the Tavern."

"Gotta go," Kris whispered, cupping her jaw with his warm hand. "I'll see you later."

"Yes, please."

Their eyes locked, and she felt a shiver snake down her spine. How many times had she said goodbye to this man? But this time it wasn't goodbye.

It was hello and I love you and I'll see you real soon.

It was I want to spend my life making you happy, because that will make me happy, too.

"I love you," he mouthed. And she mouthed it right back.

As far as she was concerned, it didn't get much better than this.

EPILOGUE

Two years later...

"Dad!" Cole's low voice pierced through the air as Kris swung the axe to cut the tree trunk up into useable pieces. Looking up, he could see Cole standing in the doorway of their ranch house, his hair too long despite Kelly's urging that her son get it cut for the holidays.

They'd built this house last year. Right after he and Kelly and Cole ran away to get married without telling anybody. She hadn't wanted a fuss, just wanted to be his wife. And he was fine with that.

The same way he was fine with Cole calling him Dad. Lyle had been in touch twice since Cole's surgery. Once last Christmas and once this summer, after Kelly had told him that she and Kris were married. He hadn't been out to see Cole at all.

It annoyed him to shit, but he made sure not to show it to

Cole. Just tried to be there for him in all the ways Lyle should have been.

Putting the axe down carefully on the ground, Kris smiled. "Everything okay, bud?"

"Mom's in the bathroom. Said to get you. She thinks it's time."

A chill went through his spine. He practically ran into the house, following Cole through the huge hallway, and even in his panic he noticed how much harder it was to keep up with the kid nowadays. Cole'd had about five different growth spurts in the past two years, the latest one had gotten him to within twelve inches of Kris' height. At thirteen he already towered over Kelly.

She was small but mighty. And she didn't need height to put the fear of god into Cole whenever he stepped over the line.

When they got to the bathroom the door was open. Kelly was sitting on the floor, Paul beside her, holding her hand.

"Okay, baby?"

"It's too soon." She looked petrified. "She's not due for another three weeks."

He hunkered down in front of her, wiping the hair from her face. "The c-section is scheduled for next week. She's ready. Let's go meet our girl." He looked at Cole. "Can you get your mom's bag?"

Cole nodded, looking almost as apprehensive as Kelly.

"I'll let everybody know," Paul said. "Oh, and I'll open up the tavern." He stood a little easier than he used to. The surgery on his knee had been a success, and he could walk without a cane once more. He could drive, too, and he'd bought a small car so he could cover some of the shifts that Kelly used to work. Between the three of them they managed the place so they all could have a life.

And the nights that he and Kelly could stay home and spend time with Cole were his favorites.

When it was just the two of them left in the bathroom, he reached down to take Kelly's hands, helping her stand. Her stomach was perfectly round. She'd joked that she'd probably give birth to a basketball, and Cole had protested, because he'd prefer a puck.

"Why are you so calm?" she muttered, still clinging to Kris.

"Because I've been looking forward to this moment for so long. I missed Cole's birth, I can't wait to be with you for this one." He put his arm around her and helped her walk out of the bathroom. "How long have you been having contractions?"

"About an hour. It's still early. Maybe they'll try to stop them."

He shook his head. "From what I've read they'll just deliver this close to your due date. It's only a couple of weeks. They'll be able to take care of her."

He'd spent most of the past eight months reading up on pregnancy and birth and childcare and everything that went with it. He'd been to every doctor's appointment, listened to her for hours while she tried to decide if she wanted a neutral nursery or a pink one. Repainted it when she changed her mind.

And when she'd cried because she was hormonal and she hated being such a flake he'd held her tight and kissed her and showed her with his body how much he loved her.

It was snowing when they stepped outside. The kind of thick flakes that clung to everything, including your eyelashes and lips. Kris had wrapped her coat around her and put his arm around her shoulders, helping her down the steps when she suddenly stopped and let out a low groan.

"Another contraction?" he asked, checking his watch.

"Yes," she gasped.

This one lasted sixty seconds. She was still in early labor. Which was good because as cool as he was trying to be he didn't want to deliver a baby in his car. Especially not a breech baby, because this little girl was in the exact same position Cole had been all those years ago.

Cole was proud that his little sister was as stubborn as he was.

When they got to the car Cole had already thrown Kelly's bag in the trunk. He opened the passenger door and Kelly got in, muttering about being huge as she put the seatbelt across her belly.

"Call me when you can," Paul said, shaking Kris' hand.

"Yep. Thanks for holding down the fort at the tavern."

"Always."

"You ready, bud?" Kris asked Cole. "You got your phone? Your charger?"

"Yep." Cole patted his backpack. They'd talked long and hard about whether Cole should be at the hospital or not when Kelly gave birth. They wanted him to feel part of this in every way. In the end, they'd agreed he'd be in the waiting room. Kris' family would be there to look after him while Kris supported Kelly.

And then Cole would be the first person to meet their little girl.

"Okay then. Let's go."

"It's a girl," the doctor said, and even though it was no surprise, tears were rolling down Kris' face anyway. He was holding Kelly's hand, watching as the doctor held up their tiny, red faced baby, her eyes screwed up as she let out a yell, protesting at her sudden entrance to the world. "And she's feisty."

Kris laughed because damn right she was. "Just like her mom."

"Shut up," Kelly said and everybody in the room laughed.

It was only a minute before the nurse gave the baby to Kelly for some skin-on-skin bonding, her tiny head resting on Kelly's chest as she blinked up at the world.

"Is she okay?" Kris asked, watching as his two girls lay together on the bed.

"She's perfect. Breathing well, a good color," the nurse told him.

"Will she need to go to the NICU?" Kelly's voice was groggy

"I don't think so. The team will examine her but everything looks good right now." She looked over at Kris. "Would you like to hold your daughter while we get mommy all stitched up?"

Kris nodded, and the nurse told him to sit. "You can take your top off," the nurse said and Kelly laughed again. Damn he loved that sound. "To keep the baby warm," the nurse added, sounding amused and exasperated at Kelly's grin.

He did as he was told, removing the scrubs, and then she passed his baby into his arms. Her skin felt so soft against his chest, her little legs curled up against him, her mouth rooting at his body as though she was expecting him to provide dinner.

"Does she have a name?" the nurse asked.

Kris looked over at Kelly. She was exhausted from the procedure. He could tell that from the droop of her eyes and the slowness of her voice. And yet she'd never been more beautiful. Her strength and capacity for love amazed him in every way.

Coming back to Winterville was the second best decision he'd made. Winning her over was the first.

She'd taught him to love again. Fiercely, like she did. She'd taught him to fight for the things he believed in and that was such a precious gift.

"Hope," he said softly, looking into their daughter's clear blue eyes, feeling a wave of love washing through him. "Her name is Hope."

DEAR READER

Thank you for reading Mine For The Winter!

If you're not quite ready to let Kris, Kelly and Cole go, check out this bonus epilogue for a glimpse of their wedding and happy ever after (plus a future take for ALL the Winter family!

TO DOWNLOAD YOUR FREE EPILOGUE TYPE THIS ADDRESS INTO YOUR BROWSER:
https://dl.bookfunnel.com/qm4xc2do6j

This is the final book in the Winterville Series (for now) but I plan to write a few outtakes for my newsletter subscribers, so make sure you join us by clicking here to download the bonus epilogue AND join my newsletter list.

And if you're looking out for your next read, why not try out the Heartbreak Brothers? Their story begins with Take Me Home

I can't wait to share more stories with you.

Yours,

Carrie xx

ALSO BY CARRIE ELKS

THE WINTERVILLE SERIES

A gorgeously wintery small town romance series, featuring six cousins who fight to save the town their grandmother built.

Welcome to Winterville

Hearts In Winter

Leave Me Breathless

Memories Of Mistletoe

Every Shade Of Winter

Mine For The Winter

THE SALINGER BROTHERS SERIES

A swoony romantic comedy series featuring six brothers and the strong and smart women who tame them.

Strictly Business

Strictly Pleasure

Strictly For Now (Available for Pre-Order)

ANGEL SANDS SERIES

A heartwarming small town beach series, full of best friends, hot guys and happily-ever-afters.

Let Me Burn

She's Like the Wind

Sweet Little Lies

Just A Kiss

Baby I'm Yours

Pieces Of Us

Chasing The Sun

Heart And Soul

Lost In Him

THE HEARTBREAK BROTHERS SERIES

A gorgeous small town series about four brothers and the women who capture their hearts.

Take Me Home

Still The One

A Better Man

Somebody Like You

When We Touch

THE HEARTBREAK BROTHERS NEXT GENERATION SERIES

That One Regret

That One Touch (Releases 2024)

THE SHAKESPEARE SISTERS SERIES

An epic series about four strong yet vulnerable sisters, and the alpha men who steal their hearts.

Summer's Lease

A Winter's Tale

Absent in the Spring

By Virtue Fall

THE LOVE IN LONDON SERIES

Three books about strong and sassy women finding love in the big city.

Coming Down

Broken Chords

Canada Square

STANDALONE

Fix You

An epic romance that spans the decades. Breathtaking and angsty and all the things in between.

If you'd like to get an email when I release a new book, please sign up here:

CARRIE ELKS' NEWSLETTER

ABOUT THE AUTHOR

Carrie Elks writes contemporary romance with a sizzling edge. Her first book, *Fix You*, has been translated into eight languages and made a surprise appearance on *Big Brother* in Brazil. Luckily for her, it wasn't voted out.

Carrie lives with her husband, two lovely children and a larger-than-life black pug called Plato. When she isn't writing or reading, she can be found baking, drinking an occasional (!) glass of wine, or chatting on social media.

You can find Carrie in all these places
www.carrieelks.com
carrie.elks@mail.com

Made in the USA
Columbia, SC
07 February 2024

31690212R00190

Made in the USA
Middletown, DE
01 November 2022